D0962069

Critical Praise for *Time of the Locust* by Morowa Yejidé

"Deftly brings together the fantastic and realistic . . . and spins them with gold and possibility." —*Washington Post*

"Yejidé is poised to make her mark with a novel that might be described as one of family connection—but encompasses so much more . . . When the father, Horus, develops supernatural abilities and connects with his son, strange and powerful things happen, but the focus is less on fantasy than on the fantastic power of love to bind and protect us."
—*Washingtonian*

"At times almost mystical in its intensity, Yejidé's prose brings lyricism to her dark subject matter and unhappy characters, eventually introducing a kind of magical restoration to her shattered fictional family."
—*Kirkus Reviews*

"Beautiful prose conveys the sadness and fractured selves of these characters, who are both strong and fragile . . . The novel is challenging and memorable." —*Publishers Weekly*

"There are characters who hook you from the second you meet them on the page. Sephiri, the autistic boy at the heart of *Time of the Locust* is one of them. In this moving debut, author Morowa Yejidé creates a protagonist who finds comfort in an imaginary world filled with sea creatures that help him cope with the 'real world.'" —*Essence*

"A superb debut work of magic realism and finalist for the PEN/Bellwether Prize for Socially Engaged Fiction, this is the book for you, your friends, and your book club." —*Ebony*

"We have needed storytellers to remind us of our humanity and our interconnectedness and stories that drill down to what we struggle with, often in silence. Welcome Morowa Yejidé, whose exquisitely written and page-turning novel, *Time of the Locust*, reminds of who we truly are."
—Asha Bandele, author of *Daughter*

"A unique and astounding debut."
—Lalita Tademy, best-selling author of *Cane River*

"A stunning, magical novel about the power of love between an imprisoned father and an autistic son. Original, compelling, Yejidé explores the human psyche in a dreamscape world."
—Jewell Parker Rhodes, author of *Douglass' Women*

"Arrayed against seven kinds of imprisonment—autism, gluttony, self-hate, inanition, racism, vengefulness, and a fiendish species of incarceration in a supermax prison—in this auspicious debut novel, stands the volitional force of unfettered love. Morowa Yejidé's depiction of the inner world of the parents of an autistic child (the father unfairly imprisoned and the mother sagging under the load of single parentage) is rendered with compassionate aplomb; her brilliant depiction of the mental weather of their autistic son is matchless. *Time of the Locust* is a rich and rewarding story of redemption for those who believe, as the poet Richard Lovelace wrote, 'Stone walls do not a prison make.'"
—J. Michael Lennon, author of *Norman Mailer: A Double Life*

"*Time of the Locust* is a brave and mesmerizing journey into the mysteries of autism, solitary confinement, and inner struggle told with dazzling imagery and passion. In this luminous first novel, the crossroads between the dream world and the physical world is a place where physical chains are of no consequence. A soaring odyssey of the human spirit."
—Kaylie Jones, author of *The Anger Meridian*

CREATURES OF PASSAGE

CREATURES OF PASSAGE

MOROWA YEJIDÉ

BROOKLYN, NEW YORK

This is a work of fiction. All names, characters, places, and incidents are the product of the author's imagination. Any resemblance to real events or persons, living or dead, is entirely coincidental.

Published by Akashic Books

ISBN: 978-1-61775-876-8
Library of Congress Control Number: 2020936133

First printing

Akashic Books
Brooklyn, New York
Twitter: @AkashicBooks
Facebook: AkashicBooks
E-mail: info@akashicbooks.com
Website: www.akashicbooks.com

For the living and the dead.
And those on their way to one or the other.

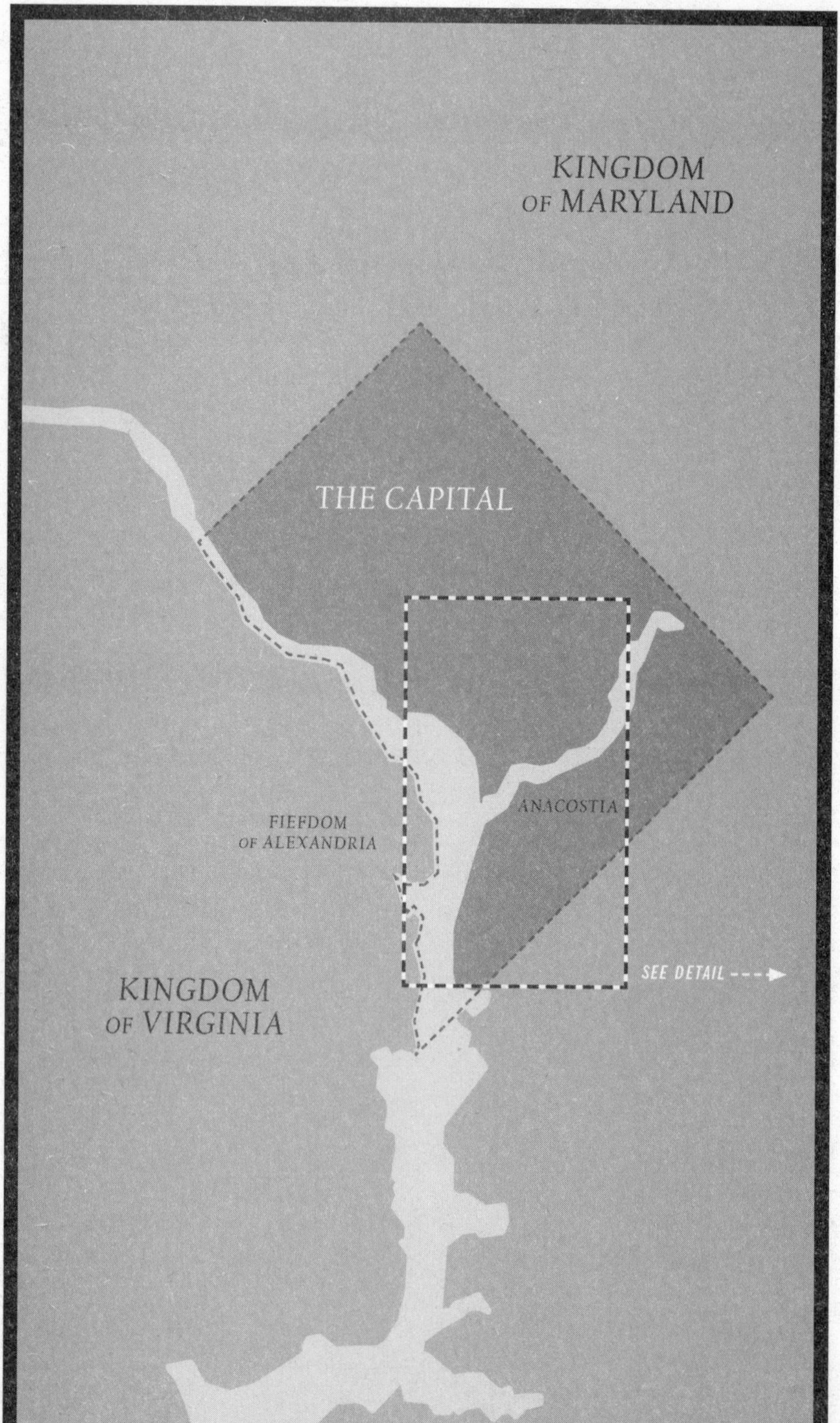

KINGDOM
OF MARYLAND

THE CAPITAL

ANACOSTIA

FIEFDOM
OF ALEXANDRIA

KINGDOM
OF VIRGINIA

SEE DETAIL

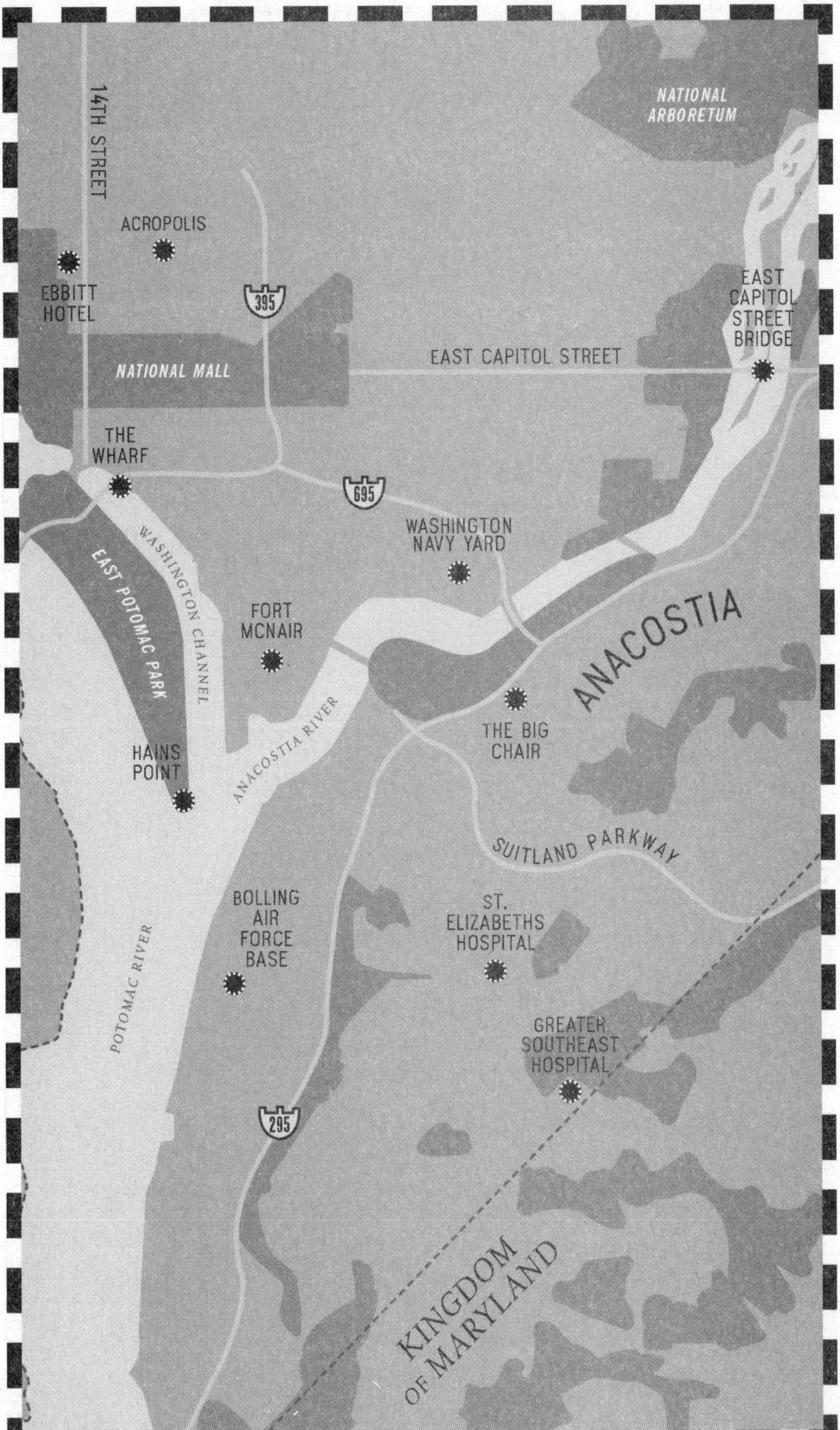

NATIONAL ARBORETUM
14TH STREET
ACROPOLIS
EBBITT HOTEL
395
NATIONAL MALL
EAST CAPITOL STREET
EAST CAPITOL STREET BRIDGE
THE WHARF
695
WASHINGTON CHANNEL
EAST POTOMAC PARK
WASHINGTON NAVY YARD
FORT MCNAIR
ANACOSTIA
THE BIG CHAIR
HAINS POINT
ANACOSTIA RIVER
SUITLAND PARKWAY
BOLLING AIR FORCE BASE
ST. ELIZABETHS HOSPITAL
POTOMAC RIVER
GREATER SOUTHEAST HOSPITAL
295
KINGDOM OF MARYLAND

CONTENTS

Life is a shadow and a mist that passes quickly by and is no more.
—Madagascan proverb

PASSAGE I

MOVING THROUGH SPACES

FERRYMAN

The goddess Nephthys ferried lost souls through the dark currents of the Great Mystery, from one isle of existence to another and out to the far reaches of fate, all the while filled with a profound sadness for her brother, the murdered god Osiris, whose power was taken by dividing him into pieces . . .

Nephthys Kinwell was not a savior of souls. That was God's charge. Or maybe the trade of the Devil. But she did ferry souls from one quadrant to another, and over the streets that now covered the prehistoric marshes of the capital of the territories. There was a certain geography to it all, she'd learned. To the win lose draw of lives. For Nephthys Kinwell knew—as all wandering hearts do—that it was not enough to know where things happened in the lines and circles of human lives, but why, since the reasons for happenings were buried much deeper than the happenings themselves. So she never had to look for the signs omens bones of creatures of passage. They found her.

The kingdoms of the land that together made the united territories had just turned two hundred years old the summer before, a fledgling in the long line of empires risen and fallen. But in 1977 Anacostia was still the New World, an isle of blood and desire. It was the capital's wild child east of a river that bore its name, a place where much was yet discovered. Anything was possible in that easternmost quadrant, where all things lived and died on the edges of time and space and meaning. It was a realm of contradictions, an undulating landscape of pristine land and dirty water, of breathtaking hills and decimated valleys. Crab apple and cherry trees flourished in the yards of abandoned houses and centuries-old oaks flanked run-down corner stores. Pushers stood watch for cars when little kids were crossing the street and junkies held doors open for old women. Paroled men played basketball and chess with fatherless boys. The unemployed sat in windows and kept tabs on the injustices of the land. *I'll tell your mama* was the universal threat, because next to God there was none more powerful. And the damnation and glory of man was forever intertwined in Anacostia, since all who lived there were faced with the unconquerable presence of both.

So the mechanics of rule and office and Congress and the four-year-old District of Columbia Council was all a vast gray mass glimpsed across the water. Fairfax, Arlington, Montgomery, and Prince George's fiefdoms were distant domains. The triumvirate of the White House and the Lincoln Memorial and the Washington Monument stood alabaster and resolute, and like the Acropolis held great dominion. But their reach was hardly felt in that east-of-the-river realm, where people lived a reality that was and was not of their own making. Where dreams came true even when people didn't want them to.

Now Nephthys Kinwell sat on the throne of a worn-out chair in a crumbling Anacostia apartment on the anniversary of her twin brother's death. Or rather, the day he was found in the river. Each passing year marked the loss of her binary existence, and this observance only heightened the unbearable inertia of one. She didn't have the strength to get behind the wheel of the Plymouth at a time like this; she had no will to help her passengers journey through the pitch black of the happenings of life, for sometimes she was the one adrift. And none of the people who got into her car could help her cope with the past. Nor could the white girl in the trunk charm what lay ahead.

Nephthys shifted in the chair. She could still remember the inexplicable feelings she had that day, even before a body was found and she was called down to the morgue. Her head felt like it was exploding. She doubled over from some agony in her abdomen, as if being cut from the inside out. She was tormented by a searing pain in her lower leg that arrested her breath. And the more air she tried to take into her lungs, the more she felt as if she were drowning. That must have been when it happened. When she lost the other half of her soul. What that meant crept deep into her in June of every year, so that she had to boil it down to something tolerable with as much liquor as she could stand. Because if she didn't drink, she had to think about the body. She had to think about the shark.

But no matter how much she drank, she could never completely wash away the sight at the morgue. The eyes bulged grotesquely out of their sockets. Clumps of hair scraped away along with the scalp, where bright-red splotches remained. The lower left leg was missing, torn away as if chewed off by some beast. Nephthys had stared at all that for a long time with disbelieving eyes. No, those couldn't be the dungarees with the patch she'd affixed on the pocket just the week before. That was not his boot. No, that was not her brother's half finger, the one shortened like her own, for they had been born holding hands. In the flickering morgue lights, she looked from one horror on the body to another and found that the world was big enough that it had to be someone else. Not her brother.

Nephthys settled deeper in her chair and reached for the small flask that lived always in the pocket of her housecoat and brought it to her lips and drank what was left. The passage of years did not make the image of her brother's bloated figure among the putrid waters of the Anacostia River any easier to bear. Worse were the seemingly pleasant, undisturbed faces of the police officers when she'd arrived at the station to file that useless report. Her brother's death was labeled "unsolved," as if his life had been a riddle, his very existence quickly called into doubt. That was why she'd spread his ashes that way, in different places. It allowed her to think of him living in other bodies of water instead, moving through other currents that gave him passage to better places: the cherry blossom–flecked currents of the Tidal Basin; the shallow majesty of the Lincoln Memorial Reflecting Pool; the slushy inflow of the McMillan Reservoir; the black tranquility of the Georgetown canal; the roiling deep of the Potomac River.

She looked around the cluttered room. It was dim and she could just make out the frames of objects at her feet. There was the tidal wash of things she'd brought in and dropped on the floor over the years, which covered the old rugs and kept the cracked tiles from view. She lost track of time and her mind drifted like ether in the gloom. Was it dawn or dusk? Or some other dimension birthed from memory and pain? She couldn't be sure. The alcohol she'd been drinking moved slowly through the slack passageways of her veins, a seething current of heat searing her nerves. In that state she could sail an ocean of her own making, tepid and stagnant. She could block out nearly everything, except the image of her brother's broken body and the fog that carried the call of other wandering hearts. Through the haze of the early-morning hours (late-evening?) she felt her half finger throbbing as it always did in dampness, the tip now dark and bereft of the topaz light it had when she was a child. The half finger didn't glow anymore. Not as it did in the casket-black nights back on the Sea Islands, where she and her brother once played in the wonderland of the Gullah marshes, when they glared at a dark world through the fearless, hopeful eyes of children. The fact that she and her brother had somehow managed to move from one island to another kind of island was not lost on her, and she placed this on the long list of things she found darkly ironic.

One of her legs was going numb and she tried to reposition herself against the shabby seat cushion. She rubbed the mangled flesh of her half finger. They were born holding hands, she and her brother, their fingers conjoined at the pointer. And they would have lived their entire lives that way, if they hadn't been cut apart soon after they took their first breath. *It's all gone now*, she thought. The Sea Islands were far, far away, a past that lay underwater. Every bit of that long-ago life was now lodged in the tubing of ancient coral reefs, disintegrating beneath the verdigris of lives once lived, folded into the happenings of other happenings. Many years later, gated communities and resorts and time-share flats would be built on top of the old black-family cemeteries and bank-seized properties of the Gullah lands. And the few living who remained would be the unwitting stars of a sort of human nature preserve, where tourists came to smile and point as if looking at the last of a species. But Nephthys had no way of knowing this as she sat in her apartment in the southeast quadrant. What she knew was that now there was only the Washington Navy Yard and Bolling Air Force Base. Now there were overgrown lots and houses that were no longer homes. Now people walked the streets as shadows of themselves, joining the ghost tribes of the Nacotchtank Indians, creatures of passage from one generation to the next. Her half finger throbbed harder still, and once more she was reminded of how life could begin and how it could end.

Indigo swirlin' round de vat . . .

Nephthys shook her head vigorously to silence the sound of the past, that old Sea Island song she and her brother sang as they helped their mother stir the indigo in the vat. She caught a glimpse of herself in the faded oval mirror that hung from the desiccated wall like a witch's talisman and turned away. She did not want to see the creases that time had ground into her walnut-colored face, her graying hair now blending with the dust. More and more, she was uncomfortable looking at her reflection in that mirror. For the deeper she looked, the more she had a creeping feeling that someone was looking back.

No beginnin' and no end . . .

She shook the song away again. Then, as if by some silent

request, the peeling plaster wall cracked and the mirror crashed to the floor. Nephthys looked down at the shimmering mess and massaged her leg. She set her thoughts aside. She would have a drink, and after that she would have another, in a committed stupor, gathering memories to cremate. And this was how she began every sunrise and ended every sunset on the anniversary of her brother's death.

More hours seemed to slip by, she couldn't tell how many, until stray sunrays burned through rips in the window curtain, and it was then that she realized it was day and not night. She reached for her flask and felt its lightness. Empty. She looked around for the bottle, the one she thought she'd placed next to her chair. It was gone. The bottles seemed to move somehow, never where she left them. She found them in bizarre places: on the broiler tray of the never-used oven; beneath the piles of clothes in her closet; under the bathroom sink. Sometimes she sat in the fog of her Plymouth and thought about how the bottles moved if she didn't move them. And what that could mean or not mean.

She stared into the din of her lair. She'd memorized every inch of the living room grid, every item among the objects spread across the floor and along the countertop of the kitchenette: scarves and dresses, newspapers and magazines, plastic containers and ripped paper bags, beaded necklaces and unopened envelopes, crumpled hats and shoeboxes. She knew all the rises and depressions of her mattress, the exact position of the falling-down furniture, the precise tilt of the little end table next to her chair where the bottle should be, the last of the others she'd already emptied. Which was why the missing bottle irritated her now, since she was certain she'd put it next to her chair where it would be within reach. But it wasn't there.

Scattered rays beamed from the mirror shards at her feet, lighting the living room walls like a mineralized cavern. Then, she thought she heard a choked voice at the front door. It was barely audible through the limestone that walled her mind and it slid through the apertures of what she thought was her imagination.

"Nephthys . . ." said the voice.

She tilted her head with the slowness of a drowsy lioness bothered by some clatter in the savanna. "Cyan't nobody be callin' me," she said, listening to the sound of her own slurred speech, thinking her mind was playing tricks on her.

"Nephthys Kinwell . . ." said the voice again.

She blinked in the darkness. Did someone call her name? That name of hers that she'd never fully understood? And yet she couldn't say her name without thinking of her brother's name too. And again, the image of her twin's body on the morgue slab flashed in her mind, the missing pieces of him somewhere else, and she only wanted to drink more.

There was a soft knock at the door.

Nephthys sat listening. Was it the children playing in the hallway again? "Not now," she mumbled, clutching her empty flask. She didn't feel like struggling up from the chair with her numb leg to hand out any candy. The children who wandered the hallways came looking for her sweets nearly every day, early in the morning when only the very young or the very old paid them any mind. Each child at her door was a welcome distraction from thoughts of another child, another time.

Now her flask was empty and her bottle was missing, and there was the muddled memory of handing out a few sour balls and lollipops. But she couldn't tell if that had been earlier that morning or the day before.

There was another knock. "Auntie?"

Her imaginings fell away at the sound of that word. She was Nephthys Kinwell. Or the Car Lady. She was nobody's aunt. "Wrong door," she said.

There was more knocking.

Reluctantly, with stiff and arduous movement, Nephthys

struggled from the chair. She hadn't bothered to change the ceiling light bulb and the light switch would be of no use. She shuffled to the window, tripping over empty bottles and shoeboxes filled with candy strewed about the floor, and inched the curtain aside. A blinding one-inch beam cut across the room like a laser probe. Was it midmorning or midafternoon? She went to the front door, heavy and cryptic like all low-income housing doors, and pulled hard. The potent smell of alcohol from her den slithered out like some phantom serpent as the hallway air rushed in.

A boy was standing under the flickering fluorescent hallway lights, staring up at her through two big eyes set in a chocolate face.

Dizzy, Nephthys leaned against the frame of the door in her formless housecoat, steadying her legs as she peered at the child. Even leaning, her head nearly brushed the top of the doorframe. In the antiseptic light, the silvery puff of her hair looked as if it had been sifted with flour. Nephthys stood over the child, squinting. And slowly, she realized that the boy was Dash, her great-nephew. His presence seemed impossible. But she'd learned many things about order and chaos in the southeast quadrant, how children of Anacostia appeared and disappeared. She glowered at the boy through yellow cat eyes scored with the bright-red lightning streaks of broken blood vessels. If she imagined the child, she would know it soon.

"Eh? Speak."

The boy seemed stunned.

Nephthys looked down the hallway, wondering (hoping?) if Amber, the boy's mother, had come there too. She heard only the sounds of other people and other lives behind the closed doors: babies crying, telephones ringing, men cursing. She looked again at the boy, squinting as if trying to see him from a great distance.

"Dash? Wuh you doin' here, baby cootuh?"

The boy fidgeted.

"Mama know 'bout you standin' here?"

"No, ma'am."

"Done left school, huh?"

"No . . . I had to leave early." Dash took out a folded piece of paper from his pocket and held it up to her like an offering.

"Wuh that there?"

"Nurse Higgins said to tell you it's a sick note."

"Wuh kinda sick?"

Dash looked away and held the letter out farther to Nephthys. "She told me to bring this to you."

"Me and not your mama?"

The boy was silent.

Nephthys looked at the paper in the boy's hand but did not take it from him. There was no use trying to decipher the words, a collection of symbols on paper. And she knew who Nurse Higgins was, knew her well. For there were some souls lost forever in the darkness, and a rush of memories about the nurse's son, Gary, flooded her mind. The grocery store and the lighter. The police and St. Elizabeths. And there were souls that she feared would soon be lost. Like Rosetta.

Nephthys pushed the thoughts away and gazed at Dash. "Nurse Higgins, huh? Well, come in, chile." She watched the boy step forward slowly, as if entering a chamber, navigating the floor of objects illuminated by the sunray's spotlight. He made his way to a radiator near the window and sat on top of it. Nephthys closed the door and turned the dead bolt. She scanned the living room for the missing bottle once more. Nothing. She looked at the boy, frozen where he sat. She was immune to the spoils of her habits and the reek of rot and ruin, but she knew that the child was not accustomed to the fumes of time. She lumbered over to the window, snatched the curtain aside, and opened it. The world's air entered and light and oxygen flooded the living room. Recoiling, she stumbled back to her chair and collapsed into it.

When her dizziness subsided, Nephthys looked at Dash clutching the letter in his hand. "Read."

Dash stared with a look of incredulity. "Me, ma'am?"

"Go on and read the letter fuh me, chile."

The boy unfolded the paper.

"And speak up, baby cootuh."

Dash blinked in the apartment's atmosphere. Slowly, reluctantly, he began:

Dear Nefthis,

Forgive me if I spelled your name wrong but I never had to write it down. Today Dash was suspended for fighting and sent home early. He took a rock to Roy Johnson's head and beat him silly, busted his forehead open and knocked out a milk tooth. It was extra bad on account of the fact that Roy is the principal's nephew. I had both of them with me after I pulled Dash off of Roy, and as soon as the principal heard what happened he wanted to expel Dash. I talked him out of it on account of I been knowing his mother at church for upwards of thirty-five years, and I said that come Sunday I'd tell her that he wasn't doing right by punishing one boy and not the other. Especially without asking no questions. He was ready to blow his top but he didn't cross me. Now he's saying if there's one more issue with Dash, he's out. Summer break is almost here. Lord knows there should be a way to deal with this before then. It would be a crying shame for the child to get all this way and then be put out of school at the end of the year.

But I really want you to know something else. I heard from the other children that the fight broke out because Roy was teasing Dash about talking to a man. Down by the river. A make-believe man. I wanted you to know about it and I didn't want to say anything to Amber about it on account of not knowing what that girl would do. But it's a strange

thing talking to a make-believe man. Odd and troubling. Maybe Dash needs a man's hand. Anyway, I think you need to see about him, even if you all don't talk. It's been a long time on a lot of things. Good and bad has passed. But you and I know that things can happen to a boy.
—Nurse Higgins

Dash stopped reading and looked out at the window-framed bright sky as if watching the words on the paper fly away. A deep silence sifted down into the room and settled over everything.

Nephthys shifted in her chair and worked what she'd heard the boy read around in her mind. *Down by the river.* There was only one river Nurse Higgins could have meant. And once more her blood ran cold and she shivered at the image of her brother's body.

She looked at Dash perched on the radiator and shook her head as if loosening the dust and moths from a dress worn only on special occasions. "Wuh happened at school?" She asked this with the innocence of a stranger, toneless and without judgment.

"Nothing, ma'am."

"Don't sound like nothin' to me."

"Just teasing."

"About a make-believe man?"

Dash was silent.

Nephthys had no plan to press the boy for an answer, for she'd seen many things in the darkened hallways of her mind and the byways of the quadrants. And in her years of ferrying souls from one place to the next, she'd learned that people were as real or as unreal as others wanted them to be. Which was one of the reasons why she drank. She reached once more for her flask and remembered that it was empty. Listless, she looked at Dash, this great-nephew whom she hardly knew. And she wished that she could conjure something matronly or mighty to say to him. What could she say? She didn't know. *But you and I know that things can happen to a boy . . .*

"Oonuh hungry? Nyam?"

Dash nodded and then shook his head, seeming to half comprehend what she meant. "No, ma'am."

"Rock candy?"

The boy sat up straight, brightening. "Do you have any mint?"

Nephthys scanned the cluttered floor for the rock candy as if deciphering a puzzle that she'd put together many times before. "Yeah, got mint. Get that Sears shoebox there," she said, pointing.

Dash stood up and moved across the jumbled floor like a blind man making his way through a crowded street. He spotted the Sears shoebox and kneeled in front of it and lifted the lid. It was filled with the colorful mayhem of every kind of candy. He rummaged through the box. And snaked in and around the wonderful pieces was a delicate strip of faded indigo cloth. He pulled it out and examined it, holding it up to the light. The cloth was made of heavy cotton, decorated with a dark-blue and white geometric pattern. "What's this?" he asked.

Nephthys was lost in her calculations of where the whiskey bottle might be. When she saw the indigo cloth Dash was holding, the tide of liquor in her blood receded. The cloth was hand dyed by her mother; a relic from another place and dimension, which like all bewitched treasures—ageless and so impossible—the ancients sought to keep from pirates by burying. Which was why she'd kept it inside an old hatbox in her closet. But how did it get in the Sears box, in the living room? She tried to make sense of it, but the tide of what she'd been drinking came in again and she was unable to do so. "Put that back," she said. Then, softer, "You can have more candy."

The boy put the indigo cloth back into the box as he was told and pulled out two more pieces of candy. "Thank you, Auntie," he said. He glanced at her and quickly looked away.

Nephthys stiffened. *Auntie.* The word ran down her back like cold water, a flash of a feeling that quickly faded into the lifelessness of a title she felt she'd never earned. But the gratitude she heard in the boy's voice resuscitated something in her heart that she thought was dead. "Welcome, Dash."

Nephthys rubbed her half finger as something else came alive inside. She was working her way around to asking about how the boy's mother was doing. There was no telling. Dash looked well enough. But Amber was capable of almost anything. And in that way that people in Anacostia ask loaded questions with loaded answers, Nephthys said: "How your mama been?"

Dash was enjoying the rock candy but the pleasant look on his face quickly faded. He shrugged. "Fine." He toyed nervously with the empty candy wrapper in his hand, folding it and unfolding it. And after a long silence he said, "I think Mama had a dream about me."

The words hit Nephthys like a rogue wave and she reeled in her chair. The old fear rose inside of her. Because Amber Kinwell knew things days or weeks or months before they happened. Sometimes years, it seemed. The woman with the peacock feather in her hat who drowned her husband's mistress in a bathtub. The six black boys murdered in a special cell of the capital jail. And who could forget the dead toddlers? Amber said she dreamed that a woman was going to kill her three children with rat poison. Two weeks later it was reported on the news that a woman named Cenna Henson had killed her three children (a two-year-old boy and three-year-old twins). It was later discovered that on the eve of the woman's eviction, she cooked an ambitious dinner and laced every delicious bite with rat poisoning. They were all found in poses—she and the toddlers—tranquil and polished, like cherub pieces in a menagerie. But there still seemed to be things that Amber didn't see, even in the horror of the ordinary. She saw the woman feeding her toddlers but not eating the food herself. She saw the little coffins but not the mother's casket beside them. Yet the dreams always seemed to come to pass, one way or another. Like her brother, the river, and the shark.

Nephthys rubbed her half finger. Could it be happening

again? Because there was only one time before when her niece dreamed about a Kinwell. Her stomach was turning and her head was buzzing. She closed her eyes, not wanting to see Dash's face when she asked the question, the same query that everyone had of Amber Kinwell whether they doubted her sanity or not. She gripped the arms of her chair with both hands, clenching her eyes tighter. "Wuh she see?"

Dash stared into the wasteland of objects on the living room floor as if the answer might be there somewhere. "She won't say. But I can tell it's about me."

Nephthys sighed. Even if the boy could tell her what the dream was about, was there anything she could do? She opened her eyes and looked at Dash. And had she been able to find her bottle earlier, she might have left the whole matter alone—the letter from Nurse Higgins and the dream—and watched them sail away with all the other reasons she drank. But now she couldn't.

Someone was singing loudly in the apartment hallway and Nephthys glanced at the grit-filmed clock on the wall, its hour and minute hands stuck in the same position for years. "School be lettin' out soon, won't it? Better get on home, Dash." What she meant was that she didn't want the boy in any more trouble for the day, because anything at all was possible in that little periwinkle-blue house at the bottom of the hill at the edge of the world. And she needed time to think.

Dash stood up from the radiator.

Nephthys watched him pick his way to the front door. And feeling helpless, she turned once more to the small things that she thought the old could offer the young, for she believed that sugar held great healing powers for the woes of any child. She struggled up from her chair and followed him to the door. She reached into her housecoat pocket and held out a red gumdrop. "Nyam. Eat."

Dash took the candy from her, staring at her half finger.

Nephthys turned the dead bolt, trying to smile, thinking of

what bothered her most about the letter. *Down by the river. A make-believe man . . .* A strange feeling crept into her and she pushed it away. "Oonuh push on through to tomorrow, baby coo-tuh," she said, and turned the knob and pulled the heavy door open.

At the threshold, each looked at the other as if their eyes could help them find what next to say. But there were no more words between them—the boy and his great-aunt—nothing to frame the door that opened to this place they were now sharing. A place that held secrets.

Dash stepped out and Nephthys watched him walk down the glum hallway of sounds until he was gone. Loud static from a record player somewhere announced the beginning of a rhythm and blues song:

Caught between infinity and life
Reachin' ever so high
Livin' it up before it's time to die
No bargain either way
Different kinds of judgment days
A million ways they make you pay
Caught between infinity and life . . .

LAND'S END

Dash headed home from his first-time visit to his great-aunt's apartment. It felt like he'd been there for days. He was energized now, proud of his excursion. He replayed the experience in his mind, remembering the strangers he approached in the hallways of the building, ignoring their startled looks when he asked where the "Car Lady" lived, as he heard people call her, for he didn't know which floor or which door. And he was riveted by the possibility of his mother walking up behind him and catching him there.

A pungent odor had blown out into the hallway and seized him at once when his great-aunt opened the door. He'd been unprepared for her height. She was so tall up close, the tallest woman he'd ever seen, and when she glared down at him with that haunted look in her red-streaked eyes, he'd lost his boldness. She towered above, asking questions in that rocking, mesmerizing way she talked. He was amazed by the dark, cavern-like apartment, the floor filled with unknown things. And there was that curious piece of deep-blue cloth buried in the shoebox. She didn't seem to like him touching it. But she was kinder than he thought she would be, and if there was so much candy readily available in a place like that, maybe the forbidden Nephthys Kinwell was not so bad. But most of all he thought about that half finger. He'd seen one like it before. On someone else.

Dash walked on. As he hurried down the street, he saw the ill-famed Plymouth parked nearby, a hulk of steel that people whispered about. From the weird distances that places like Anacostia can create, he'd seen his great-aunt many times in that car. His mother forbade him to speak to or approach this blood relative without ever explaining why, and in his ten short years of life he'd never been able to understand the bitterness between his mother and Nephthys. Others in the neighborhood seemed to know something about what it was, but it was like they were privy to some lurid conversation that had been going on without him. And there was something about the way folks said *those people* when they talked about the Kinwells, something that didn't seem good. But *those* people were *his* people, and something about that inescapable fact made him call the Car Lady he visited in the apartment "Auntie." Was that all right? He didn't know.

He walked on, hastening his stride through the spectrum of positives and negatives that places like Anacostia wrought: mothers handing treats to toddlers in strollers; policemen roping off alleyways with yellow tape; men waving to friends in passing cars; SWAT vehicles parked in front of buildings. He passed by the corner store he sometimes snuck out of the house to get to, thinking about the nurse's letter and having to read it. Reading came easy to him (a teacher once talked of skipping him a grade). But reading the letter aloud made him feel like he was on display. Why couldn't Nephthys read the letter on her own later? After all, it was addressed to her. And the lengths Nurse Higgins seemed to be taking to get to the bottom of his behavior troubled him. *But you and I know that things can happen to a boy . . .* What did that mean? Did the nurse know about what he saw on the day he opened that door at the end of the school corridor? He pushed the image of it away as he had so many times before, for it was still too big to fit into his mind.

He passed some men talking on a stoop. "What's up, shorty?" one of them said. Dash nodded to him and walked on.

There were other things that lingered in his thoughts about the letter. Like when he read "man's hand." People murmured that phrase when his mother insisted that he stand close to her on the rare times they came out together to run errands. He heard the men in the barbershop mumble it when she dropped him off every few months and waited outside. And he heard it again after the fight with Roy, when the principal was pointing his finger in his face, saying his mother needed to have him dealt with. He had always wondered if a *man's hand* somehow referred to his father, and this bothered him for reasons that he could not explain. He walked on, tired of trying to understand the things that people said. That was why it felt so good to shut Roy Johnson up, to bust his mouth for breathing a word about the River Man. And for talking about his mother.

Just before the fight broke out, Dash had been eating his lunch alone on one of the school benches when he heard his name.

"Dash Kinwell is crazy!" Roy Johnson announced. He was strutting around the schoolyard as if it were a stage. He'd skipped school earlier that week and hung out down by the river, and by chance he'd witnessed one of Dash's exchanges. He was so flabbergasted by the sheer luck of his discovery that he waited three days to share the juicy news. "Dash Kinwell is crazy!"

The schoolyard quieted as the other children grew silent. The Kinwells were long the subject of witchcraft and legend, and when they heard the Kinwell name they gathered as if warming themselves around a campfire.

Roy's eyes lit up with the thrill of the spotlight. A scrawny boy with a big mouth inherited from his gossip-mongering mother, his small stature would have made him an easy target. But he was the principal's nephew, and he took every opportunity to remind others of this fact. He relished pulling the ponytails of girls and throwing dirt on their dresses, sassing the teachers, and stealing coins from his classmates and then claiming that they were just jealous of his riches.

Roy waited for the other children to fully assemble and join him in the jeering. "That's right. I caught him talking to himself at the river. Talking to the air!"

A hush came over the children, for that meant Dash was *off.*

"Oooh . . ." a little girl named Lulu said. "You *crazy,* boy."

"And they gonna be bringing Dash up to St. Elizabeths soon," said Roy. "Because I saw him steady talking and steady nodding and wasn't nobody there." He looked over the heads of the children at Dash on the bench, laughing and pointing. "Hey, Dash! Tell 'em! Tell 'em! Yeah, you was just talking and wasn't nobody there. Jabbering and saying something to somebody. What you call him? The River Man, right? And who's the River Man? Nobody. Because Dash Kinwell is as crazy as his witch mama!"

The children gasped at the revelation that confirmed the things they heard their parents say. How Amber Kinwell's coiled hair turned to snakes with deadly venom when she got angry. How she had cephalopod ink coursing through her veins instead of blood. How her garden grew by the power of black magic. How she put roots on people she didn't like and "worked the moon" on anyone who looked her in the eye.

Dash was listening as he sat on the bench, his face growing hot. There were many things about his life that he'd learned to tolerate, but someone calling his mother crazy was not one of them. He stood up from the bench and headed toward Roy.

"Crazy as your mama! Crazy as your mama!" Roy was jeering. He was about to back down when he saw the look on Dash's face, but then he remembered that he was still the principal's nephew. And he knew—as all children of Anacostia do—that to show fear was to show weakness. He looked at the children watching, electrified by the bloodlust he saw in their eyes, and continued: "Yeah, that's why your mama got that head of snakes and your drunk-ass auntie drives that ghost car."

"Take that back," Dash hissed.

"And now you talkin' to yourself."

"Shut up!"

"The evil black Kinwells. Everybody knows all about that witch at the bottom of the hill and that drinking, demon-car-driving—"

"I said shut up, you little rat!"

"And a jive turkey who talks to himself by the river when *ain't . . . nobody . . . there.* I ain't see a soul but—"

That was as far as Roy Johnson got. Because by then Dash had picked up a rock and tackled him to the ground and was pummeling his face.

Dash continued his walk home from Nephthys Kinwell's lair, avoiding deep cracks in the sidewalk and the glass from broken bottles. He stepped over an exposed water main pipe jutting through the concrete. He heard the distant chimes of an ice cream truck, which told him that school had let out. Children seemed to come out of nowhere at the sound. A group of preschoolers appeared on someone's porch, and together they began a happy chant. Some dropped their toys and ran inside to ask for money.

An ambulance siren screamed by and Dash sped his stride. He was about to cross the street when he saw Lulu, one of the girls who'd joined Roy Johnson in taunting him earlier.

"You crazy, boy!" she shouted from across the street.

Dash walked on, ignoring her.

"Hey, crazy boy! Crazy as hell like that witch bitch."

Dash heard that word again. *Crazy*. And now the word *bitch*, referring to his mother. Boys weren't supposed to hit girls, he'd been told. But he thought about slapping Lulu into the sidewalk if she kept on.

"Crazy boy! Crazy boy!" the girl chanted. She had learned very early from her big sister Rosetta that there were two kinds of people in Anacostia: hunter and prey. *You be the hunter, not the prey,* she'd told Lulu before she ran away across the bridge. But later on, when Lulu saw her prowling the streets or getting in and out of cars, she caught a glimpse of some frightened thing that seemed to have crept into her big sister's eyes, so that she wondered if the hunter and the prey took turns being the other. "Witch bitch!" she shouted now with more fervor, until she crossed a woman sitting on her porch.

"What you say?" snarled the woman.

"Huh? Nothing."

"What you say?" asked the woman again, louder. "Ain't you Rosetta's little sister? I know your mama, girl. And I'ma tell her about your damn filthy mouth."

Lulu smirked, but she felt a chill inside. She wanted to tell the woman to kiss her ass, but she was not sure if what she'd said was true (about telling her mother). That could mean a whipping. She glared at Dash once more. "And plus . . . plus . . . your daddy was that crazy niggah from the war who used to be in your mama's garden! My mother said so!" She stuck out her tongue and ran back the other way.

Dash watched Lulu run off. *What was she talking about?* She didn't know his father. No one knew his father. But there were times when he looked at the picture of the blond-haired family in the unit chapters of his schoolbook (mother, father, little girl, little boy, golden retriever) and wondered who his father could be. He could think of him only as an idea or concept. Or a shadow coming down the hill. But his mother never spoke of him, not even his name. And no one ever asked how it was that Dash Kinwell came to be, since children born of Anacostia appeared and disappeared from one day to the next.

He walked on, passing an abandoned lot filled with weeds like tall wheat. He crossed the street and went by a row of boarded-up houses, the yards overgrown with an explosion of dandelions. Now he came to the hill that led to home and it was time to forget all he heard and saw on the street and empty his mind. He couldn't worry about Roy Johnson or Nurse Higgins's letter or Lulu's wild talk. Because now he would need all his strength for his mother.

* * *

Dash arrived at the edge of the world, the brink of a steep hill that dropped to a small valley where a lonely house stood dwarfed in a vast tract of mud, which from that distance looked like a slow, heaving river. The blanket of clouds that hung always with varying thickness over the little valley coated everything below in cerulean, so that the long-faded and chipped paint on the house appeared all the bluer. He knew that his mother was somewhere under that roof and gathered his strength.

Because she hardly left home unless pressed by the greatest of need. When she did, she was met with odd reactions that Dash had only noticed as he got older. Shopkeepers and vendors refused to conduct any business while standing directly in front of her. They collected money for their wares from a special basket kept on the edge of the counter for her payments. All things were sold to her at discount and always in ample supply, lest she need to make a special order or request that required them to look her in the eye. Every bus ride was free. What was harvested from her garden was bought at the price she asked, without inspection or negotiation, the money placed neatly in an envelope and left for her retrieval. There was the old Polish postmaster who answered yes to anything she said to him when she came in once a month to handle the mail. A telephone had never been installed at the Kinwell house. No one from the electric company ever came down for service calls or to disconnect the power line. And even in the blackouts of midnight thunderstorms, the single bulb hanging from the porch roof burned like the North Star.

Dash sighed, preparing for his descent. Because it would all start again when he reached the bottom and went in—his mother acting like something was going to happen to him. And he knew it had something to do with the dream about him, this dream that breathed always on their necks and gripped them both in the quiet of the rooms. He could tell by the way she looked at him now. It was the same way she looked at the people she talked about in the Lottery. And sometimes when he was hostage to her mania (heavy sleeping, insomnia, questions, silence), he wondered, reluctantly, if the things people said about his mother were true.

He trekked down, landing in the mud at the bottom. There was a garden on the side of the house, and in the microclimate of the valley, the soil was as rich as it had been since the Paleozoic era. The garden exploded with the most feral of produce many times larger than the normal size. Massive collard and kale leaves spread in Jurassic splendor. Mammoth carrots and turnips shot from the ground. Huge tomatoes and watermelons proliferated in a burst of shapes like a colony of boulders. In the rear was a gigantic stand of cornstalks that rose to the second floor of the house, and fat yellow cobs yielded early, so heavy that they dropped to the ground like apples from a tree.

Dash walked by the jungle of vegetation and reached the wood-planked porch, slippery with sediment like the teak of an old ship, and it bobbed and buckled as if it had been long overtaken by flood. The rotting shingles around the single windowpane saluted him with the usual dreariness. And as the air drained from his lungs, his body tightened and compressed with each step closer to the door. He looked up to the top of the hill once more, a kind of last-rites habit. The edge where he'd stood just minutes before was now obscured by the cloud coverlet. He took one last deep breath and turned back to face the entrance.

Dash looked into the translucent glass of the doorframe. The realm behind it waited. He put his hand on the doorknob, cold and slick with moisture, and pushed the door open with a *whoosh*. He stepped in. There was the oppressive density of the interior, which rushed over him immediately; a colorless odorless tasteless substance that filled the house for as long as he could remember, something that seemed thicker and more difficult to breathe than air. He stood in the drift and listened. Nothing. But he knew his mother must be somewhere in the depths. He looked around and cocked his ear. "Mama?" He ran his hand along the dew-coated wall, walking from room to room. What filled the house muffled his steps so that his movement was nearly soundless. He listened again. Nothing. "Ma?"

"You're back," said a sudden voice.

The acoustics of the house let Dash know that his mother's voice came from somewhere in the kitchen and he headed there. "Yes, Mama," he called out. "I'm home."

When he entered the kitchen, he saw a large cast-iron pot on the stove with bluish steam rising from beneath its heavy lid. On the table there were three enormous carrots that stretched across its top entirely, and a green pepper the size of a pumpkin squash. His mother was at the sink pulling the bones from a tray of rockfish with a pair of pliers. His heart skipped. Fish meant that she had gone shopping at the market—today of all days—and his stomach dropped. Did she see him creeping around town before school was out? Trying to stay calm, he reminded himself that he'd made it back in time to dodge suspicion. The visit to his great-aunt's apartment didn't delay him long enough to appear as if he was coming from anyplace else. His mother didn't know about the letter from Nurse Higgins. And she didn't sound upset with him.

Amber turned around and looked at him. Her eyes glistened with warmth but she did not smile. "Heard you come in."

Dash made a stoic face. The window above the sink filtered in light that accented his mother's long, coiled black hair, which clung to her thin frame like thick ropes of seaweed about some sunken statue. The birthmark between her eyes was obscured and only her full lips and chin were visible in the marine shadows. Even without a smile, Dash thought that she was beautiful, some enchanted waterborne species. He nodded. "I'm back."

"Thought I'd make some fried fish for dinner. I know it's your favorite."

"Sounds good. Do you want me to wash off the carrots?"

"After a while. Better start your homework, if you got any."

"No homework today."

"Really? Then come sit and help pick out the bones." She brought a tray of cleaned fish over to the table.

Dash pulled out a chair and sat down.

Amber handed him a slippery rockfish that was already halved. Dash held it in the light and looked at the skeleton sunk into the flesh. The splayed fish, with its delicate vertebrae, not yet seasoned and crispy with cornmeal, reminded him that it had once been a living thing. Now, like everything else in the house, it had been taken over and would be turned into something else.

"Just pull out the big bones," his mother was saying. "I'll come behind you and get the little ones."

Dash got into the rhythm of pulling away fins and skin and bone from the fish and dropping the flesh into the tray. But he knew the solace would soon end. Because he could feel the doom forming again, the enigma at the heart of everything between them: the dream. He braced for the ritual to begin, one of many.

"How was school?"

Dash didn't look up. "Ma'am?"

"I said was school okay today?"

"Yes."

"Was the walk all right? You came straight home, right?"

"Yes, ma'am."

"Nothing different?"

Dash dropped a piece of fish on the tray with the expressionless face that years of having Amber Kinwell for a mother had wrought. There would be more questions if he didn't keep his answers short. Nothing in his response could be out of place, the unmentionables kept hidden. The suspension and the letter. The mystical danger of Nephthys Kinwell's chamber. But more than that, as hard as it was to quarantine it at the edges of his mind, he had to shroud what he saw (imagined?) at the end of the school corridor. Behind that door in that other dimension. But if he'd imagined that, then he feared that he was also imagining the River Man, and he was not prepared for what that could mean or not mean. "Nothing, Mama."

VESSEL

Nephthys set out over the longitudes and latitudes of the Great Mystery, the ironclad vessel her only means, the shifting fog her only guide . . .

In the archipelagic dawn, Nephthys sat at the steering wheel of her car parked under a broken streetlamp outside of her apartment building. For the past three days, she'd been in her living room letting time slip by, drinking and raging at memories, searching for missing bottles and finding them again. She fell into slumber and came to, and in between she thought about the visit from Dash, which was difficult because that meant she had to think about Amber. They hadn't spoken in so long—she and her niece—and even though she lived just on the opposite side of Anacostia, it might as well have been the other side of the galaxy. Nephthys never had made up her mind about how to deal with the canyon between them, a divide that started with dreams and death. And she splashed and swam in what she'd been drinking to ease her feelings of guilt and the unbearable inertia of one.

Now she turned the key in the ignition and the steel beast sputtered to life. She opened a little container of Vaseline from her bag and dabbed a bit on her lips. She took out the flask from her pocket and looked at it, saying what she always said to herself before lifting it to her lips: *Biddy taste. Just a biddy taste.* She sipped and put the flask back in her pocket. *Shouldn't be drinkin',* she said to the dashboard as she'd said a thousand times before. She turned on the headlights, startling a rat in the street that quickly skittered back into the shadows. Someone turned on the light by a window in an apartment above and the silhouette stood frozen and then the light was turned out. She looked into the darkness and shrugged. Her services were needed. She charged what she wanted and people paid what they could. She never had to make what she was providing known, since anyone who required special transport knew who she was, what her car looked like, and what she did with it.

Nephthys watched a police cruiser speed by and turn into the mazes of the alleys and disappear. She took another drink from her flask and heard the familiar thump of the white girl in the trunk. Then she rolled the window down and waited for it to happen. And after a while, as always, the fog drifted into the car and Nephthys had that feeling once more. The feeling that made what she did with the Plymouth possible.

It started with the stillness, an arthritic feeling that had settled into her at the sight of her twin's body at the morgue. She stiffened bit by bit from that day forward and she found it harder and harder to move, as if her joints were calcifying. There were mornings when she awoke and thought that she was paralyzed. Her body creaked as she went about, and she felt wooden and brittle. Her blood thickened and her cells flagged as she tried to live as one in the world and not two. And every time the image of her brother's body flashed in her mind, she felt like she was slowly turning to stone, struck as she was by the unbearable inertia of one.

That was when the drinking started. She could find relief from the stillness; she could drift and float away. All the while she watched Amber grow and spread through the house on her own, without her, for the watery realm of the dwelling seemed keyed to the girl's every want and whim, and she germinated like some unknown underwater species and did what she wanted of her own accord. Nephthys struggled through the affliction of stillness as the days went by. She fed Amber from the feral garden and sent her up the hill to school. But each time Nephthys looked at this strange child of her brother, she'd fought back the question of how the girl could know and yet not know of her own father's demise. And she had stared out to the fearful unknown, wondering what they were going to do. They needed money. Her brother's income was gone and she'd left one island without the skills to function on another. *Gotta do*, she'd thought. *Gotta move.*

That was when the wandering started. And it was on one of her long walks, excursions to cope with the unbearable inertia of one, that Nephthys ended up on the edge of the southeast quadrant at Earl's Scrapyard. And in accordance with constellations, circumstances, and events, she roamed and rambled about the debris, until she came across a lanky man called Find Out.

He was tall—nearly seven feet—and grossly underweight. He was completely bald, and his dark and leathery skin wrapped about his skeleton like some bizarre jerky. The cartilage and joints in his body seemed fused as if by cement, and he walked unnaturally upright, his head bobbling atop his spinal cord. He wore black excrement-spattered rubber boots that came up to his knees, and in the firelight and shadows of the high stacks and spires all about, he looked like an embalmer, a great Anubis guarding some vast plain of pyramid graves. And it was said that he could find anything in the entire world. He brought Tahitian pearls to high-rolling poker games in basement bars on U Street. He delivered a blue boa constrictor to a blind woman living in the clock tower of the Old Post Office Pavilion (she wanted a pet to match the eyes she could no longer use).

As Nephthys approached, Find Out glared with the dark and sunken eyes of some creature drawn in a comic book. "What you want?"

Nephthys looked into the countless piles behind the tall man. There were massive stacks, tunnels of scrap that seemed to lead to other tunnels, and she wondered what it might be like to enter and move through yet more places and spaces. *Gotta move*, she thought. She looked back at the imposing man. "Somethin', maybe."

"Lady, if what you lookin' for was here," said Find Out, scowling, "I would know about it. I'm Find Out and I been knowing everything." Because aside from the cause of the haunting image of his wife's face in the raging bonfires of the night, he knew all that could be known about what was lost and what was found. He even kept a tin can hidden deep in one of the junk piles. It was filled with what he called "last things," those final items that a lost soul possessed. Like the last Nacotchtank Indian's leather cord and a runaway slave's silver coin. Like the gold necklace he found in that trunk and the little pink hair barrettes he found in a creek. There were those last things and more. But no matter how desperate he was to relieve the pain of losing what he could never find by selling or trading what he collected, once he put something in his secret tin can, he never touched it again. Because for reasons that he could not explain, he felt responsible for the safekeeping of these last things in a kind of cosmic escrow, until those who lost them came looking in this life or the next.

"Just want to pass on through," Nephthys said, looking into the skeins of the scrapyard. She was feeling the onset of the stiffness again, and she grew anxious as she stood talking to the stranger. "Gotta do. Gotta move."

"Ain't no way to pass through this place, lady. All's you can do is move around in it."

Nephthys shrugged, intrigued. "Long as I can keep going, I aim to move around forever."

"Look, lady. Leaving is all you can do." Find Out was getting aggravated by her being there, an interruption of his fixation, for the substance he needed to stay dead was calling him again. But then he saw a swirl of blue smoke form and rise behind her and gather about her head. It was an unusual sight—the smoke showing him someone he hadn't been searching for—and he looked at the woman carefully. "What's your name?"

"Nephthys."

"What?"

"Nephthys."

"What you want, Nephthys?"

"Ain't sure."

The blue smoke of his trade had trailed down a tunnel of flattened and stacked steel, and Find Out thought of the Plymouth he'd found by the Anacostia River and parked back there. It was just where he left it all those years ago. And now he wondered, as he watched the blue smoke curl above this woman's head, if she was who the car and its occupant were waiting for. Like the last things in his tin. "You wanna see it?"

"Wuh?"

"The car."

Nephthys shrugged again, eager to get moving. "All right."

They walked deep into the metal cavern, each tunnel of refuse tunneling into another, one pathway dimmer than the one before it. On they went, until they came upon the car like the discovery of an eighth wonder of the world. A 1967 Plymouth Belvedere, blue like the sky.

Find Out pushed away the steel bumper of a truck that had fallen on the hood without leaving a single scratch. He stood by the trunk and waited, listening.

There was a low thump.

He looked at the blue smoke circling, thinking about how the car had once served one purpose but now might serve another. The key was still in the ignition. "Try it."

"Why fuh?"

Find Out watched the blue smoke swirl about the car. "You'll know. All I know is that it's yours."

Nephthys looked sideways at Find Out. "Cyan't drive. Never learned."

"It won't matter."

The stiffness was getting worse but Nephthys hesitated.

"Go ahead. It's your car."

Nephthys looked at the Plymouth, incredulous. "Cyan't be no car of mine."

"But it is. Go on."

Nephthys got into the car and sank down into the seat.

"Turn the ignition."

"Wuh?"

"Turn it on."

Nephthys fingered the key and turned it. The car roared to life.

"See, like I told you."

Nephthys listened to the engine rumble, thinking of the places she could go, how she could keep moving with such a vessel. If only she could drive.

There was a loud thud from the trunk.

"One more thing," said Find Out. And here he paused, thinking about that night when he passed out in the tall reeds of the Anacostia River, and awoke to two men pulling a body from the trunk of the Plymouth. Through the smog of the substance he'd been consuming so as not to feel alive, he watched the men carry the body to the banks and throw it into the current. He found what traces were to be found after they were gone, including a gold necklace he fished out of the trunk and put in his tin can. "The car is haunted," he said. "But she won't hurt you."

"Who?"

"The white girl in the trunk."

Nephthys blinked. "Oh."

There was another loud thud.

Find Out watched the blue smoke swirl and dissipate slowly. "Look like she been waiting for you."

Nephthys then felt an inexplicable comfort as she gripped the steering wheel. She looked at Find Out. They would later engage in another transaction—she and this man—the likes of which could not yet be imagined. But as she stared into the dashboard, she knew what was next. And without having to be taught any steps, she released the brake and put the car in drive, pressed her foot on the gas pedal, and maneuvered out of the tunnels of the scrapyard.

Nephthys took the haunted Plymouth wherever her wandering heart carried her, the ghost in the trunk a kind of charm it seemed, for she was never stopped by the police, nor did the car break down for any reason or ever run out of gas. The fuel gauge remained in the same position since its trunk dweller's fateful night—three-quarters full—and never moved again. But one dawn, as she sat in the Plymouth near the banks of the Potomac River, a fog formed over the surface of the hood. It grew thicker and rose higher. Nephthys stared through the windshield as it moved toward her, and it snaked into the car and coiled around her thoughts, giving them voice and eyes and skin.

The truth was that Nephthys wasn't the first, for there was one of her kind in each epoch. The last one was an enslaved woman who hailed from the Ashanti Empire. She once lived on the campus of Columbian College (which later became George Washington University) with the wealthy college steward who owned her. And she too looked into the fog and heard the cry of wandering hearts. For in that low visibility of the fog's atmosphere, where the living felt around as if blind, the fog tried to help men realize that they were but creatures of passage, pointing the way from one destination to another. So that the enslaved woman snuck off the Columbian campus each dawn and moved in secret from one quadrant to another, helping those she heard in the fog to escape elsewhere.

But Nephthys had no way of knowing this as she sat in the Plymouth in Foggy Bottom, staring into sentient mist. What she knew was that every phosphorous dawn after that, the fog came to her, and she heard within it the eerie call of wandering hearts. And that was when her unbreakable bond with the fog began.

* * *

A dog barked in the dawn and Nephthys shifted in the driver's seat, feeling stiff. She looked at the timepiece on the Plymouth's dashboard. She'd been looking at it for years now, not because she needed to know the time, for she had her own sense of the passage of minutes and hours. She looked for the assurance of knowing exactly what the pointing arrows indicated. They read 5:35 a.m. She nodded, comforted by the surety of the hands. Because numbers were more certain to her than words. And in her decades of living, she had learned that she knew more than what letters and words and sentences could describe, and she saw and felt and spoke of things that such glyphs were too limited to convey. What the alphabet formed in little combinations had never held more importance to her than the happenings of those who lost their way. Or found it.

She peered into the dawn and waited. And after a while the fog came and thickened around her. Now she could feel it. *The colonel's wife*, she thought. *It's the colonel's wife today.* She put her foot on the gas pedal and disembarked, coasting down the street.

MESSAGES

Nephthys heard things whispered over the water in the stygian nights, and she gazed across the fathoms deep, wondering where that solitary black began and ended . . .

Nephthys drove downtown toward the Ebbitt Hotel in the northwest quadrant once more, where the fog told her the colonel's wife would be waiting. She passed street signs and highway signs and posters plastered on street poles. She recognized some words more easily than others, but only if they came with a place where she had experienced something. She knew residential signs not because of what the letters indicated, but because the spot where the signs stood marked indelible places in her mind. The Safeway grocery store on East Capitol Street, for instance. That was where a young man she'd taken was hauled away to St. Elizabeths. And each time she drove by, the memory played in her mind.

Besides, there was always help if Nephthys needed it. There were nice black office girls in Dupont Circle who were still living with their parents until marriage. There were proud young men from Howard University who answered her questions or offered instructions in lengthy orations, asking her, "Ma'am, can you remember all of that?" In fact, Nephthys could remember what they were saying and the color and pattern of the shirts they'd been wearing if she spoke to them five months before. Words were but a calling out of symbols that held purpose only when put together, but meaningless apart. Images were files in her head. Sounds and conversations were permanent, recordings grafted onto her mind. And she'd always felt that the lettering, the glyphs that other people seemed to need to use, was a lower form of communication. So there was no need to say the words *I can't read.*

As she approached the Ebbitt Hotel, she saw the colonel's wife sitting in the familiar black car parked in front. Sometimes, in the wanderings of her own heart, she wondered where else the destinations of her passengers might lead, and she stared at the woman and through her and out to the reaches of the territories.

The colonel's wife felt her pulse quicken when she saw the Plymouth coming down the street. She'd risen well before dawn that morning in the Kingdom of Virginia, where she lived in a beautiful home in the fiefdom of Alexandria. She knew that her husband, Colonel Piper Abramson, lay silent in their rosewood-framed bed each time she left for her covert passage, pretending to be asleep. She'd watched him spend thirty years of his life in the sunless moonless airless rings of the Pentagon, and she knew that he was prepared to spend thirty more roaming the pathways of denial. Because she'd learned, among the long list of things ascertained from her appalling in-laws, that children of respectable families did not have mental illnesses. And there were times when she wondered if her husband was right, that their son's condition had somehow come from her own savage beginnings, for she hailed from the Nordic outback of the Upper Peninsula in the Kingdom of Michigan. And each time she sat in wait for Nephthys to arrive, she stared into the dawn, contemplating the role she played in their son's biological demise.

Nephthys pulled up in front of the Ebbitt and stopped, the Plymouth idling softly.

The colonel's wife got out of her car and locked it and came over and slid into the backseat. She handed Nephthys a crisp one-hundred-dollar bill, a small fortune she felt worth paying for the important task at hand, for she was uncomfortable with boarding a bus, where everywhere she turned there seemed to be eyes questioning her reason for being there. Nor did she want to catch cabdrivers stealing looks at her through the rearview mirror in judgment of where she asked them to take her. So it was no surprise that the colonel's wife thought it fitting to ride to Anacostia in the safety of Nephthys Kinwell's Plymouth to see her son in one of the psychiatric wings of St. Elizabeths Hospital. It was where she and her husband had him committed six years before, so that their neighbors and the rest of the family could go on thinking he was studying medicine in Europe. Many years later, another son of privilege would make his own living film by attempting to assassinate a movie-acting king, but instead end up entombed in the same walls as her own son. And like other mothers who crossed into that wild realm of the southeast quadrant, each time the colonel's wife entered St. Elizabeths she left a piece of herself there.

The white girl in the trunk rattled the crank of a broken car jack and Nephthys pulled off.

"Morning, Neph," said the colonel's wife. She'd never been able to pronounce that peculiar name in all its fullness—Nephthys Kinwell—and they'd agreed without ever saying aloud that the abbreviated "Neph" was acceptable to each of them for different reasons.

"Mornin' it is," said Nephthys.

They rode on, pausing for motorcades and funeral processions and pulling over so that fire trucks could pass. In the usual silence that ensued, the colonel's wife listened to the bump scrape tap of the white girl in the trunk, thinking about what such dark lingering could mean or not mean. For she made her clandestine trips to St. Elizabeths not only to see about the well-being of her son, but to also see how close he was to death. She thought about death more often as she grew older, as the reality of not having any grandchildren settled into the foundation of her opulent colonial home. But more than her own fatal musings, she thought about her son's ravings. On her last visit, he spoke of the long conversations he had with Death when it came to his room in a black robe and sat by his bed. And he talked matter-of-factly about the five ways that Death told him creatures of passage die:

1. Moving through spaces
2. Staying in one place
3. Resigning life to another
4. Surrendering one's life
5. Entering the Void

Her son confessed to her that he knew the last one well, since the Void called to him through the expanding kilometers of his madness long before he strangled his girlfriend to death. And he was certain that the Void would obliterate him on his thirtieth birthday. The colonel's wife was terrified and intrigued by the things her son said to her, and in her long, empty days in the catacombs of the family mansion, she read books on the mysticism of astrological patterns and tarot readings of death and theories of the afterlife.

So it was no surprise that the colonel's wife made a point to pick up a copy of the *Afro Man* newspaper in the lobby of St. Elizabeths on her last visit, for she'd heard that the Lottery section was all about death and who was next. And it was through the guarded conversations she'd had with the orderlies who checked her purse for weapons and contraband that she discovered the Lottery had been in print for over ten years, and that its author was Nephthys Kinwell's niece.

They waited at a stoplight, listening to the Plymouth's engine clack and the white girl in the trunk drum the spare tire. A man standing on the corner was humming a popular song to himself, and when he saw the unmistakable Plymouth he stopped and walked the other way. The light turned green and Nephthys pulled off.

The colonel's wife watched Nephthys take sips from her flask, never worrying about her ability to drive. But sometimes she paused at other things about her, like the curious lilt in her voice. Not quite Southern. Not quite Caribbean. "Where are you from?"

"Sea Islands."

"Oh?"

"Uh-huh. My people were Gullah."

"What?'

"Gullah."

"Gullah . . ." said the colonel's wife, baffled. "And your name, what's the origin?"

Nephthys shrugged. "Don't know the whole story."

Because the truth was that the twins were named by a butler on the old Sea Island plantation where their parents had been employed as servants. The butler was an ageless man brought to the island on a pirate ship as a child, his own given name and lineage long lost. And in accordance with the dark irony with which creatures of passage live, his ancestors and descendants were folded into the pages of time, hidden as they were in the convoluted bloodlines that land conquest and slave auctions and breeding rapes brought. For unbeknownst to the butler, he was both a descendant of the Ethiopic scribes of Geez and a distant Kinwell forefather. And he had secretly taught himself to read and write without ever understanding his burning need to do so, nor why he knew the gravity of names. So it was no surprise that when he'd heard about the birth of twins holding hands—that their fingers were fused at the tip—he snuck into the parlor where the plantation owner's old African expedition letters were kept, for there he knew he would find the requisite signs omens bones. He sifted through them until he was obliged to write two names down on a scrap of paper, his own kind of papyrus: Osiris and Nephthys. And in the naming of the Kinwell twins, he satisfied his ancient urge to scribe something on the wall of being that was undiminished, everlasting.

But Nephthys had no way of knowing about the butler's indelible hand as she drove through the streets of the quadrants with the colonel's wife in her car. What she knew was that her mother told her that the old plantation owner liked to say that niggers came from a place called Nowhere, and in that place there was nothing, because what made them and the things that they made held no value at all. That they had no part in the treasures of a dark continent, being just animals among many in the kingdoms of those lands. And her mother had said that the butler told her this was not true.

Nephthys turned onto the bridge and looked at the colonel's wife in the rearview mirror. "From wuh I know, a man from the old days gave my mother the name."

"Oh." The colonel's wife would have liked to talk more about that, outlandish as it sounded, for their exchanges were without praise or scorn. But she had a more pressing question. "I heard that the woman who does the Lottery is your niece. Amber Kinwell, right?"

Nephthys reached for her flask, bracing as if a box had been opened that she preferred to keep closed.

"Such a gift."

"Don't know if it's a gift."

"How can she *live* with such a talent?"

"Talent?"

"Ability. How does she live with it?"

"Don't know how much livin' is possible." And here Nephthys thought of Amber in that realm where she'd left her.

They rode on, the colonel's wife now silent in the backseat as she gazed out the window at the quadrants. Over a century before, from his controversial appointed post, Frederick Douglass had signed the deeds of Washingtonians still believing in the dream of owning something that had already been taken out of so many hands; places marked by the blood absorbed and bodies buried beneath the quadrants. Many years later, the quadrants would be consumed by a neoplasm of surveyors and developers, a superstate of cranes and constructs. Neighborhoods and vestiges of other eras would vanish into the folds of time. Little old ladies and cane-walking men would amble the city in a state of stupefied grief, pointing at unrecognizable places made more unrecognizable by the Lego-block stacking of pricey loft apartments and the sprawling offices of government agencies and their contractors.

The colonel's wife peered out the window. The closer they got to the brick-faced institution, the gaunter and more wide-eyed she became, so that by the time Nephthys drove down Martin Luther King Jr. Avenue and turned onto the medical campus, she felt her body stiffening as if struck by rigor mortis.

Nephthys stopped and turned off the car. In the silence she felt that familiar unease each time she made this passage, for its destination made her think about Nurse Higgins's son.

At last the colonel's wife put her hand out and gripped the door handle as if it might keep her from falling through the floor of the Plymouth and into the colorless bottomless chasm of the Void. "A couple hours," she said hoarsely, and got out of the car.

Nephthys watched the colonel's wife walk to the entrance slowly. Two orderlies were waiting, receiving her as if she were first in line at a wake. The large door closed behind her, where she would be locked in the space-time continuum of St. Elizabeths until she came out again. Nephthys looked away from the entrance and stared at the dashboard. Now the Alexandria woman's questions loomed in her mind. She shook her head, trying to make the thoughts forming dissipate. The river and her brother. The dream about the shark.

She recalled that Amber had been twelve years old when the dreams started. They seemed unstoppable by the time she turned seventeen, and her prophecies pelted the house in an endless drip of water. Nephthys remembered that final day clearly. She was sitting with Amber on the deck of the front porch, listening to her talk of a man who would freeze to death in front of the Morton's Department Store and the little girl who would fall down an elevator shaft in a code-shy building in one of the quadrants. And that was when Nephthys realized that she couldn't take any more. She couldn't bear the constant death tolls that only deepened the bitterness of her own grief. And every time she looked at Amber, she wondered how it was that she seemed to know so much about the downfall of others and so little about what had happened to her twin. How could Amber not have known what was to happen to her father when she seemed to know so much about everyone else? And when Nephthys looked at her niece, she loved her and hated her too.

So there were reasons why she left Amber at the bottom of the hill, Nephthys reminded herself, staring at the cold facade of St. Elizabeths. Reasons why she drank. She took a sip from her flask and noticed an orderly staring at her from one of the windows. When he seemed to realize that she saw him, he stepped away quickly. Nephthys knew it would be several hours before the colonel's wife emerged from the labyrinths of the building, her face sheet white from listening to the messages of her son's madness.

She turned the key in the ignition. Her half finger throbbed and she looked into its lightless tip. It bothered her that there might be other kinds of messages. Like the long-ago song riffs she sometimes heard in her head. Like the bottles that moved of their own accord in her apartment. Like what she thought might have been in the wall mirror, now broken on the floor. Or who.

She gripped the steering wheel, put her foot on the gas pedal, and drove away.

SORCERY

At the site of the hit-and-run accident that left a pregnant woman in a pool of blood on a street in Anacostia, an infant splashed inside her mother's cooling fluids. As the woman moved from one plane of existence to another, the preborn lay quiet in her amniotic water, listening to the sound of her progenitor's heartbeat slowing to a stop. And in accordance with the law of reciprocity, where nothing is taken without something granted, Death whispered the star recordings of lives into the infant's ear, gifting her with the vision of another life's end. With each tale of reckoning the infant's eyes widened anew, unblinking in the darkness of the womb. And when finished whispering the register of fates, Death touched the neonate's forehead lightly with its finger, leaving a mark.

Amber stood at the kitchen sink, staring through the window at a small stand of old trees. She was doing this more and more, and each time she felt like someone was staring back at her, waiting. But everything was as it had been the day before, with the lily patches and tree gnarls and knobs unchanged. The places where lightning had written its name on the bark remained. There was no one there.

Puzzled, she turned away from the window and finished washing the breakfast dishes. Now that Dash was off to school, the house was quiet, save for the creaking of its hull. She stood listening to the silence, feeling listless. Unlike so many other days, she didn't want to idle away her time washing and cutting the spoils of the feral garden. She was not in the mood to fill the long hours with endless tasks: shaking out the sediment-covered blankets; wiping condensation from glass; scraping the verdigris from the kitchen chairs; gouging mud from the hallway floor planks; collecting salt from corners.

She poured herself a glass of water and sat down at the table, watching particles float by in the cool, interminable current like phytoplankton. But even in that calm, flashes of the dream about Dash took hold and she began to fret once more, for the dream seeped into everything. She stood up from the table and paced the floor. She thought about going up the hill but couldn't decide why. Was it to look for the unknown man in the dream? But how? It all played in her mind. A forest. A dead cardinal falling through the trees. A faceless man, lurking, then chasing. Then Dash running through the trees. She could see him lying in a creek.

Her blood ran cold at the last image. It maddened her that she couldn't see more. Just flashes. The only thing that was clear was doom. Nothing like that first dream when she was a girl. Nothing like the shark. Her mind raced. Who was the faceless man and why was he chasing Dash? Maybe she should be walking him to school and back from now on? Or just keep him at home? Then she would sleep better and watch him more. *I could keep him in the house . . .*

A knock at the door startled her and she jumped. But then she remembered that it was the second Monday of the month. That meant it was time for the Lottery, the last thing she wanted to think about now.

There was another knock.

Sighing, she made her way to the front door and opened it.

Mr. Johnson was standing on the porch, stomping and scraping his feet, a feeble attempt to remove the thick mud from his shoes. He held the elegant air of a jazzman in his sand-colored suit and brim hat. He ran the storied *Afro Man*, a local independent newspaper that featured stories about the state of black people in the territories. On the second Monday of each month, Mr. Johnson came to the bottom of the hill to personally speak with Amber Kinwell. A tenacious businessman and one of the few people who ever dared visit, he understood the dollar value of Amber's dark gift to the sales of his newspaper. He'd been listening to the stories about her for years. The sea breeze that preceded her wherever she walked. How her wild black hair held a supernatural tint, and how her shoulder blades were dusted with salt crystals. The warnings never to look her in the eyes, the only protection against her glare of ruination. People said that the birthmark on her forehead was the thumbprint of the Devil. He heard these things and more and didn't believe most of it. But he was never sure about her eyes.

Mr. Johnson smiled without looking up. "Good morning, Ms. Kinwell."

"Morning," Amber said, holding the door open.

"Thank you. I'm glad we meet again." The newsman's eyes traveled up slowly, stopping at the wonderland of her hair.

Amber nodded. She knew that he made a point never to look at her directly like everyone else, but she liked his warmth and ordinariness. And he didn't seem to fear her.

Mr. Johnson took off his hat and stepped over the threshold into the foyer. Once inside, the lighter palettes of the outside world just steps away melted into deeper hues. No matter how many times he'd been to the house, he was never prepared for that darkening. Gradually, his eyes adjusted as he stood in the vestibule, and he felt his heart slow in the thickness of what he now had to breathe. "Appreciate you having me over."

"Can I offer you some coffee?"

"Awfully kind, but no thank you." He followed her down the hallway. "Drank a whole pot last night and haven't been to sleep yet. Had a problem with a story and almost missed our deadline. Nearly knocked me down. But we got it straightened out." He let out a nervous chuckle as he followed her into the kitchen.

"Please have a seat," said Amber. "Water?" She took a pitcher from the pantry.

In the heaviness of the house, water was the last thing the newsman wanted. "Sure, I'll have some." He looked into the pantry. The shelves were crowded with rows of mason jars filled with the bounty of the garden, he supposed. But in that beryl light, the contents looked like huge globules in lava lamps. And although he'd been to Amber's amphibious lair before, the spectacle of her astonished him every time. The floating vines of her hair like ropes of seaweed. The black sheen of her orca-like skin and her thin, chiseled limbs. He stole looks from the corners of his eyes and watched her pour water into a glass, fascinated.

Because the truth was that the newsman believed in Amber's ability and power, for he hailed from the mystic bayous of the Kingdom of Louisiana. He was raised by a grandmother whom even the rulers of that land consulted before making any serious decisions. His grandmother was a magic woman, a seer who spoke of what she called the Great Loop, and he thought about the things she said each time he was in Amber's presence. She talked of how damnation was the inescapable circle one made around oneself. How payment would come due for the plunder and ravage of the earth, for there would be superstorms to drown millions and pathogens crawling from one place to the next. She spoke of the cycle of happenings in the empires of the world, with each century marked by the same gall of deed and outrage of talk. But more than anything, he remembered his grandmother saying: "We just going round and round, we creatures of passage. And we gonna keep going round till we understand the Loop." And sometimes when he looked at the glint of Amber's dark skin, he thought of his grandmother's tale about the black wolf whose coat was slick with the elemental oils of the spaces through which he passed, and how the wolf knew the start and end of all stories. So it was no surprise that the newsman was inclined to take Amber and the Lottery seriously, since from his grandmother he'd inherited the tremendous strength to record the happenings of the ages and then watch them repeated.

"Make yourself comfortable," said Amber.

"Don't mind if I do. Hope you've been well."

Amber rubbed her eyes. She hadn't slept much again. "Well enough."

Mr. Johnson looked at the flower print on Amber's dress. He'd been visiting her each month for a long time, except for that brief period years ago, when she asked him to stop. He'd heard gossip that it was because she had a man around then, but he could never confirm who it was. And then he'd heard she had a baby, so that must have been the son's father. What happened to him? He didn't know. The newsman smiled and looked into the tendrils of Amber's hair. "Appreciate your time today, Ms. Kinwell. Can't believe it's June already. The year has just been flying by. How's your boy?"

Amber filled her own glass with water and didn't respond.

Mr. Johnson cleared his throat in the awkwardness of the moment. "I thought we might discuss the Lottery in the usual manner today. As you know, folks take an interest, and I never was one to dismiss the powers of the spirit world."

Amber looked beyond him to the window over the sink that framed the trees. She felt that strange sensation again, as mysterious to her as the origins of her ability. She gazed back at the newsman from across the kitchen table. "You know, my mother died before I was born."

Mr. Johnson was looking at the angles of Amber's collarbone, prepared for anything she wanted to discuss, but he was yet unsettled by her sudden statement. He scratched his head. "Childbirth?"

"They say it was a hit and run."

"Goodness gracious. They ever catch who did it?"

Amber shrugged.

"Mighty heavy load, not knowing." He was curious about

something else now. Because although he'd heard of the tragedy of how Osiris Kinwell was later found, he'd always wanted to know more about his twin he saw driving around sometimes; if what people said she did with that Plymouth was true. And why she and Amber seemed to have nothing to do with each other. He shifted in his chair and began carefully. "Some terrible things have befallen your family and I'm so sorry. Must have been hard on your aunt too."

The house creaked and a wave of silence rolled into the room.

The newsman looked at the glass of water in front of him and suddenly it was all he wanted. He drank it down in one long gulp and the heaviness in his chest eased.

"Yes," Amber said. "My aunt Nephthys." And here she waved a hand as if the gesture would clear the subject away. Because talking about Nephthys meant she had to think about the very first dream she'd ever had. She had to think about her father, the river, and the shark. "Let's get the Lottery done now."

Mr. Johnson didn't press the matter further. He took out an envelope containing her payment from his jacket pocket and placed it gingerly on the table. Then he took out a pen and a small pad. "I'm ready when you are. Say the word."

Amber leaned back in her chair. As always, a kind of nausea washed over her like seasickness. She didn't have to conjure the flashes of her dreams, since they came to her of their own accord. But each dream had different details. And now she was too exhausted to say anything but the basic elements, since the one dream worrying her took up most of the space in her mind. She tilted her head and began:

1. Police raid. Green house with the big philodendron on the porch. Body in the closet.
2. Pink pacifier and bottle. Box buried in the yard. Frederick Douglass house. Study cottage in the back.
3. Red, white, and blue beads on the ends of braided hair.

Train tracks. Washington Bullets T-shirt. Kingman Lake.
4. Wires on fire. Apartment on Dotson Street. No numbers on the doors. Windows nailed shut. Woman can't breathe.
5. A mother. Five children. A man named Wilson holds his arm and loses his heart.

Amber stopped and twirled a lock of hair around her finger and let out a long sigh.

Mr. Johnson was writing furiously on his notepad, recording every word she said, and he put his pen down when she stopped. As always, her death dreams were ghastly, more so because he knew they came true. Young women killing themselves when they'd fallen on hard times. Houses burning down with families in them. Shootings and stabbings and poisonings. Boys hung in jail cells and that sort of thing. Despite the fortitude inherited from his grandmother, the death dreams bothered him long after he wrote them down and had them printed. He had stopped confirming the gory details of Amber's foretelling in the television reports and obituaries, for this interfered with his ability to sleep at night. He stared into the green lines of the table. "Is that all?"

The floorboards of the house creaked as if buckling from some unseen pressure.

There's more, Amber thought, staring at her guest's empty glass. There was so much more in the five visions than what she'd described. And there was the dream about Dash. But speaking of that meant acknowledging what she couldn't bear to accept. "Yes, that's all of it."

Amber stood topside on the wood-warped porch like the deck of a ship, watching Mr. Johnson drift into the mist until he was out of sight. Her legs grew tired and she sat on the step, weary from the doldrums of precognition. Once more she thought about that first death dream when she was twelve, a bizarre and horrible vision about her father. And once more she tried to understand the reason why she'd seen him eaten by a talking shark but was unable to do so. *It's just a dream*, she'd told herself back then.

And she'd believed it for a while too, until her father's body was found. When Nephthys came back from the morgue with the news, Amber ran around the garden, screaming. Later on, she told her aunt the dream she'd had about the shark. She remembered Nephthys telling her that it didn't mean anything and should be forgotten. "Real be worse than any dream," she'd said. But from that moment on, there was something about the way Nephthys looked at her: an accusatory gaze, a silent rebuke. The dreams were more frequent after that, and they got worse as she grew older. Different people with different deaths. More chilling in clarity, more terrifying in accuracy.

Amber stared into the thickening cloudcap. Neither she nor Nephthys had ever found out the particulars of her father's undoing from the autopsy or the police; how he ended up in the river or who put him there. But the facts of the chewed-off leg and ravaged body followed them wherever they went, floating about the rooms of the house, festering and poisoning everything between the two of them, until her father's death drowned them both.

Amber got up and went back to the kitchen and cleared the table. At the sink she looked into the small stand of trees. Again, they seemed to stare back at her, full of the enigma that places like Anacostia create. And once more she asked the silent wood what she'd asked a thousand times before: *What happened?*

PARABLE OF THE DREAMER

The great white moved through the water like a submarine on watch for the enemy, his icy glare matched only by his cold will. His bleached underbelly was as massive as that of a whale, and his serrated teeth jetted from mammoth jowls that sucked in water like some wild sinkhole. The beast powered through the currents he'd marked as his territory, magnetic north guiding his dorsal fin from one point of the horizon to another. He swam on, an unrelenting patroller, until he spotted a man in a boat and rocketed toward him.

The great white circled the craft and said to the man, "You're in my waters."

The man sat calmly in his boat. His dark and bare legs spanned almost to the bow, and he braced them as he adjusted the line of his sail, anchoring it around the half finger of his hand like a hook. He looked at the shark. "Waters can't be yours."

The shark surveyed the miles of briny deep he had already cleared and turned a glacial eye to the man. "These waters are mine and I'm going to kill you."

"Why?"

"Because I can. Because I am."

"I am too."

"You exist only because I am looking at you."

"You really believe that?"

"I do."

The man peered over the water at the peopled land and back at the shark. "You can't kill us all."

"Makes more to hunt."

"But more to come."

"True," said the shark. And he opened wide his great orifice and bit into the side of the boat with the force of a bomb, dragging the man under.

ISLE OF BLOOD AND DESIRE

Anacostia, that isle of blood and desire, was its own kind of cay. For those who dwelled there sometimes forgot where the southeast quadrant ended and the other quadrants began, and the happenings of their small spaces was the world entire. And because of the spells of fortune and misfortune cast down on that wafer of earth through the eras, each year compounded the consequences of the next, so that one Anacostian scrutinized another as if looking at the last of his kind.

Amy Riley had this feeling of obsolescence each morning when she stared across the kitchen table at her husband, Brandon, in their childless, brick-faced home on Alabama Avenue. She hailed from a bleak floodplain in the Kingdom of Delaware, where roads appeared and disappeared on maps, and struggling farmers prayed for rain to stop, each vying for the crop of another or none at all. When she could no longer bear to look her husband in the eye, she stared instead at the shark tooth dangling from the chain around his neck, a reminder of her malice and loathing, for it seemed that the possession of his trinkets—she among them—was the only thing he cared about.

Well into middle age, Amy adorned herself in the young party dresses of the day, her bluish varicose veins peeking through her nylon stockings. She felt her long blond hair was still her best feature, and she spent hours brushing it with their three dogs at her feet. But there were times in the boredom or fright that filled her days when she drifted into thoughts of the man who worked at her husband's furniture shop. Osiris Kinwell. For reasons she found difficult to explain, she was intrigued by him, filled with primeval feelings that went beyond the limits of her sensibilities, for when she heard the dollop of some exotic nameless place in the lilt of his voice, she thought of swamps and cotillions and whips.

But even now, the way he reacted when she first introduced herself to him was puzzling. Because she expected him to be nervous in her presence since she was making a point to address him directly. But he wasn't. Weren't her eyes blue like the skies? Didn't her hair stream down her back like the ladies in the Sears catalog, and wasn't it golden like the dolls in the store windows? Despite her unfortunate circumstances and the disappointments that life had brought her, she believed (knew?) that she represented the ideal woman in the kingdoms of the land. For the television, radio, movies, and all the magazines had told her so. There were history books brimming with pictures in her image and museums filled with paintings of wars fought over women who resembled her. And there were riches made and lost with jewels snatched from dark people in dark continents and bestowed on the pale décolletages of centuries past.

Still, she wondered if he found her interesting. Different. She heard that he was a widower. Alone, except for a daughter and a sister. And she never saw him with any of the black women around there. Maybe he was lonely too? It was the loneliness that fed what was beginning to grow inside of her each time she tended a black eye or a bruise on her arm. And as her fixation on Osiris deepened, she resolved to let him know that she was accessible, a forbidden thing now within reach. She made up reasons to visit the furniture shop, where she feigned inspection of the merchandise, working her way around to the reason she was there.

Amy visited the shop for the third time on a blazing-hot Tuesday. It had to be a Tuesday, like the times before, because that was the day Brandon was not at the shop, busy as he was with his appointments with suppliers.

She began with a simple word when she saw Osiris manning the establishment: "Hello."

Osiris looked up and nodded, surprised to see her so often lately when she'd never come into the shop before. "Afternoon, Mrs. Riley. How you been?"

Amy smiled. "Doing well. Seems like today must be one of the hottest days on record. If this heat and humidity keeps up, we might have to close earlier." She looked up at the dust-filmed ceiling fans as if surveying the conditions. "Brandon says that maybe he'll see about getting a new AC unit installed in here. Hope so, for your sake, with you being in that back room working."

A regular came in and looked around and Amy waited until the customer left.

"You must be parched," she continued. "You know if you like, you're always welcome to a little iced tea at our house sometimes on Saturday. Brandon goes out to the country with his buddies most Saturdays, and I don't have much to do."

Osiris felt like something was starting that shouldn't. For he sensed he was being hunted and handed a plate at the same time; given an offer without a choice. "Awful nice of you."

"I know you can't be too busy to enjoy a cool drink," Amy said. She gazed at him, waiting for a response.

In the pause that followed, Osiris listened to a siren roar down the street.

Amy leaned against the counter, tossing her hair. "I make a mean iced tea."

Osiris saw the message in Amy's eyes, for it was impossible to miss. "Thank you kindly, Mrs. Riley," he said, smiling a plastic smile. "Be sure to 'member and keep in mind."

Amy smiled too, trying to read his expression. "You do that."

Another customer came in and looked around and Osiris

waited for the patron to leave. He picked up a piece of plywood and put it back.

"Better get on with some things here before closin' time."

"Well, have a good day," Amy said, and she turned and walked out of the shop.

As the days went by, Amy sat through episodes of *All My Children* blaring on the television, thinking about her last encounter with Osiris, an uneasiness settling into her. She didn't know if it was the look on his face or how he said what he said. *Be sure to 'member and keep in mind* . . . Like *he* was tolerating *her*. And she thought she saw a thin lining of something around the edges of his eyes, and this bothered her more and more. Because if she couldn't set her value against his desire to obtain what was beyond reach, what she had been told in a million ways was forbidden and therefore superior to all, then what measure could she use? What way was there for her to be?

She rubbed the fresh bruise on her wrist and felt its pinch, her anger growing. *Because the way to be can't be this*, she thought, and slowly, a lie as old as the kingdoms of the land began to take shape inside. Many years later, the same lie would form in the minds of others who stood in front of television cameras, on courtroom witness stands, and before campus review boards. But Amy had no way of knowing this as she stared at the commercials on the screen, fidgeting in her brassiere. What she knew was that the lie made the intolerable contradiction of what Osiris said and what she felt go away.

So it was no surprise that later that day, when her husband slapped her into their bedroom wardrobe, demanding to know why she was seen visiting with this nigger three times in a row, the lie inside swelled with her reddening cheek. Amy held her palm to her face and looked at Brandon with the unchecked resentment of an animal paired in captivity. And now that this new humiliation was happening, as raw and exposed as the beating, she couldn't have Osiris around—couldn't allow him to be around—knowing that he would only *keep her in mind,* could she? She let the tears flow down her cheek, warm and familiar, her outrage enriched and rectified by what she was about to say.

She looked squarely at her husband. "I was just trying to be nice, a good Christian. But Osiris wouldn't leave me alone."

Sometimes in the troubled waters of his mind, Brandon Riley thought of how his family had left the blood-soaked lands of Ireland for better places, and how now he felt that one faraway island had merely been traded for another. Anacostia used to be all white and full of the promise of fortunes, and this point was never lost on him whenever he heard the songs of Earth, Wind & Fire pouring out of car windows or smelled soul food cooking on someone's stove. He once prided himself on having survived, thrived even, when so many others had left. Over the years he had tried to smile at the black children around the neighborhood, but found it increasingly difficult to do so as they grew older and bigger, for each one of them meant more encroachment on the spaces of his mind, his sense of position and property.

That was why he revered the shark. And ever since his first visit to the Museum of Natural History, where he viewed the great white exhibit in all its horror and glory as a child, the image of the creature was an imprint on his soul. Each time he went back to see the elegant gallery photographs or skeletal reconstructions of the magnificent beast in subsequent years, he was thrilled again by the power of the water monster. And later in manhood, when the circumstances of his life unfolded, the image of the great white was a balm to his angst, a reminder of the imperative of dominion. For he reasoned that the shark's terrible and fatal bites in the waters of the world were justified, since others had no business being in places deemed its territory. The great white was an alpha predator, he'd learned, a survivor through the act of being what it was. And every year Brandon bought a shark tooth in honor of that untouchability, a reminder of what kind of creature he was meant to be. So that he moved about the dominion of his house, his shop, and Anacostia with the precise disposition he felt was required.

But like all frontiersmen bound by the unpredictable happenings between newcomers and natives, he felt a ceaseless unease, a permanent emergency. It was in this constant state of martial law in the confines of his mind and his home that Brandon glared at his wife when he slapped her. And as he watched the tears roll down her cheek, on time as always, on cue, he knew that she was lying about Osiris. Because it seemed that the desire which still overcame him when he watched her dress and sit in the morning sun, or when he took her in the bed, had never been mutual. That all along she seemed to want something else. And as he looked at her crouched on their bedroom floor staring at the wall, it seemed that she held yet another desire, this time for an ape with eyes too clear and a back too straight for his kind. Brandon looked upon her in full hatred of the betrayal he sensed, and prepared to untie his belt. For he'd already accepted that this was why it was not the first time he'd beaten her, nor would it be the last.

SHARK WATERS

Brandon Riley told three buddies from his youth his version of events between his wife and Osiris Kinwell, the only version he felt mattered. Amy stopped at the shop to pick up some carpenter's glue for a small project at the house. She was alone with Osiris in the back of the shop. When she was about to go, he wanted to talk and was friendly. Too friendly. He looked at her in such a way that made her uncomfortable and she wanted to go. He made a pass at her and she tried to leave. But he grabbed her arm. She told him to stop and still he kept on. Finally she broke free and ran out. "I think he tried to rape her," Brandon said. "Amy showed me the bruises on her arms."

His friends fumed as they listened. For they came down from the backwoods of Prince George's fiefdom in the Kingdom of Maryland, wanting something to punctuate what they believed was more evidence of an end to a way of life. Because from the land bridges of Marlow Heights and Oxon Hill, they had watched the places around the Anacostia River morph into something no longer their own.

"See, I told you not to deal with 'em," one of the men said. "Told you not to hire 'em."

Another man nodded. "Give an inch, they take a mile."

"Like I been saying, something was bound to happen," said the third man.

Many years later, there would be other foot soldiers and commanders in race wars that never started and never ended, just as in centuries past. And there would be latter-day nationalists and citizen circles and patriots, who from the forgotten fiefdoms of the territories heard the claxon bells of an orange-skinned king. And they would clamor ever louder to end the bloodlines of others to stem the end of their own. And those of the priesthood of social science would try to devise ways to keep score of which groups had the right to spaces and which did not, while researchers tried to figure how to make one plus one equal six in heat-controlled labs. So that the people of earth would be locked in an unending game of math, where empires sought to add or subtract the numbers of the other, all of them unaware that their efforts equaled the zero-sum total of nature's design.

But the men listening to Brandon Riley had no way of knowing this. What they knew was that one black man was one too many.

"What do you want to do?" asked the first one.

Brandon looked at his friends, feeling better. "Meet me in the back of the shop."

They didn't intend to kill Osiris. Not at first. Just teach him a lesson before Brandon fired him. Just remind him of the land he was in, the world he was inhabiting. And they agreed that there was no safer place to do what they at first intended than inside the shop, behind closed doors. In the daytime. Certainly not at night, when what they called the "elements" came out in full force. And definitely not out in the open where they might be seen. The police couldn't always be trusted to see it their way if things got out of hand. And they were outnumbered now.

So it was no surprise that when they blew through the entrance of Riley Furniture Shop one hot afternoon, the heat from their rage staggered even the flies.

Brandon was waiting for his friends in the back of the store after he'd cleared out the customers, Osiris unaware of his design.

"Kinwell!" one of the men barked as he burst through the

entrance, his face a bright strawberry red that clashed violently with the lime-green shirt he was wearing.

The other two men entered behind him, the last one closing the front door and locking it.

When his friends came to the back, Brandon Riley glared at Osiris with a face of satisfaction, of triumph. Because he had hit Amy with the clear understanding that this man—that black manhood—must be put to death. They formed a hunting circle, Osiris at the center.

"You're in my waters," Brandon said quietly.

Osiris looked from one man to the other, puzzled. "Waters?"

Brandon nodded, fingering his shark tooth.

"Meanin'?"

"You gave my wife quite a scare."

Osiris could feel what was next, the beginnings of something familiar that might somehow end with his demise. "You really believe that?"

"I do."

Brandon's friends wore smiles that made their faces indistinguishable.

"We hear you've been messing with Mrs. Riley, boy," one of the men said.

"Yeah," chimed the two flanking him. One of them moved closer.

Osiris tightened his hand around the hammer he was holding. He looked at Brandon Riley steadily, ignoring the others, and after a beat he said: "Wasn't much talkin' on my end."

Brandon laughed, appalled and electrified. "That so? Well, it's good to know we got some of you who ain't much for talking." He felt the power of his realm now, the dominion of his depths. He picked up a screwdriver from the worktable and tossed it playfully from one hand to the other, thankful he had no legal forms with Osiris Kinwell, nothing signed on paper that said he was his employer. This handyman could be any handyman.

Paid in cash and no questions asked. Whatever was about to happen, he could always say that Osiris tried to rob his shop, that he caught him in the act and had to take matters into his own hands. He fingered his shark tooth, thinking of the way Amy had looked at him from across the kitchen table.

Osiris watched Riley and his men move closer and prepared for what was next. Events played out in the time-lapse rendering that happenings in Anacostia wrought: the clanking sounds of nunchucks; Osiris punching the men flanking him and breaking a nose, then a jaw; Brandon punching him in the stomach; the other men dragging him down to the floor; feet and fists; explosions in his head and the demolition of his chest.

It was the blaring buzzer, made especially loud to ensure that anyone at the back of the shop could hear it, that snapped Riley and his friends out of the trance of their feast. Someone was at the entrance ringing the buzzer. And they were reminded that they were at a place of business in the southeast quadrant and not in the humid magnolia groves of the Kingdom of Louisiana or the dusty hamlets of the Kingdom of Texas. Each looked at the other, and down at what they had done.

Retired Howard University professor Gordon Evanston was standing at the locked entrance of Riley Furniture Shop ringing the buzzer, anxious to have his son's wooden music box fixed. In his wife's increasing confusion and belligerence about who and where she was, she cried bitterly, saying that he had broken their boy's cherished possession. Dr. Evanston tried in vain to help his wife understand that she'd dropped it herself as she stood in their son's room, untouched since he reported for boot camp at Parris Island.

And even now, in the daytime at least, it was easier to try to handle his wife's condition than to allow himself to think too deeply about the fate of their son. The boy he took to get his first haircut at Look Sharp Barbershop. How the professor smiled when he watched him wash and wipe the family car down in the driveway on Saturday afternoons. The pride he felt when he saw him drive off to the prom with his school crush. But the nights were different. They were filled with dreams of his son being held in a nightmarish jungle camp west of Da Nang, where he was curled on a bamboo slab, half-starved, his back crawling with leeches. Or he envisioned him cold and stiff, in repose on a field of grass under a star-filled sky. It was the ceaseless trauma of not knowing. It was the glaring "MIA" on the letter from the army. The promise of the open-ended "missing" tolled in his mind. *What if (when?) his son came back from wherever he was someday and found his cherished music box broken?* So the repair at Riley Furniture Shop was important, and he rang the buzzer repeatedly, wondering why the store wasn't open. "It shouldn't be closed this early," he was saying aloud to himself. Frustrated, he returned to his car.

Police tape had blocked the parking area nearest to the shop entrance and he'd had to park on a side street and walk around to the front. He shuffled back, grumbling to himself. When he reached his car, he got in and sat, oblivious to the oven-heat temperature, wondering how he would get his wife to understand that he couldn't get the music box fixed. It was so hot that afternoon that there seemed to be no one around, except for a few pigeons searching for food. So it surprised him when, gazing through the windshield and pondering his predicament, he saw some white men coming out of the back of the shop. They were gingerly helping (carrying?) a black man into a car pulled up close to the door. The man didn't seem to be able to walk on his own and it looked like there was a bloodstain on his shirt.

The professor watched them place the man carefully into the backseat. Two of the white men got in the car on each side of him, and a third jumped in the driver's seat as Riley got in the front passenger seat. And since the professor knew that he was no longer in the countryside of his youth in the Kingdom of Arkansas, where such a sight meant only one thing, he looked upon the scene with unassuming eyes. An accident, perhaps? A trip to the clinic? *Maybe that's the reason the shop closed early*, he thought. The private cataclysm he was suffering did not mean that business affairs had stopped. He wiped his dripping face with his monogrammed handkerchief. "Things happen," he murmured as he watched them drive away.

They parked the car in an abandoned area under the bridge, got out, and waited until dark, not looking at the body in the backseat, no longer concerned about the elements, since now they were most in need of finishing what they'd started.

"We'll dump it in the Anacostia," one of them was saying. "I heard nobody's ever down there. The current will take the body away."

Brandon Riley nodded. Many years later, when he entered his own living death and was on his way to the Void and encountered the wolf, he would ponder his own happenings and what retribution could mean or not mean. But now he stared into the shadows, feeling that he'd turned the bend that going too far required. And as he began the long and useless process of trying to bury happenings in the pages of time, he wondered if there really was a hell as described in the biblical verses of his youth, or if the question hung unanswered in death as in life. But he pushed such thoughts aside and nodded again in the gathering darkness, for in his mind he was already writing the third act of a script in which what he was about to do had never happened.

Osiris hit the water. In the footprints that memory was leaving in what remained of his mind, he thought of the flower prints on Amber's sundresses and her impossible eyes. And he heard his sister's laughter when they once played together on the dunes.

And he thought of the beautiful sight of Gola when he first glimpsed her on the docks of the wharf. He bobbed and rolled in the current. And he tried to call to Nephthys in the symbiotic language of twins, but it was too late to stop what was happening to him and too early to tell her from the other side.

UNBECOMING

The death of Osiris, like the death of a star, was brought about by the inexorable pull of gravity toward the Great Terminus. Matter caving in upon matter, pressing tighter and tighter into itself, collapsing into antimatter. In the last quantum moments of his living body, the pulsing of his cells slowed like a signal drum, each beat as if in step with the passage of a thousand years. The river current flowed swiftly and his lungs filled with water. His limbs were useless and he drifted along in the brackish waters with the trash of years past and the black slag that floated always on the surface. The flow carried him on, the debris in the water delivering blows to his body and tearing about his head. His foot was pulled into the blade of a dumped factory shear on its way down, and it chewed through the soft flesh of his lower leg, taking the limb with it.

The current carried him, and a large piece of driftwood from a dying forest far upstream caught the pant cuff of his other leg and dragged him into the undertow. In the seconds minutes hours, he sank into the blackness of the depths until he landed at the bottom of the river. The driftwood settled across his chest, pinning him there. He would later bloat and float to the surface and be dredged to the banks and taken to the morgue for Nephthys to behold his bulging, half-eaten eyes, scalped head, and torn limb. But now as he struggled in the metaphysics of the moment, he tried to free himself but was unable to do so, not yet realizing that he was dead.

All around him lay the discarded sunken things of years past, and he was immobile among the river rocks and fish-egg beds and elemental plants that would remain long after the last human passed from the earth. The driftwood lay over him like the lid of a sarcophagus, and he pushed and pulled to no avail. He cursed his predicament and the dark irony of being submerged in water and yet at the mercy of a tree. He lay still and blinking in the drift. Slowly, he understood that his death was over but something else had begun. The grotesqueries of his loss flashed through his mind's eye like the hydrogen blasts of stars. His wife, Gola, and her impossible death. *Would he ever see her again, now that this was happening?* His chance to watch his daughter bloom had been stolen. And there was the unbearable tear from his twin; the aberration of being one when there was once two. He was filled with a forlorn chill and he felt the interstellar cold of his solitude.

It was a pandemonium of revelations. The weight of one loss pressed into the weight of another, and Osiris felt the rage inside spark and begin to grow. It gained in magnitude from one dark realization to the next, swelling beyond the limits of its bearing. On it grew as he counted and recounted the four corners of his death until he burned with the heat of the chromosphere. The rage fed on the antimatter of his unbecoming, searing through the riverbed and down into crust and mantle and core, and out through the bottom of the world and the layers of the multiverse, where at last it reached the point of all points. And that was when all that Osiris was and all that he would ever be exploded.

Freed by rage, his spirit beheld itself in all its horror. And it knew—as all angry spirits do—that ruination was its only nourishment and destruction its only birth. It reveled in this knowing and embarked on that apocalyptic journey to the domain beyond all others. It traveled to the wasted territories of the absurd and out to the far reaches of chaos, until it crossed the apex of the enraged, the anguished, and the damned. The Twelve Hours of Night.

THE TWELVE HOURS OF NIGHT

Osiris arrived livid and howling in that red realm of time and fire. Where signs omens bones transpired in infinite ways and indefinite outcomes, shape-shifting according to the reality and unreality that angry spirits desired. And in that realm of the Twelve Hours of Night, each hour was a day year decade, and time moved forward and back according to its own reckoning.

He was on his back. And when he stopped roaring and opened his eyes, he saw all around him an infrared night. He sat up, blinking in the red mist. He saw that he was on the banks of the river in which he'd just died, except that the black slag traveling its currents now seemed a thick floating mass of coagulated blood. In the distance, ominous storms raged in crimson plumes and lightning streaks lit up the sky in spectral reds beyond the range of sight. And all about and within him was the fugue of fire. Small formless creatures rife with mange skittered across a ground littered with carrion and the sheen of spilled viscera. A dog ran past him toward the river as if to hide from doom in the gelatinous waters, and it stopped at the banks and growled and turned back.

Osiris stood up. To the east he saw the wasteland of Earl's Scrapyard, but in that bloodletting light the field of junk metal was a jagged-boned graveyard of gutted dinosaurs. The scrapyard appeared and disappeared in the flares of lightning, its silhouetted piles of refuse reaching skyward in great towers of waste where huge black crows populated the peaks in wanton rookeries. At the foot of the spires were blazing bonfires, and he saw the elongated figures of fiendish men gathered in their glow as if at some altar of pyrolatry.

A thunderclap shook the night. To the west the bridge out of Anacostia snaked into the stained horizon, and beyond that the adamantine monuments hulked in the dark. Osiris began walking, not yet realizing where he was going but moving in one direction assuredly, like an animal onto a scent. He passed the scrapyard and headed toward distant lights reminiscent of the glimmering eyes of preying reptiles through a black absolute. And from every corner and shadow the sounds and smells of those hunting and hunted abounded. The rip and tear of flesh and crack of bone. Drunken singing amid frightened shrieks. The boom and thump of one being dominating another. The scream and squawk of unending retaliation. He walked by the Big Chair, that infamous structure on the corner, empty as if awaiting the return of the king of ogres from a night of man hunting. Under the glower of streetlamps, he saw rats in their thousands crawling the low mounds of trash and unburied things, fallow and stinking. The windows of dwellings were black and some were aflame, and each door seemed an ominous invitation to another door behind it, where one place led to another.

He walked on. And once more he recalled what he'd lost at the hands of the Rileys. And the more he thought of these things the hotter he burned, and his only desire was to set everything on fire. With each step his anger increased and his bitterness grew in the wild like a pubescent child. And then he knew at once where he was heading and why. He tore off into the night.

Osiris crept through the red mist which floated always about him and found Brandon Riley lying in a hospital bed with acute pain from end-stage lung cancer jolting him from sleep. He moved closer and loomed over him, staring at each strand of hair and watching the man's chest struggle to rise and fall. Osiris was concentrating so much that it was a long while before he noticed

Amy Riley. She was sitting in a chair by the bed looking at her husband, dry-eyed and silent. Osiris was sickened at the sight of her in one moment and giddy in the next, and he drew near and mimed the act of strangling her to death, jeering a singsong ode to her ruin.

Guess who? Guess who?
Somebody got you.
'Cuz dark be deep.
And death be long.
Guess who? Guess who?
Guess who it be?
Look see. Look see.
Nobody but me.

But Amy did not seem to see or hear him, and when he touched her forehead with the intensity of his hand, she rubbed her cheek as if coping with a hot flash. He watched her riffle through her purse for a napkin and wipe her drenched face.

He turned back to Brandon Riley, walking toward him slowly, staining the white floor tiles red with every step. He stretched the walk to the bed out for miles, savoring what he was about to do, not smiling or scowling, but with a look of satisfaction and absolute knowing. He climbed onto the bed and onto Riley's chest and sat like a great vulture come to collect long-awaited bounty. He listened to the man's labored breathing. With each rise and fall his rage grew still, and Osiris pressed down hard into the man's mucus-filled air sacs. He thought of his last living day at the shop and his ordeal in the river and pressed yet harder, thrilled that in this way he could drown the man without a single drop of water.

The monitors connected to Riley rang with a burst of biometric sound as his body began to heat up.

From atop the man's caved-in chest, Osiris caught a look of

fascination in Amy Riley's eyes as the medics rushed in and drew the curtains. The temperature monitor surged. A wave of fire rushed over Osiris with each monitor uptick, and in his mind's eye he pictured the slow roasting of penis, liver, lungs, and heart. And as he sat so for minutes hours days, he looked into the man's terrified face and spoke words into his ears that had no sound but went on living in one's head forever. His fury rose higher, engulfing the bedridden man in flames that ran down the sheets and up the walls, so that Riley's ceaseless screaming was to him a deep and rich splendor. One of the doctors said something about cardiac arrest and then there was the even tone of the flat line. Osiris basked in the finality of that sound until the supremacy of silence ensued, and he was nourished and fortified and the pyre inside grew.

Each time-click forward and back drew Osiris into further depths of doing and undoing. He roamed decimated spaces until he found Riley's murderous comrades in the blood-soaked hills of the Kingdom of Maryland. He prowled with the owls and the nighthawks, watching the men for weeks months years in their falling-down dwellings riven with rot and ruin. One by one he burned them. Smoking in the bed. Electrical fire. Gas oven explosions. It was not so much that their deaths excited Osiris in the same way that the broiling of Brandon Riley made his spirit soar. Rather, it was the prospect, the ongoing and everlasting inevitability of their death by his hand, that only made him want to destroy more.

And this was how Osiris spent the first three hours of the Twelve Hours of Night.

It was the dark anticipation, the just-over-the-horizon feeling of the promise of death, that led Osiris to Amy. Because the lie had outlived him and she with it in the rooms of her mind. He crept upon her as she opened a bag of dry cat food for the twenty-seven tabby cats that lived with her in that Alabama Avenue house. He sauntered around the feces-covered carpet and urine-sprayed walls. He walked from room to room and through the rotted wood paneling and watched her soak in the green-rimmed tub. He terrorized her endlessly, setting fire to locks of her hair as she cooked bloody things at the stove. He took every chance to singe the fur of the cats so that they mewled an incessant chorus of agony. He triggered the smoke detectors in unending succession, and when she tore them all down, he toyed with the furnace in the basement, flicking it on and off and heating up the water tank to watch the pressure gauge rise. With his half finger he lit candles everywhere, and in the flickering shadows of a house made darker by the layers of filth and the passage of time, he laughed at her every jump and start and cry in the night. He invented countless games to worry and frighten her in infinite combinations, relishing the long list of time-consuming and exotic ways to kill her.

Osiris raged on, taunting Amy and listening to her talking to herself about her husband. His decline. His burial and the final destruction of what had taken the Riley clan generations to build. How he could never hurt her again. How she alone was standing at the zenith of what was left: almost nothing at all. She talked about the shark-tooth necklace that lay buried at the bottom of her purse where she'd kept it in spite of all the times her husband had asked her where it was. And one day as Osiris was listening to her talk about her matrimonial victory with a gray-haired tabby sitting on her lap, he laughed and then realized that she was staring at him.

Hello, he said, smirking.

Amy gazed with seeing and believing eyes; a look of feeling guilty but not sorry, and a reckoning that happenings were now swinging the other way. And after a while she said: "I did what I had to do."

You really believe that?

"I do."

Osiris went on tormenting her for months years decades after that, until she broke all the mirrors and nailed the windows shut. At last, the boredom and pointlessness of considering and reconsidering all the possible ways to murder her held less excitement, and the satisfaction of knowing that she would go on suffering and decaying held more.

And this was how Osiris spent another three hours of the Twelve Hours of Night.

It was in the Hour of Seven that Osiris turned back to what he'd lost, and the pain of it reduced him into yet smaller denominations of himself. He thought about his wife. *Where was she, now that he was here?* Images of Amber picking vegetables from the garden filled his head. *Who would protect her now? How would she and his sister carry on?* In the miasma of his despair, he tried to reach Nephthys in the symbiotic language of twins but was unable to do so. He rocked and quaked in the interstellar cold of his solitude until it became unbearable, and he headed deeper into the night.

PYRE

Osiris sought the company of his kind, angry spirits, whether living or dead. Not only out of restlessness, but from a need to feed what drove his rage, and in this way celebrate the brilliant pyre of destruction. Those angry spirits were everywhere in the kingdoms of the land, and they lit up the dark pathways of existence like stars illuminating the black canvas of space.

By the Hour of Eight, Osiris was drenched in the sanguinity of chaos he found in the quadrants and had burrowed deep into the red-hot depravity of others weighed down by the heaviness of being. He made merriment of cause and effect at the scene of crimes. He perpetrated and denigrated and stole last hopes, and he was newly nourished by helping others to their downfall.

By the Hour of Nine, he delighted in dastardly deeds done in threes. He roamed spaces filled with the excrement of all that could be harvested and defiled. For weeks months years, he splashed in lascivious filth, lauding each blaze in the night. He nourished the fancies of child psychopaths, and indulged the depravities of dirty old men, and rubbed raw the loneliness of women in bars. And he savored the crackle and sizzle of souls.

The singular fires of ruin were alight everywhere like jack-o'-lanterns in the dark. And it was in the Hour of Ten that Osiris found he was drawn to the fierce fire of one who drove around chasing down others in constant games of cloak and dagger and chutes and ladders. Osiris found that he kept crossing this man's path, and as he watched him burning alone in his police cruiser, he wondered what it could mean or not mean. *What was it about this one's fire, when there were so many others to see, to douse, to burn?* But he was drawn to the singular soul nonetheless, and he floated into his police car, the backseat crowded with the trapped spirits of those whose living lives had ended there.

Osiris watched the man look this way and that, as if sensing someone was there, and then take a gun out and hold it to his head and put it back, the fire burning from within him yet brighter. *Should I help him along?* Osiris wondered, feeling giddy. But his smile quickly faded, and he suddenly felt a need to weep. Because now he had a familiar sensation, like the feeling he had in that hospital room and in the hills of the Kingdom of Maryland and in the house on Alabama Avenue. The feeling grew stronger as he stared into the man's flames. And he saw Gola's face in the pyre, and that was when he understood who the man in the car was.

The truth was that in his decades in the force, the policeman had done a lot of things, incidents he couldn't talk about in a confessional booth or write in a report or ever allow to be filmed. But sometimes in the privacy of his power, he wondered about the difference between law and order and good and evil, since each changed according to the circumstances of his time. *We're the good guys,* he told himself. The ones he arrested or shot were just monkeys, troublesome creatures to be dealt with from one day to the next. But there were things that bothered him still, moments he couldn't shake. Like that time he was speeding down the street in his cruiser, in hot pursuit of dealers who owed him some money. And it seemed that a pregnant woman appeared out of thin air and stepped off the curb to cross the street. He didn't see anything, focused as he was on his pursuit, until it was too late. And the farther away he drove from that pool of blood, the more he affirmed all the reasons why tearing down the highway to somewhere—anywhere—at one hundred miles per hour was better than staying.

Later, out of a morbid curiosity that he could not explain, he learned her name: Gola Kinwell. He found out that the unborn baby—a girl—had survived. That her widower, Osiris Kinwell, was found in the Anacostia River some years later. That her sister-in-law, Nephthys Kinwell, drove that sky-blue 1967 Plymouth he saw so often. He had a thousand opportunities to pull her over but he could never bring himself to do it. And more and more, in his solitary moments, he had this feeling of being watched, like someone was standing behind him. He had increasing bouts of an inexplicable fever, and he was unable to concentrate or sleep for more than two or three hours at a time. And now as he sat in the cruiser, sleepless and sweating, he knew only that each fitful night felt like an eternity, and in every one of his nightmares he was on fire.

Osiris looked at the lingering spirits trapped in the backseat of the cruiser and they looked back, seeming to sense what he was about to do, understanding the part they would now play without having to be told. Two by two, eight by eight, twelve by twelve, they combined to engulf the man in a coefficient of destruction and a multiplying factor of outrage, and they pressed in tighter until the police cruiser exploded.

Shouts roared onto the scene and into the night. The freed spirits dispersed from the rubble of the car and wandered off into the red eve to live out the rest of their deaths. Osiris watched the body burn in the vehicular inferno, the fused image in his mind's eye of Gola and Nephthys and Amber an accelerant to his anguish. Once more he thought of his own terrible end, how his living life was gone. And he tasted the bitter char of hopeless helpless hate for all living things. He looked at one of the few trees left on the street near the burning carcass of the car, recalling the driftwood that had pinned him down at the bottom of the Anacostia River. Now nature was only a reminder of his death, and he railed once more at his state of being, striking his half finger like a match and setting the tree alight. From there, he moved on to find more trees, setting each one on fire, and then from one wooded place to another. He spread far and wide, burning as much as he could, for with each dying ember he wanted to destroy more.

He raged on. All through the Hour of Eleven he watched living things perish in his wake and he laughed at the drama of ruin, igniting and razing all in his path. And it was at the height of this burning, at the inception of the Hour of Twelve, that Osiris encountered the wolf.

RIDDLES

The wolf shimmered in his fine black coat, slick with the elemental oils of the spaces through which he'd passed. His goldenrod irises pierced the opaque darkness. And because of his extraordinary sense of direction, he easily found entrance and egress through the serpentine pathways of the earth and from one plane of existence to another. He traveled the southernmost and northernmost landmasses and trudged through primordial snow. He traversed ancient land bridges and moved from one hemisphere to the next, around geysers and through mountain ranges and lakes and rivers, and into primeval timberlands.

So it was no surprise that many centuries ages epochs later, as Osiris was spreading a huge fire in the remnants of the Algonquian forest on the edge of Anacostia in the Hour of Twelve, the black-furred wolf was there. He was lying in repose under the last beech tree in that region, his thick coat gleaming in the firelight.

The wolf was relaxed even as the blaze grew. He looked at Osiris as if picking up a conversation from where they'd just left off. *You're right, you know.*

About wuh? Osiris thundered when he noticed the wolf. The animal's tranquility in the presence of his fury insulted him, since until that point he'd terrorized all manner of beasts who lived and died by fire.

Saying nothing, the wolf looked at Osiris and beyond him and back again.

About wuh? The blaze was spreading and the possibility of

frightening the wolf excited him, and he flicked the flame at the tip of his half finger.

The reason you're here, said the wolf.

Osiris didn't understand what the wolf was saying and this only made him angrier. *You wanna talk before burnin', huh?* He flicked the tip of his finger again and moved closer.

The wolf yawned and glanced around at the hellfire.

Osiris moved closer.

The wolf turned over on his side to relieve one of his legs that had fallen asleep. *Can't you feel it? You must feel it by now.*

Osiris felt the pyre inside rise and recede and rise again and was silent.

The reason beyond the fire, said the wolf.

Osiris lit a patch of holly and watched it burn. *You ain't sayin' nothin'.*

The wolf gazed at the new fire, sighing. *Either way, you're going to have to stop what you're doing. Otherwise, you will be doomed to the Conundrum of Three.*

Osiris thought about all the dastardly things he'd done in threes, and the growing and inexplicable hunger to do more. *So?*

The wolf brushed his paw over the singed grass and peered at Osiris with the wisdom of one who knows the ending of a story that another has just started. *The Conundrum of Three. It's the mind seeking the memory of a body long gone, and the body withdrawing from the mind and the spirit, and the spirit chasing the echo of the other two.*

Osiris stood speechless. Because sometimes in the interstellar cold of his solitude he wondered how he would carry on, for he could not tell which of his mind, body, or spirit held reign. He thought about killing the wolf as he tried to find a reason why engaging him was pointless, but he was unable to do so. Unsure of what to think, he gazed into the flames.

The wolf's goldenrod eyes twinkled. *Walk with me.*

* * *

They walked together in that Hour of Twelve. The red realm fell away. Sound itself disappeared and the crackle and sizzle of souls could no longer be heard. The fires dissipated with each step they took and all things burning were reduced to dust. All around were tornado-like cones of smoke that reached high into the unknown altitudes of oblivion. They trekked for miles clicks parsecs through wasted landscapes and the spaces of their minds.

They walked on, entering an ashen realm, a vast and pale pan of emptiness where wind and rain did not exist. Neither was there sun nor moon, and in all directions of the flattened, pumiceous terrain, the thin line of the horizon marked only where starlight met shadow.

Where are we?

The wolf stopped walking. *The Gray.* He pointed with his paw. *Through there.*

Wuh?

Go. You'll find your way forward. And back.

Osiris looked into the blank expanse and back at the wolf. *Ain't nowhere to go.*

The wolf was silent. For he knew that crossing over could only be a lone act; embraced when the cost of not crossing became greater than going to the other side.

Osiris stared into the uninterrupted space made emptier by the preponderance of nothing. His eyes traced the endless range and he searched right and left and from one formless space to another. He looked up at what might have been sky, trying to decipher horizontal from vertical, and when he looked down again the wolf was gone.

CROSSING

Osiris awoke on his back in an ultramarine light where before there had only been the pallor of the Gray. He lay still listening to the emptiness, not knowing what to do next, not yet sure how he felt, now that rage was not the only thing he could feel. And more than this disorientation, he was shocked to now feel cool. How was that possible? He tried to concentrate, to remember. The infrared realm. The flames and the burning. The ash and smoke. The wolf. A walk. And then . . . what? He felt a sting and jumped. He sat up and looked at his hand. The tip of his half finger glowed with the sunset colors of cooling glass. Except for that, the fire was gone.

He stood up. All around was a wide plain that seemed to go on into infinity, and a blue mist floated down. He looked from one undefined place to another and found no form or trace of anything.

Through here . . .

But where was here? He started walking, checking his half finger over and over, as if the seething amber tip might somehow act as his compass. In the distance the drift tricked the eye, so that the sapphire shadows that formed in the bends of indiscriminate light stood like headless creatures beckoning him. He camped at intervals that had neither pattern nor reason. He went on, trying to negotiate the vast plain with his footfalls and the ebb and flow of the mist, until he tired of the monotony of not knowing where he was going, and he stopped and sat down on the featureless ground, rocking back and forth. At times he closed his eyes, hoping that when he opened them again the blue reaches would be filled with something more than the inexplicable mist. But nothing changed.

He stood up and walked on. The drift advanced and retreated and the more he moved the more it seemed he was standing still. He was beginning to fear that he was already doomed to the wolf's warning of the Conundrum of Three, with the mind seeking the memory of a body long gone, and the body withdrawing from the mind and the spirit, and the spirit chasing the echo of the other two. *The reason beyond the fire* . . . What did that mean?

He walked for miles eons clicks, until at last he came to what seemed like the edge of the ultramarine realm, because a great wall of water appeared suddenly out of the mist. It was alive with the roll and crest of waves that traveled vertically, crashing and receding and traveling up to heights beyond reckoning. He looked back at the cheerless pan behind him and thought of the Gray and the red realm of time and fire.

Through here . . .

Where was he to go? And if he stayed in all this emptiness, where would he be? He turned back to the wall of water, not knowing if the cost of moving through another space was greater than staying in one place. He stepped forward into the up-down waves and plunged into the wall of sea.

The water carried him into the unfathomable deep. He was churned and whirled and spun in a great water wheel, and in the delirium of vertigo he sang a song riff from his long-ago living youth:

Indigo swirlin' round de vat
No beginnin' and no end
Circlin' round de ring shout lap
No beginnin' and no end . . .

At last the spinning stopped, and he drifted into yet a deeper current beneath the one that first carried him, and he moved from one side of the great blue to another. He saw the depths as they once were and shall ever be, filled with extinct mammals, other creatures from other passages. The deep grew deeper still and he looked into the cauldron of mystery and the brew of ages looked back. He dove thirty-five thousand feet to the bottom of a great trench, where ancient rock glowed in the dark and iridescent organisms with sentient eyes moved like floating stars. Sulfuric acid–eating crustaceans drifted on toxic plumes and flatfish frolicked under crushing hydrostatic pressure. Colonies of creatures talked to each other in photonic tongues, blinking in the black like some great light show.

And in his voyages on the waterways, he came upon the Empire of Ashu, where sunken Africans in their millions lived a death frozen in time. They greeted him like a lost cousin come to visit, and they shared with him the unthinkable happenings of their age. The women offered bowls of pearls and the children showed him the toys they'd fashioned out of ancient coral. The men invited him to sit on mounds of primordial rock mantle, where together they spent long hours contemplating the cataclysm they'd endured—what they called "the white ravage"—and they told Osiris what they'd learned in the centuries of a living death: that no matter the happenings folded into the creases of time, the Pendulum of Ages was bound to swing the other way. The drowned people shared these things and more with him, so that he had a knowing greater than the knowing he had before.

He bade them goodbye and moved on, traveling from one nautical realm to another, and he lay at the bottom of the waters without the fear he'd felt in the Anacostia River. It was so quiet there that he could hear the Great Heartbeat. And that was when he knew—as all ghosts do—that death is just another kind of living.

* * *

Osiris awoke on his back. Beneath him were the warped planks of an empty dock. He was surprised to see the sky above, full of the pastel watercolors of night passing into day and the geometric formation of birds moving as if they were stenciling on a great canvas. The water lilies floating near him had already opened their hearts at first twilight, brazen in their early glory, their cores beating with the life force of Cassiopeia. He held his half finger up once more. The fire glow remained. He lifted his head and saw the dark obelisk of the Washington Monument slicing the sky, and that was when he understood where he was. The wharf. Southwest quadrant.

He felt something crawl across his hand. It was a single blue crab escaped from some fishing boat yet unloaded, he guessed. He turned to watch it skitter across the dock and into the water, and when he turned his head, Gola, his wife, was there.

In the privacy of the empty dock, they acknowledged each other with the gravity of one ghost to another, staring for seconds minutes hours and with the same passion they'd had in their living lives. Each remembered the other at the height of life's vigor, not as they came to be after its fall. And in their lost and found love, they conversed as if their twenty-fifth wedding anniversary approached, amusing themselves with the idea that they could board one of the boats and drift away. They rejoiced in the mystery of their reunion and had sex in the sapphire light. It was the kind of love that anthropomorphic beings make, and they broke the sound barrier and bent space and time, and in their ecstasy made $\pi - \pi = 1$ and each the other became.

When they calmed down, they relaxed under the watercolored sky and listened to the Potomac River's current. They talked like aged parents, wondering about the fate of their daughter, Amber.

I never saw her, said Gola, and she started to cry.

Osiris held her closer. *But I got him.*

Who?

The one who took you from me.

Gola smiled a thin smile.

They talked on, and Osiris shared with her the twelve years he knew their daughter. How she picked what she wanted from the garden. Her amphibious nature and peculiar understanding of things unexplained. How he and Nephthys felt like they were merely watching her grow. And here Osiris grew silent.

Gola felt his woe and she tried to balm his distress about being unable to reach his sister in the symbiotic language of twins, now that he was dead. She kissed him and played in his hair, pulling strands apart and twisting them together like the twirled black licorice of her living days. The more she pulled, the longer his hair grew, until ropes draped down his shoulders like heavy yarn.

They lay together, Osiris tracing the areolae of Gola's breasts and she toying with the tendrils of his hair. They watched the birds in flight and the colors of the sky deepen in splendor.

And after a while Gola said: *You're right, you know. The reason you're here.*

Startled, Osiris sat up. In the time drip he stared at Gola, trying to wrap his mind around her utterance, and then deciding (hoping?) he didn't hear her right, for such words had been spoken to him before. *Wuh you say?*

Gola was silent.

Osiris jumped up. In his wondrous time with Gola, he was beginning to think that all he'd endured was behind him, that he'd dodged the Conundrum of Three. That somehow the Hours and the Gray and the misty realm were all dreams to be forgotten. *Say again?*

Gola said nothing.

Osiris turned from her and walked hurriedly to the edge of the dock. In the illogic of what he thought he'd heard, he was about to tell Gola that she shouldn't taunt him with the mystery of said and unsaid things; that if she understood what he had been through, she would not play tricks of the ear. But when he turned around, all he saw was a lone blue crab skittering across the dock.

RIVER MAN

Osiris stood on the banks of the Anacostia River. Even from a great distance, he looked much taller than the average man, muscular, the sheen of his skin like onyx. His hair fell around his shoulders and partially covered his face in thick black ropes. From the curtain of tendrils across his wide forehead, he looked through bold, glaring eyes that shifted his countenance rapidly, so that it seemed in one moment he smiled and in the next he scowled. He wore layers of dark fabric draped over his towering wiry frame like that of a monk's robe or a cape, the flaps of cloth shimmering. His half finger was stark among the other long digits of his hands, an amber light at the tip shining brilliantly in the darkness of his presence.

Ever since he left the wharf, he'd been wandering the cherry blossom–flecked currents of the Tidal Basin, the shallow majesty of the Lincoln Memorial Reflecting Pool, the slushy inflow of the McMillan Reservoir, the black tranquility of the Georgetown canal, and the roiling deep of the Potomac River. He moved from one quadrant to another, thinking about his unsettling encounters. The Gray and the misty realm fused and separated in his thoughts, and the wolf and Gola and the crab jumbled together in his mind. Gone were the crack and sizzle of souls and the unrelenting desire to burn, and in their place was a haunting hole that filled his being. In the interstellar cold of his solitude he reached out to Nephthys but received no response. And now he lingered at the river, not yet sure where to go next.

And there was the boy. At first the child seemed familiar to him for reasons he could not explain. But slowly he recognized his daughter's likeness in the boy's face like an ingredient he'd finally been able to name, and that was when he understood that he was looking at his grandson. Should he tell him who he was? He didn't know. For when he thought about his time in the Hours, his treks through spaces, and that dawn on the dock, he had yet to understand how it was that he got to the river. But each time he came to the banks to contemplate what this lingering could mean or not mean, it seemed that Dash was there. And in his wonder, he could not tell if he had conjured the boy or if it was the other way around.

WORDS AND DEEDS

Dash headed to the river. Just a while before, he had to wait for his mother to fall asleep so that he could sneak out of the house once more. It seemed that she was up walking the crypts of her dreams in the night more often, and she could barely keep her eyes open in the day. Now it seemed that she only looked at him in that new way, like how she looked at those she spoke of in the Lottery when she saw them on the street. He'd learned that asking his mother what was wrong was futile, since she would only ever say "Nothing." But her face said something else.

He walked on, thinking of what he might like to talk to the River Man about this time. And as he neared the water, Dash was sure that he would be there like always, a figure of mystery at the banks. Sometimes Dash thought about how odd it was that when he looked carefully at that face behind the thick ropes of hair, he resembled Nephthys when she'd first opened her door and he saw her up close for the first time. It was curious, too, that they both had a half finger, and Dash marveled at how there could be two such odd things in the world. But one half finger glowed and the other one didn't. Nephthys was a woman and his rock-skipping friend at the river was a man, and Dash's child logic told him that one could not be the other. *They just look alike*, he thought, and he put this among the things he noticed but found difficult to understand.

Besides, there were other things he wanted to know. So it was no surprise that Dash looked forward to talking with the River

Man, and he asked him about things he thought might help order his thoughts without ever realizing that he was speaking to his grandfather.

The River Man and Dash greeted each other with the same silent salutation as they had so many times before, and each picked up a rock and skipped it across the water.

Dash stared at the glowing tip of the man's finger, never tiring of its wonder. Maybe he would ask him about it next time. There were more pressing questions now. And after a while he began: "If you're not sure you saw something, does it mean that you just imagined it?"

The River Man looked at the boy. *You believe you saw it?*

The more Dash thought about it, the more confused he became. "I'm not sure anymore."

Was it good or was it bad?

"Both . . . I think."

The River Man flicked his half finger as if shedding cigarette ash that had collected there. *Cyan't be both. One and then the other. One or the other. But not together as the same.*

Dash thought about his comic books, where everything was clear. Right or not right. Yes or no. "Can't be both . . . like good and evil?"

The River Man looked as if he might laugh, and just as quickly as if he might cry. Because he'd done a lot of things in that red realm of time and fire. There were his escapades on dark streets and bright strips, his deep dives into orgies and massacres and debaucheries that had no end. He had killed and helped others kill and saved yet others so that they could kill again. There was so much more, things he could never bring himself to tell the boy. For it seemed that evil had infected him like a virus beginning with his own murder, and once it took hold, he was stained by it and reveled in it and smeared it across his face. But now that the fire inside was gone and he could feel what was good again (like watching his daughter at the kitchen window or looking at the sky), he was not sure which of the two would keep rule. He took one of the prehistoric rocks he kept in his pocket and skipped it across the water and looked at Dash. *Good be a lot of things. Evil too.*

Dash was watching a cluster of aluminum cans bob and bounce in the current. An oily film surfaced where the cans submerged and disappeared, and the slick glittered iridescently in the light play on the water. "Like bad words?"

The River Man squinted at the sun. *Depends, I guess. Sometimes bad words just be bad words, like cursin'. Other times they don't match the face, and that makes 'em bad.*

Dash nodded, thinking of how his mother's face didn't match the word *nothing* when he asked her what was wrong. Or the phrase that other man said that didn't match his face when he opened that door. And once more he tried to balance what was said with what he saw happening in the utility closet and could not reconcile the two.

The River Man stopped to watch a hawk circling something below. *Or bad words can be when you get a certain feelin' about somethin' bein' said.* And here he thought about the doomed feeling he had when the wolf talked about the Conundrum of Three.

"Yeah, that's what it is. A bad feeling."

Wuh was it?

"Huh?"

The bad words.

Dash kicked a piece of broken glass into the water and watched the splash it made. "*I am not a beast.* That's what I heard him say."

Who?

Dash hesitated, for among the many things he did not understand, it seemed that the man in the utility closet looked like the janitor Mercy Ratchet. He looked like the man who mowed the lawn in the summer and shoveled the snow in the winter and decorated Saints of Eternity with all those lights at Christmastime. But now when he saw the man smiling at him in the school corridors—the widest smile he'd ever seen—it was like he was looking at someone else.

And then there was the other thing more disturbing than the words and the smile. Which was why he couldn't seem to form the question about it. Because he still wasn't sure if what he saw in the utility closet was *doing it*, like he'd heard the other children say grown-up people did. Because Annie Porter was a kid and the grown-up man was not, and one could not be the other, could it? He wanted to ask the River Man more about that—how one thing could not be another—but it was like it was all mixed up in his head. And he had no way to match the words with the deeds, unclear as he was about what *doing it* looked like. Which was just as well, he thought, picking up a rock and pushing the riddle away, because the door he'd opened was gone.

PASSAGE II

STAYING IN ONE PLACE

BITS AND PIECES

Having been so recently made by God, Dash's mind was a delicate, elegant machine. And when he saw something too big to fit into that divine creation, his mind tried to break it down into smaller parts that could be more easily handled. For children of the ghetto—like children of war—learn to see the world in bits. They hear it in segments. Life happens before them and moves into them and through them in pieces. So that a murder can be witnessed with a laser-sharp recollection not of the blood, but of the newness of the Converse Chuck Taylor All-Star sneakers on the body. The reason a woman is on the corner at night is not thought about; only that her daughter is a classmate. The wino singing at the entrance of the neighborhood corner store is merely part of the gateway to the happy purchase of candy. The tracks on the addict's arms as he sits on a bucket are eclipsed by the sound of the genius inside of him as he plays the trumpet in his hand. Used needles and weed butts on the sidewalk are noticed only in proximity to the penny that someone dropped: *Find a penny. Pick it up. All day long you'll have good luck.* So that Dash lived in and around a traumatized world, and he experienced it much like the candy that defined his childhood: in smaller bits and pieces that could more easily fit into the fragile spaces of his ten-year-old mind.

On the day that Dash saw *it*, he was sitting in class fighting the tedium that the last weeks of school can bring. It was not that he was a poor student. Rather, he found it difficult to care about the workings of the three branches of government (legislative, executive, and judicial) that were said to rule the kingdoms of the land, since they were parts of an empire that seemed far, far away. Nor was he inspired by the decrees of the four-year kings down through the decades, who all looked the same to him and were interchangeable with the photographs of the farmer king now in his textbooks. Many years later, there would be a king with skin as brown as his own, and many times over he would be compelled to rise to power and relinquish power in the same breath, for the land he envisioned was not the land he was charged to lead.

But Dash had no way of knowing this as he sat restless at his desk. What he knew was that he had to go to the bathroom. And it was with great relief that when he raised his hand, he was granted permission to do so by the teacher. Annie Porter, the girl who sat in front of him, went to the bathroom too, thirty-five minutes ago. But since it was already so hot in the airless building and the end of the day was more than half the day away, and since the teacher was so tired of the frustrations of teaching and the children tired of listening, no one noticed that Annie Porter had not returned to her desk.

Dash wasted no time leaving the classroom and entered the hallway. Moving about the school felt like an odyssey through two different realms. One was a realm where the corridors were filled with children, where they traveled in a band of noise from one place to the next like flocks, changing direction according to threat and opportunity. The other was a realm where the corridors were empty and eerily quiet, where gold-filled trophy boxes and dark doors could be portals to other dimensions like in his comic books. Dash was thinking this on his way back from the bathroom when he noticed a sweet scent that reminded him of the caustic delight of Lemonhead candy. He followed the scent to a door he'd never noticed before at the end of the corridor. It was shadowed by a blown light bulb above it that had never been changed. Years of handling and countless coats of shellac made the door's pine facade look like a slab of fossilized wood. He tried to peer through the keyhole but could not see anything beyond the black world it held. An entrance to some secret tunnel, perhaps? Instantly, he was driven by the allure of the unknown that only children know. He turned the knob and was surprised to hear a click. The door was unlocked and he opened it . . .

Long after Dash saw what he saw, he thought about the Memorex commercial—*Is it live or is it Memorex?*—where one had to try to understand if what one was seeing was really what one thought one was seeing on this plane of existence, or if it was a recording of the same thing in some other dimension that existed on the tape. Dash saw the commercial many times on the TVs displayed at the five-and-dime stores, since his mother insisted on not having a television at home. She said there were episodes more real than the ones depicted on the television. That what happened in the weekly installments of *Good Times*, *Sanford and Son*, and *All in the Family* existed only in somebody else's world and not the one people lived in. But Dash kept on thinking about the Memorex commercial because it was something like how he felt about what he saw behind that door. The school utility closet. Annie Porter. And wasn't that the janitor?

After Roy Johnson had taunted him about the River Man because he heard him trying to ask about something for which he couldn't find words to describe, Dash wondered more and more about what he saw, for it was too massive and confusing, too impossible to fit into the psyche of his child's mind, and he began to fear that maybe Roy Johnson was right. Maybe he was going to St. Elizabeths after all. Because what he saw was a sprawling thing that stretched across his cerebral cortex. His mind tried to break it into bits and pieces to flash in his head like the fourteen-slide reel of his View-Master toy, moving fast at some parts and slow at others. He had even changed the scene from the school utility closet to a field of grass in one of his early-reader books . . .

A little girl playing in tall grass, practicing her counting and chants as she hops. Five plus five equals ten. Ten plus ten equals twenty. Fifteen plus fifteen equals thirty. A long shadow in the field of tall grass. The man moves toward the girl. The man starts laughing. The girl starts laughing. The man dances around. The girl dances around. The man pushes the girl down in the grass. The girl stops laughing. The man starts laughing. The girl starts crying.

It was all stamped onto his mind like a watermark. But Annie Porter was gone now. He heard, among the many things the other children said about her now, that she'd gone somewhere down south because she had stopped talking. He heard Roy Johnson brag about how his uncle, the principal, was fed up with Annie Porter's mother constantly questioning the school about her daughter, and he was glad to be rid of the whole thing.

But somehow, now there was a white wall where the utility closet had been. *How was that possible?* He didn't know. And when he mixed this puzzler in with the rest of it, he wasn't sure if anything had ever happened. Because he couldn't check if Annie Porter had really been there (was it live?). Nor could he tell if he actually saw someone who merely looked like that janitor (was it Memorex?). And he couldn't match what he thought he saw with what he thought he heard: *I am not a beast*... But more than anything, he couldn't find a way to understand what kept burning through his thoughts: *What were they doing?*

So it was no surprise that the divine machinery of Dash's mind tried to break the enormity of a thing into smaller, more palatable bits and pieces whenever he thought about the keyhole, the door, and the dimension. There was no door, just a wall. There was a girl who was there but now she was gone.

INTENTIONS

Mercy Ratchet stood in the quiet of Anacostia's Saints of Eternity, a structure built in defiant response to the white parishioners at St. Emma, who thought it more fitting for the black congregation to praise God in the church basement. He wiped the bottom of the porcelain holy-water bowl clean with a towel, one of the many caretaker tasks he did so often. Because of his enthusiasm he was left alone to do his work. In addition to his job as a janitor at the elementary school, he performed duties necessary for the fulfillment of the rites and sacraments as well as any member of the papal family, his dedication unmatched. So no one ever asked him to excuse himself when spiritual matters were taking place. Guilt-ridden parishioners who threw themselves on the mercy of Christ's court did not take offense to Mercy Ratchet looking on as he polished the altar brass. If Mercy broke the sacred silence by rattling the stained glass or disturbing the candles during a prayer vigil or christening, it was assumed that he was taking care of something important for God. And who in their right mind could ask him to stop such a thing?

No matter how many years he'd been at Saints of Eternity, he still thought about Sacred Heart of Patapsco, the Baltimore church of his youth. And sometimes when he smelled the old wood around him or heard the foundation creaking, he saw himself trapped once more in that other basement, where a thick and coveting garden grew. At such times he was overcome with the sensation of his cataclysmic childhood, and when he closed his eyes and opened them again, he sometimes felt like he was still there.

He looked into the bottom of the porcelain holy-water bowl, reminding himself that all of that was gone now, a world away. Now there were only tasks and intentions. And since it was June, he savored his favorite Catholic observation. For he'd meticulously studied all the devotions over the decades and found the June devotion to be the only rite long conducted in secret. He read that its practice spread undetected to various dioceses throughout the centuries, and it wasn't until 1873 that Pius IX officially gave his approval. Certain devotees were even said to have witnessed apparitions of Jesus, allowing the chosen to rest their heads on Christ's heart, at which time marvels were revealed. And to his great wonder, Mercy read that when a soldier pierced the side of Christ, a stream of blood and water flowed. *A pure stream means a pure heart*, he thought, every time he read it. Because he felt that if he could practice that one thing—always and forever having only good intentions—then what came out of his intentions would necessarily be good. Like what he was beginning to think about every time he saw Dash.

I am not a beast . . .

Mercy shook the dust from his cleaning towel. It was a small saying but one that held great power, for everything that came after its utterance meant nothing. He looked into the colors of the stained glass and pulled that termless phrase from the crypts of his mind as he'd done a thousand times before, wondering what it could mean or not mean. And why it still rang so loudly in his head.

Even in the flickering pale light above his head and the rat droppings at his feet, Mercy delighted in the basement wonder of the kitchen at Sacred Heart of Patapsco, for it was well stocked with sugar. And like any boy of twelve, Mercy reveled in the privilege of eating as much of it as he could stand. This was possible because it was his task to make the lemonade. Other boys of the church had other tasks, but his was special and liked by everyone at the fish-fry dinners. He loved how the scent of the squeezed lemons perfumed the stale, mildewed air, transforming it into a garden. Every Sunday, Mercy squeezed the tart liquid into a glistening crystal bowl atop a huge steel table. When he thought he had enough to spare, he brought a wooden spoon to his mouth, lost in sweet and sour ecstasy. Which was why on that one Sunday, Mercy didn't see Priest Abernathy standing behind him like a piece of heavy kitchen equipment suddenly come to life.

The priest pulled a handkerchief from his pocket and wiped his brow and put it back, smiling. "Smells awful nice in here, doesn't it?"

"Yes," said Mercy.

"Like the Garden of Eden."

"I s'pose so, Priest Abernathy." He had read about the garden often in Bible study.

"I can see why you were picked to make the lemonade. Nobody does it better."

Mercy stirred the mixture vigorously, looking into the yellow whirl. He was proud of his creation. "Thank you, sir."

"Let's see what else about you that's better."

"Sir?"

The priest breathed deep of the sweet air and turned to lock the door behind him in preparation for what was next. And after a silence he said: "It's all right, son. Don't you worry. I am not a beast."

As the happening was happening, Mercy couldn't remember the sound of his father's voice or his mother's face, or how many years it had been since he was born. He couldn't move. Nor could he speak, for thought and word were taken from him, and he was left only with sight and touch. Many years later, there would be more happenings within happenings with other children in the kingdoms of the land, stories of pilgrimages to the Void that would burn through what took centuries of cardinal law to create. But Mercy had no way of knowing this as he stared into the dark corners of the kitchen in the basement of the church, wondering if the rats were watching. What he knew was that he felt himself transforming. And in that slow morphing, he learned that hell was not a place. Rather, it was a state of becoming and he was made a changeling to molt into what he knew not.

The priest had backed away after finishing his feast on Mercy's soul, which he had swallowed whole. "Get yourself together, son," he said. "The fish fry starts in about an hour, and we have to be ready for the flock coming in. You know that the saints are depending on you to do your part." He went over to the crystal bowl and turned the wooden spoon up to his mouth. "Now, this is good lemonade! Fit for the angels." The priest looked at Mercy and squinted, as if seeing him for the first time. "Are you sick? Speak plainly."

Mercy shook his head, as if responding on behalf of someone else. He no longer knew what sickness or wellness was, and he felt a numbness that came with slowly disappearing.

Priest Abernathy threw a handkerchief at Mercy and looked away. "Clean yourself up and finish this good thing you got going here. Come on now. Time waits for nothing. Now tell me, are you sick?"

Mercy shook his head.

"That's a good boy," the priest had said. "Because we can't have problems with you being sick, not on a day like today." He'd had problems in a Boston church in the Kingdom of Massachusetts and then other problems in an Albany church in the Kingdom of New York, certain things that made it impossible for him to stay. He straightened his frock and gave the boy a look that sires of ruin give. "And we're never going to have problems with you being sick now, are we?"

Mercy was immobile.

"That's right. Because a strong young soldier like you can

withstand the sun and the storm. You understand, don't you?"

Mercy nodded, pieces of himself somnambulating through the place he'd vanished to, where light and darkness melted into heat and cold, where all questions merged into one: *Why?* And from that distant place, he looked into the priest's face and found an enormous smile, and in his delirium, Mercy thought of the Cheshire cat in the storybooks on his bookshelf at a home now long gone. *We're all mad here. I'm mad. You're mad . . .*

And something took root inside of him and grew.

From that place of vanishing, Mercy tried to forget the happening and plunged into all sorts of distractions: staying awake for two days at a time; killing squirrels in the park; eating the feathers from his pillow and pieces of soap; punching holes in the wall of his closet. He started pushing other boys into urinals when they were peeing and peeking under the stalls when they were sitting on the toilet. But he found this a source of grave retaliation, such as black eyes and sprained wrists. On the other hand, he found that the girls were much easier targets, for they screamed and jumped when he smacked their behinds or pulled the ribbons from their hair. He got a warm and satisfying feeling when he made them cry.

For long before that Garden of Eden Sunday with Priest Abernathy, he'd felt the beginnings of that vanishing with each of his passing birthdays and in the quiet chill from his father that never waned. The report card with hard-earned grades received with lukewarm acknowledgment. The curt responses to his questions (*Did you like storybooks when you were my age? What was my grandfather like? Will I be tall?*). But what had revolted Mercy most, what would forever live in his memory, was the image of his mother's eyes, dull and lightless, staring at him as if through jars of formaldehyde when he finally got the courage to tell her about the Beast. And when he'd finished his accounting of his terrors, she reached for the Bible on the table and leaned her head to one side as if trying to see a painting from another angle, as if attempting to understand what was being depicted. She opened her mouth as if to say something but said nothing and lifted her hand as if to touch him but withdrew it. He would later freeze the image of her lightless eyes in his mind and understand why he wanted the colors he saw in the eyes of girls.

And in the loneliness of his thoughts, Mercy knew—as all the neglected do—that indifference was an insidious poison, a slow drip into the mind and the heart. And each act of cruelty to himself or someone else was a hopeless helpless cry to the Void that the indifference and the lightlessness made: *I am. I exist.*

Finished with the holy-water bowl, Mercy wiped a panel of stained glass depicting the Last Supper with a damp towel, smearing his fingers across the rendering of the apples, thinking of his intentions. The garden had been defiled and could never be visited again. He easily made up a reason to wall it off and paint it over (leaking inside the utility closet that there would never be funding to repair), and the school principal agreed to the remedy with no questions asked. So it was no surprise that when he finished the project and packed up the drywall and paint materials he'd used to erase what he'd been doing, it was like the door that led to the garden was never there.

Which would have been enough, Mercy was thinking as he looked at the smears he'd left on the stained-glass panel. Except there was still the matter of the boy.

WITNESS

He saw it.

And Mercy Ratchet knew that what Dash Kinwell saw had to be called *it* because there were no words, no mythology, no construct to describe what it was made of, and it defied all reason and scripture except in the chaos of his mind. He had her all picked out, the thirteenth one. Annie Porter. She was quiet. Indeed, her silence made her special. It made her worthy. And he'd prepared the utility closet and everything was perfect: no mildew-laden mops, stagnant water, or rat droppings to ruin the setting. He'd scrubbed and polished it and even fragranced it with lemon verbena. And it was going so well—the counting game and all—until Dash Kinwell opened the door he thought he'd locked and saw it and ruined everything. It wasn't only that the boy saw it that bothered Mercy. It was that there was a familiar trinity in the boy's eyes (one part innocent, one part believing, one part disbelieving) that made him rage and grieve when he recognized it, because it was so much like the other boys he touched, so much like what the Beast must have first seen in his own eyes on that Sunday all those years ago.

And more and more, Mercy thought about what he would do. Because now it seemed that something inside of him was getting worse. Or better. And in the usual manner when things had to be contemplated, he needed that special elixir. Lemonade. The drink that would bring that day back to him and make it all make sense again. Something that would make remembering merely an evocation of image and sound, not dismemberment and loss of being.

He walked back toward his crumbling abode, twirling a twig. He lived in a falling-down frame house on the edge of Anacostia near the hinterlands of Prince George's fiefdom in the Kingdom of Maryland, where flocks of red-breasted robins and marauding gangs from the Appalachians once ruled. And as he stepped onto his porch and opened the splintered door, he could almost taste the lemonade, feel it sliding down his throat. But more than the taste of it, there was the actual making—the science of it becoming what it was—that excited him.

Mercy reached in the old refrigerator and pulled out a fat jug. "Good and cold," he said aloud, placing it on the table. Now he would make more, for he wanted always to have lemonade ready. Lemonade on tap. Lemonade forever. From the pantry he selected ten of his finest lemons from shelves that were otherwise empty and cut them into perfect halves. He loved to use the sterling silver knife. He sliced each lemon slowly, deliberately. He ran his fingers across the spiderweb of lemon membranes and squeezed the juice from the halves into the pitcher as the remembering began. It was a funny thing how something with such simple ingredients could combine to form the most sublime of elixirs. And he'd always believed that it was the lemonade that had drawn the Beast out to the church basement that day.

He held up a slice of lemon and smelled its aromatic wonder and set it down again, feeling energized. For June heralded the great season of summer when the wrath of snow and ice and the chilled petals of spring were distant memories. When the grounds outside of the schoolyard had to be cut regularly. And recess was longer—twenty extra minutes in addition to the usual forty. Time enough to watch the girls. As long as it didn't rain, Mercy had a clear view and he could enjoy the sacredness of his private scrutiny—sixty minutes of bliss—in the company of his fantasies as he walked the schoolyard perimeter. It was hard to concentrate and harder to wait for the bell to ring each day before recess. He would watch the children filing out in various degrees of jubilation, blanketing the schoolyard like a frothy tide. Games of double dutch assembled rapidly and girls shouted for boys to move aside, and within seconds the still air filled with a symphony of shrieks, giggles, insults, and cajolery.

Mercy got the sugar tin from the sagging kitchen counter and poured what was left of its contents into a large mason jar. And when the excitement of his memories was too much and the endless possibilities of opportunity dizzied him, Mercy thought about the others. There were twelve in all, not counting Annie Porter, each an expression of his good intentions. Each girl encased in a jar on a shelf in his mind. Such eyes of light! Nothing like the formaldehyde-soaked cow eyes of his mother, for Sarah Ratchet was the exception, not the rule. Mercy only touched some of the girls. He did more with others. Like the one with the cream soda–brown eyes. He watched her for months, fish fry after fish fry, Bible study after Bible study, Sunday mass after Sunday mass. On the chosen day, he bought her a cream soda to celebrate his choice. He'd just finished his regular handyman chore of preparing the church hall for dinner and waited for those eyes near the refreshment table . . .

"How come they never have soda, Mama?" he heard the girl say. Her mother was busy discussing the heathenry of her neighbors and ignored her.

The girl was trying to get her mother's attention when Mercy said: "I got something you'd like better than this old watery stuff." When she looked up at him and smiled, Mercy imagined her eyes dropping out of her head and into the punch bowl, where he could fish them out and keep them in his pocket forever. "I got something much better," he repeated, smiling. He was thinking of the kitchen pantry downstairs. It was ready and waiting. "Got some cream soda down in the pantry. The best you'll ever have. You think you'd like some?"

The girl nodded.

Mercy put the sugar tin back on the counter. He remembered now very clearly how he took the girl's hand and how the ease of it was almost more than he could believe or stand. And since he was the handyman, groundskeeper, caretaker, and provider of all things great and small (tissues, lost wallets, missing watches, choir robes, and more), no one noticed him leading the girl out of the banquet room and down the hall. While they were all consumed with the business of planning trips to heaven, he walked right by. There were six more Sundays of cream soda, eyes, and bliss after that, Mercy remembered. He later heard that the girl was sent to Chicago to stay with an aunt. Or was it Detroit to stay with her grandmother? Somewhere, anyway. He never saw or heard about her again. Occasionally, not out of fear but curiosity, he wondered if she ever said anything. But what could she say? There was nothing to say. He'd taken the words from her too.

Mercy poured the squeezed lemon juice and some water into the mason jar with the sugar, got a bag of ice from the freezer, and dumped in some of the cubes. *It hasn't been all perfect*, he thought. He'd made some mistakes. Like Hazel Eyes. She was a toffee-colored girl who had been abandoned on the steps of Saints of Eternity by her white mother when she was just a baby. An old woman who'd lost all her children to the South took her in and raised her. And when he'd led her into the forest, he knew that she would make a perfect addition to his collection. She would have been a beautiful jewel in his crown. But he'd miscalculated her mouth on the day he chose her. "I'ma tell!" she'd shouted. And when he tried to get her to understand that there was nothing to tell, she got louder. He had to choke the sparkle out of her eyes to quiet her screaming. He had to bury her in the semishallow ground near the creek where he drowned her that nobody but the amphibians paid any attention to. And as he watched the pink barrettes that slipped from her braids float away, he vowed never to deal with a running mouth again. And since children born of Anacostia appear and disappear from one day to the next, no one ever found her. After that, after Hazel Eyes, he had to make concessions, modifications. Like the addition of the substance.

Still, there was the girl in the snow, Mercy recalled. Rosetta. She was one of his triumphs, even with the issues he'd had. She was his favorite, a masterpiece. He could still feel the crisp chill of that day and see those bloodred winterberries. He figured that she was about fifteen years old by now. He'd noticed that her little sister Lulu was the same age she was when he chose her. He heard that now the girl in the snow was working at the Butterfly Club, a pit of wild animals. But back then, when she was just the girl in the snow, she was something to behold.

From the porch of his house he saw a small hooded figure, little limbs scurrying and little hands picking winterberries and dropping them into a plastic bucket. He marveled as he watched her out there all by herself, standing in all that white, collecting all that red. *Little Red Riding Hood,* he thought, laughing at his luck that the girl was so near. He figured that she had to be one of Shanita Jefferson's children wandering about, since everyone knew they were all scavengers. When he looked closer, he realized that it was Rosetta. Little Rosetta. He knew from watching her play stickball with the boys that her head was hard enough to be so far out of the way. All the way out here.

He stepped down from his front porch to get a better view of her flittering around. *I know the Little Red Riding Hood story,* he mused to himself. *I know it well.* He stood watching her dart about the white mounds. Then he went back inside to quickly get things ready. That way, when they got to his favorite part of the story, he wouldn't have to stop and fix anything. He was thankful that the wood-burning stove was already crackling. He threw a hunk of pine on the flames. He filled a small pot with milk, stirred in large dollops of syrup, and set it aside. Then he headed out to the winterberry picker with a bucket he kept by the door. He stepped off the porch and felt his feet sink into the deep white. It was his favorite kind of snow, silky and secretive. He padded silently up to Rosetta in such a way that she would not see or hear him until he was right upon her—chameleonlike.

"Look like you got a good thing going here, Ms. Little Bits," he said, smiling.

Rosetta was engrossed in her foraging and the man's voice startled her. But when she turned around and saw who it was, his smile so wide and bright, she only laughed. "Hello," she said. Because it was only the man who raked up leaves and helped people carry sacks of potatoes and lift boxes. Mercy Ratchet handed out tissues to screaming women during wakes and funerals. He put up the tables and chairs for raffles, bakes, and Easter candy sales. This was the man who guarded the coatroom during baptism ceremonies. Thanks to Mercy, the schoolyard was always shoveled and salted after the first snow. He kept the grounds green and manicured in the warm months. He mopped up the messes the children made. *It's just him*, Rosetta thought, relaxing.

Mercy smiled wider. "What you doing out here? Ain't you supposed to be in school today?" He knew that guilt always worked best. It was an emotion he'd long lost the ability to feel, but he knew the concept well.

Rosetta looked around casually. "Oh, I . . . uh . . . didn't have to go to school today." Her eyes twinkled with deception.

Steel gray. In the winter light, Mercy thought her dark eyes looked steel gray. But he knew that this wasn't the true color. Those eyes needed the glow of warmth. Then he would know what color they really were. And staring at her then, he was proud of his patience. He'd let it alone for a while, hadn't he? Between extra odd jobs about town, he really hadn't had the time for new eyes. New light. But the snow and the winterberries had practically brought Rosetta to his door.

"No school today, huh?" Mercy said, patting Rosetta on the

head. "Well, that couldn't be all bad. Good girls like you know how to keep busy with something to occupy the mind instead of foolin' round."

"That's what I was thinking," said Rosetta, proud of how she was sparing herself another unbearable day. The eldest of five children, Rosetta was cursed with having no resemblance to her mother, as her younger siblings did, and was told that she looked exactly like that "no-good dog." That was what her mother called all the absent fathers collectively. And every time Rosetta looked in the mirror, she saw the proof that there was someone else—a no-good dog somewhere—who she, helplessly, resembled. Was it the way her eyes were set? Her thick brows and complexion? Maybe it was the short hair that her mother cursed and sucked her teeth about when she styled it? And when her mother scolded her for some small, unexpected offense, Rosetta thought of her as she thought of the weather: it was necessary to check her mother constantly because she could shift at any moment. Precautions had to be taken. But never knowing what her biological crimes were had always made Rosetta sad, so that she held a demeanor of cheer in order to mask her despair.

Many years later, the kingdoms of the land would be filled with children like Rosetta, fatherless girls on the poles of clubs and in front of the cameras of computers and at deserted train stops and in relationships where rules were made and broken according to insult and fist. And to their own outrage and disgust, they would grow up to be just like the mothers whose attention they craved, and with as many children, each of whom they loved unevenly and according to the circumstances of the child's conception and the part that they themselves had played in it. But Rosetta had no way of knowing this when Mercy Ratchet found her in the snow. What she knew was that at last she felt understood.

Mercy nodded at Rosetta. *Clever, clever girl.* "I got a bucket here too, and I can help you get all the berries you like," he said.

"Can't eat 'em though. You know that, right? Bluebirds love 'em but they're bad for us. Taste awful too."

"Don't I know it," said Rosetta. She was grateful that at least one grown-up appreciated her world. "Thanks, Mr. Mercy."

"The one and only." He walked alongside her, filling his bucket.

"I wasn't going to eat 'em," Rosetta continued. She held one close to her face. "I tried it once and it was something terrible. I thought I'd die of poisoning at first, but I was all right."

Mercy glanced around while she was talking to make sure that no one was paying any attention. And in the juxtaposition of joy and pain that places like Anacostia bear, he saw only a mangy German shepherd defecating on the exposed roots of a seventy-five-year-old elm tree, a woman walking with a small bag of groceries from the corner store, and a smoke-billowing Mercedes puttering by. He looked at the girl and smiled. "You way out here all by yourself?"

"Uh-huh. Ain't no winterberries round my way and there ain't no car oil or trash in the snow out here."

"Oh," said Mercy as he looked around once more, satisfied. He turned his attention back to the girl. "So, what you gonna use all them berries for?"

Rosetta was excited. She had plans. "Pretend stuff. Cherries. We never get no real cherries. My baby sister Lulu is always getting the best treats and tearing my stuff up so I sure am glad Mama had to take her to the clinic today. It ain't too bad when we play pretend cherries, though. I'm gonna set up my dolls and some cups and plates and maybe later we gonna have a pretend-cherries party together."

Mercy's blood was pulsating. "Pretend is my favorite too. Say, the wind sure has picked up. It's getting mighty cold. I was just about to have some sweet milk when I saw you out here picking your cherries. Got some real good syrup too. Good maple syrup. And honey. What you say we go on back and get some?" He winked at the girl.

Rosetta thought about that. Sweet maple syrup, milk, *and* honey? It sounded like something only angels drank. Angels with wings and extra money. And this treat could be hers alone, not something she had to share with her brothers and sisters like the last Popsicle or bag of potato chips. "Yeah, thank you, Mr. Mercy," she said, gathering a few more berries dotting the ground. "Ready."

As they walked along it had started to snow again, and Mercy thought about what her eyes would really look like in the soft light of his shack. When they got inside, they sat at the splintered table together, sipping and smiling. *Blackstrap molasses*, he thought. In the warm light, that's what color Rosetta's eyes were. He gazed into the glow of it all for a while. Then he began.

"Do you know where milk comes from, Ms. Little Bits?"

Rosetta was stirring extra syrup into her mug. "Huh?"

"Milk."

"Yeah. It comes from a cow."

Mercy laughed. "No, silly. I mean mother's milk."

Rosetta had to think about that one. What was it her elementary schoolteacher said? Baby cows drink the cow milk from the tit, and baby people drink baby milk from their mama. When the baby is ready to eat the milk squirts out. Or something like that. "Comes from the mama," she said.

"Yes. That's true. But did you know that girls have it, even before they become mothers?"

Rosetta was filled with wonder. Her teacher didn't mention that part. The world was always trying to keep her in the dark. And her mother never seemed to have time to tell her anything. "Really?"

Mercy feigned surprise. "Sure. You didn't know? It's right there in your two little spigots," he said, pointing to her young chest. "Right there all the time."

Rosetta looked down at herself.

Mercy refilled her mug. "You ever see a cow being milked?"

"Yeah, I saw it in a picture book one time," said Rosetta. "And on *Sesame Street*."

"Well, it's almost the same with people," said Mercy. "Womenfolk, I mean. I used to watch my nana do it all the time, even without a baby. Just to empty 'em out from time to time. Sometimes I even helped. They get too full if you don't, you know." He shook his head. "But then if you don't start milking them early, they'll never fill up. I thought a big girl like you knew these kinds of things. I mean, it's all right if you didn't but I thought you did." He looked at the girl steadily and after a beat he added: "If you unbutton your shirt a little, I can show you. Like I said, it's just as simple as milking a cow."

Rosetta looked down at her flat chest and back at Mercy. She was a little surprised at what he was saying. But he looked at her like it was just one of those things that was part of living and doing. Like when the man at the pharmacy put his hand on her fevered forehead and told her mother that since she didn't have insurance, she could only get some horehound hard candy. Or like when the man had picked her up by the hips to set her off the bus with her brother when they tried to ride without paying the fare. And she was feeling funny now sitting at the table in Mercy Ratchet's overheated shack. Fuzzy and light, as if she were sailing on a boat. Or floating. Still, it all sounded so medicinal and official—he said "womenfolk"—and she wanted to affirm that she was not a baby like she'd been trying to tell everyone. And she was curious about how this thing the world withheld from her worked. Besides, flat as she knew she was, maybe this would help them grow like the big girls. And in the warm yellows and creams that the room seemed to take on with the wood-burning fire, she unbuttoned her shirt and bared her small chest for Mercy to examine.

Mercy began touching her, forgetting all time and space, transfixed before the Void. And he reaffirmed to himself once more that he meant well. His intentions were good. And he knew—as all deceivers do—that trust given willingly was the only trust worth taking.

In the strangeness of this new sensation, Rosetta wondered if her mother and sisters milked themselves. More than that, she was enthralled by the unfolding discovery of this womenfolk thing that the world had tried to hide from her.

They sat drinking sweet milk and milking until the snow falling outside piled on the roof in heavy drifts.

Mercy fantasized about keeping Rosetta there longer and doing more, but the promise of additional moments was more valuable. It was hard to let the moment go, and he began throwing dirt over the fire burning inside of him and after a while said: "Better head on home." For the preservation of those future opportunities, he packed Rosetta off with her winterberries—new discovery discovered—and convinced her that telling anyone about it would only make them wonder why she hadn't started sooner.

Now Mercy cleared the squeezed lemon halves from the table and dumped them in the cardboard box he used for a trash can. Getting caught was the furthest thing from his mind. Because he knew that once the lights in their eyes stopped dancing and started to dim, when the chosen ones realized that he'd taken their trust, they would also realize that they could never get it back. And this secret realization would fester (as it had festered in his own boyhood days) long after the girls understood what had happened to them, long after they'd stopped smiling or speaking or their families moved them to other places. Or they ran away. Like Rosetta.

Mercy stirred the lemonade and then poured it into a glass and looked at it as he had done a thousand times before. He would not drink a drop. It was an ablution, an offering fit only for those who were worthy. And once more he worked the chaos around in his mind and came to the same conclusion: It was not his soul that the Beast wanted that day in the church basement. It was not him, not his body and spirit that the Beast had chosen to destroy. No. Mercy figured long after he told his mother, after all feeling and grievance and memory had poured from him like the great deluge, that it was only the lemonade that the Beast wanted.

He stared at the sacrosanct glass and into the yellow liquid and thought of Annie Porter. The counting game had been going so well. And slowly, regretfully, he thought of what he'd left undone in a moment of haste. Or maybe in the comfort of arrogance? The lock. He'd forgotten to lock the utility-closet door behind him. It was so unlike him to neglect so small and critical a detail. What had caused him to slip? The footnotes of things forgotten loomed large. The boy had walked in, seen it, and ruined everything.

Mercy lifted the glass of lemonade up to the light and peered into its golden wonder, then set it back down on the table. Dash Kinwell. He would have to do something about that boy.

WATCH

Mercy was in the hallway outside of the closed classroom door pretending that he was mopping, watching Dash through the rectangular glass window. From that angle in the corridor he could make out the boy sitting at his desk. Other times he watched him in the schoolyard, sitting alone eating his lunch. Sometimes he saw him coming out of one of the corner stores and followed him to the top of the hill, where he stood watching him descend into the blue mist until he was obscured from view. He'd noticed, too, that the boy went down to the river by himself. And more and more, something else seemed to be growing inside when he looked at Dash, and he wondered what it could mean or not mean.

Because he didn't do boys. Not since Gary Higgins—the school nurse's son—and only then because of the special-friend game he could play with him. Only because of Slim Willy, Baby Cakes, King Catfish, and Slide Dog. Because doing boys meant he'd gone the way of Priest Abernathy, the way of the Beast. But girls meant the search for the light, for a spirit illumed and never to be extinguished.

He moved the mop as if he was getting a spot on the floor. He couldn't remember what the first girl he'd chosen was wearing. Was it a paisley sundress with a matching scarf, or a red wool sweater and black tights? Perhaps she had pink barrettes in her hair, or maybe it was arranged in cornrows? He couldn't recall. But what he could always remember were the eyes in all their glorious color and light, how they danced in response to being chosen once the choosing began. It was all in the eyes. And when he touched the girls and watched their lights flicker, everything made sense: perfect elixirs in basements and good intentions in Gardens of Eden. And he partook of it and reveled in it and made meaning out of the chaos of his mind.

He dunked the mop, feeling troubled. "Something has to be done," he whispered, looking at Dash through the glass. Because the boy saw *it*. And *it* had to be kept pure, the riches he found in the eyes of the chosen ones protected. But he had to have faith and remember that the garden would create the chance he needed as it had each time before. And he would know what to do when the chance came. What was growing inside of him grew stronger. He dunked the mop again, calming himself. Until then he would watch Dash like he'd watched the others, waiting for the right time, patient for the opportunity. *And who knows?* he thought, staring into the filthy water in the bucket. *I might even make another masterpiece while I'm at it.* Like Rosetta.

DEAD MARIGOLDS

Rosetta stood waiting in stilettos on the curb of 14th Street in the dawn, thinking about her little sister Lulu as she often did, wondering whether she was hunter or prey. There was a soft, warm breeze, and the bumper curls of her jet-black Farrah Fawcett wig blew softly, completely covering the cornrows she was wearing beneath it. She pressed her lips together so that the thick layer of lip gloss she was wearing would make them stick together as if with glue and she could enjoy the sensation of slowly pulling them apart. The effects of the quaaludes she swallowed earlier were beginning to wear off, so that she felt like she was splashing in the thick sludge of a bog lit with neon lights, and she stood in the damp dawn air in a semihypnotic state, biting listlessly at her chipped red nails, a habit she developed instead of smoking cigarettes. Now she felt the shooting pains more and more from the stilettos, and tried to distract herself by stroking the rabbit-fur vest she was wearing over her purple polyester minidress.

She could barely recall the events of the hours before, and when she closed her eyes and opened them again everything around her was edged in a thin band of color, like a rainbow barely visible after showers. The things that happened to her blended together in time. For instance, she recalled that one of her johns, the bald one who lived with his mother, had taken her to see *Star Wars*. But she couldn't remember if that was a few weeks back in May when it opened in theaters, or the night before. She did, however, remember the pretty flashes of the blue and red lightsabers and the fact that he'd felt her up the whole time and eaten an entire bucket of popcorn (extra butter) without offering her one bite. She remembered that later he bit her breast, saying how much he liked chocolate, and only when she cried out did he stop.

Rosetta looked into the ionized dark of the Strip, that realm of encrypted objectives and coded gestures, where people moved as if suspended in a thick and viscous oil. Big shiny cars with darkened windows glided by, and now and then one of them stopped. From inside an invisible hand opened the car door like an invitation to the ice-blue reaches of Neptune, where subzero air jetted out of black vents and steel thumped with the pulsating cosmology of Parliament-Funkadelic. She looked into the dark alleyways across the street, the glow of cigarettes flittering about like saffron fireflies.

She knew the Car Lady would be along soon. Dawn was closing in. She had figured out that at that hour it took Nephthys about thirty minutes to leave her apartment, cross the bridge, and drive the blocks to the exact point on the curb where she was now standing. Sometimes she needed a ride. Usually she didn't. But the Car Lady always seemed to show up when she wanted her. Getting a ride from Nephthys Kinwell meant she didn't have to worry about the bus driver ignoring her standing at the stop around the corner. Or the cabdrivers expecting a blow job for their fare instead of money. Besides, when she told them where she was going (Anacostia) they often said they didn't go "over there." Oftentimes, the farthest they would take her, especially in those wee hours, was the corner of 11th and M Streets in the southeast quadrant, near the Navy Yard, and from there she had to get out and walk across the bridge.

And she suffered a certain distress on any bridge. She hated the trust she had to put in the structures not to break as she walked across them. Because she'd learned that anything could collapse at any moment, split or crack or crumble and take her with it.

But more than her fear of having to hold on to something bound to break, it was a troublesome thing that the rivers beneath the bridges called to her sometimes.

The last time Rosetta dared cross a bridge on foot was in the early-morning hours on the East Capitol Street Bridge. It was renamed the Whitney Young Memorial Bridge in 1974, but like many things in the quadrants, renaming something did not change what people called it or what it was. And as she advanced, she saw a young man sitting on the ledge, his legs dangling over the currents of the Anacostia River. When she neared him, he turned to her, his blue eyes an unnatural shade in the dawn.

"One nation . . ." the young man said when he saw her.

Rosetta stopped. "What?"

"Under God . . ."

A seagull soared above and Rosetta watched it glide over the water. Her eyes were drawn down to the river. *Jump, and you won't have to feel anything anymore . . .*

"Indivisible . . ."

Rosetta looked at the young man's dangling legs, his loosened shoelaces drifting in the wind. She gazed into the river again. *Jump, and I will catch you . . .*

"I thought it mattered," said the young man.

Rosetta looked at him with the innocence of one doomed animal to another. "What?"

"This place."

What the young man meant was the dream of the territories. For he hailed from the distant Kingdom of Iowa, where from his elementary school desk he chanted the Pledge and believed it to be true. And when he arrived at the capital gates, he was driven inside by the magic that images of amber waves of grain can invoke. That the colors of the flag can inspire. But instead he found himself steeped in the filth of covering and uncovering the deeds of his superiors and coworkers: drug-fueled nights in the brothels of 14th Street and Georgetown; bribery at the Hay-Adams Hotel and the Mayflower; theft in the appropriations committees; data manipulation in the national laboratories; report bias in the think tanks; informants on the payroll. There was the support and sabotage of legislation—each in equal measure—based on shifting and sliding interests, and a game of wits and thrones. There was the pointless wheel of win lose draw. And many years later, there would be tribes of the young man's kind (Gen Me, Gen Z, Gen No) who would come to the same conclusions that he did, but at increasingly earlier ages, and they would resign themselves to wander the wiles of the times, unable to reconcile the story of the united territories they'd been taught and the world that existed.

But the young man, sitting on the ledge of a bridge in 1977, had no way of knowing this. What he knew, as a campaign adviser who whispered in his ear earlier that week assured him, was that digging down through the dream to unearth the truth (like those missing funds in the line items he'd found) meant he had to disappear. "We'll find you wherever you go, Iowa Boy," he'd said. "Might even take you to see the bottom of one of these rivers." And since the young man, already nursing a cocaine habit, had only now discovered that he had so little control of how his life could be lived, he thought about directing how it could end.

So it was no surprise that he'd arrived at his desk in the corner of the Iowa congressman's office well before dawn that morning, cleaned it out, and walked from the Capitol building down East Capitol Street (it was a straight shot) and climbed onto the bridge. He dangled his legs over the side now, not only because what he believed had been vanquished, but because he felt he had nothing to replace it with. *What do I stand for?* he asked himself, staring into the current. *I don't know.*

He looked at Rosetta. "I thought it mattered."

She stared back at him from the place in which she was living—a world away even from the one the young man imagined and could no longer face—and said nothing. For there was no solution to what the Revolutionary War and the Civil War and the Civil Rights Movement and amendments and riots and marches had not resolved in the kingdoms of the land, and they agreed on this without saying so. She left him there and walked on, not waiting to see what he would decide to do, not wanting to listen to the river call her too.

Rosetta shifted her weight in the stilettos and winced. If she couldn't get a faster ride over on the bus or with one of her johns, she tried to find another way to cross the bridge. So it was no surprise that her wandering heart called to the Car Lady, for Nephthys would not leave a lost soul without passage. Now it was nearly six o'clock in the morning, and Rosetta waited patiently for her approach. Time did things to her mind at that hour. Standing there in all that blue, the distant white marble monuments and administration buildings seemed washed in watercolor and the dark asphalt streets looked like some fantastic immobile sea.

She stared at a bright-orange neon sign flashing above an adult store across the street. She'd had enough of orange. Rosetta figured that most people thought that orange was a harmless color, but she knew it was deadly. Yellow with a little red mixed in, and it was deadly. Like a doomed fetus in the first trimester. Like the sun going down over 14th Street. Like the dust of Las Vegas. She couldn't do orange after Sweeney, with his million-dollar patio and his orange potted marigolds dying under the sun in the Kingdom of Nevada. She figured that most people didn't know that marigolds (especially the orange ones) give off a scent when they die that can be smelled even through the stench of armpits, arthritic cream, and cigars. And every time she saw anything orange, she thought of when she was lying on Sweeney's patio under a hot southwestern sky surrounded by marigolds, choking on the smell of death mixed with the funk of sex.

Sweeney had picked her up from the curb in front of the Butterfly Club six months ago, yelling "Black Beauty" from his car window. "You're exotic," he said. She knew that was bullshit, but she got in the car with him anyway because she hadn't yet made her pimp's quota or eaten. "Dark meat is the best," he said, rubbing her leg. He offered to take her to Las Vegas. "You need somebody to look out for you."

In her time on the streets, Rosetta had learned that most people didn't know how strong a fifteen-year-old girl could be. And they also didn't know how weak she could be; when the worst that can happen to her has already happened and she knows all there is to know about the rise and fall of women down through the ages and doesn't need anything else explained. "I'll take care of you," he said, staring at her small breasts.

And he did take care of her—if it could be called that—for a while. Until the men whom he owed some money came for a visit and left his headless torso on the chaise and his fingers floating in the toilet. She sprinted down a flight of steps and broke the door lock to get out. She had to leave her French Chanel pumps, all the Gucci slingbacks, and even the high leopard-print platforms that rubbed her ankles raw. She tricked and hitchhiked her way back to the capital. When her pimp spotted her again, he broke her wrist and then bought her a hamburger. "Daddy missed you," he said, handing her a bottle of painkillers and squirting ketchup on her french fries.

Rosetta looked away from the orange neon sign in the dawn light. The last of the quaalude effects were wearing off and she remembered more. She'd been dancing on the pole at the Butterfly Club after scoring some johns, then she did peep shows in the back of the triple-X theater for fifty cents a peep before coming out to stand at the curb. Sometimes when the things she swallowed or snorted wore off, she could still see his face. Mercy

Ratchet. An apparition in the winterberries and snow, who appeared out of thin air that cold and bright day so long ago. That was when the beginning and ending of everything happened. She knew that now. It was when she first learned that some filth could never be washed away.

So much of that time was still blurred in her mind and so much was clear. She could still smell him, could still see him in his faded dungarees and oil-smudged shirt. His rust-colored face was a map of pockmarks, scratches, razor stubble, blackheads, and rashes. But he had a remarkable smile, a dentist's dream of glistening white rows of teeth. Then she remembered a feeling of floating. Or sailing. There was more, things she couldn't remember clearly, and when she tried it was like peering into murky water.

But she remembered what he said very clearly: *I am not a beast.*

And every time she pulled up her shirt or pulled down her panties or pulled off her bra, it was as if she were still in Mercy Ratchet's shack. For years she wondered what she had done wrong—or right—to make him pick her that distant cold day, that day of picking winterberries. And she wondered what it was about that nameless bottomless endless thing she felt inside that made her keep it all a secret. Except it festered out in the sun like a rotting carcass each time she saw him going into the church parking lot or mowing the school grounds, and he seemed to look at her without seeing that she was there. And ever since she ran away from home, time had fashioned for her a new reality, and it was hot in the peep-show boxes and cheap motels and the backseats of cars—as hot as it had been in Mercy Ratchet's shack—except now there wasn't any milking going on. Only the ongoing drain of her soul.

Rosetta was thinking about these things when she spotted the 1967 Plymouth coming down the street. The car was as legendary as its driver. Nephthys Kinwell, heavy drinker and aunt to Anacostia's very own Death Witch, drove a haunted car that was never stopped by the police, never broke down, and never ran out of gas.

SONAR

Nephthys heard the eerie dirge of wandering hearts across the unbroken ripples of the sea, and she knew where they were without having to be told . . .

Nephthys was coming down the street slowly. She'd started that morning like she started all the others: with the feeling that told her the whereabouts of a wandering heart. She looked around as she drove along. The Strip was as alive as it had been at eleven o'clock the night before, with the dawn marking a shift from the women who worked the nights to the women who worked the days like some crazed changing of the guard.

She spotted Rosetta, as she'd been spotting her since she was thirteen, and pulled up to the curb where she was standing and stopped. Through the window they gave each other a look, and Rosetta got in the backseat of the car. Her legs buckled as she lowered herself down. She pried off the red stilettos and sank deep into the leather and sighed with a watershed of relief. When she recovered, she reached across the seat and handed Nephthys three dollars. It was much less than what she had in her purse but more than she could spare.

Nephthys took the money and stuffed it into the ashtray. She would leave it there until the next time she picked up Rosetta and the girl didn't have any money. She studied her face through the rearview mirror. "How you been?"

Rosetta offered a thin smile because she knew—as all Anacostians do—that a question was just as loaded as its answer. "Been fine," she said.

Nephthys reached into the glove compartment and took out a little brown bag filled with candy and held it up, for she believed that sugar had great healing properties for the woes of any child.

Rosetta took the bag and stuffed a piece of caramel in her mouth, and it was then that she realized she hadn't eaten since the morning before. She chewed it down quickly, grabbed a piece of saltwater taffy, and rolled up the window. The June dawn was warm and balmy, but now that she was in the car and leaving the Strip, she wanted to breathe as little of its air as possible. As Nephthys pulled away from the curb and went down the street, Rosetta watched the outrageous display from the window as they rolled by. There were the Jell-O and mud-wrestling joints. There was Adam & Eve and the burlesque acts. There was This Is It? and the bathhouses. She saw Benny's Home of the Porno Stars, the opium dens, and Casino Royal. She saw musicians, transvestites, and drag queens streaming about. And she watched the legions of sex workers trolling up and down the streets. Many years later, there would be a vast webbed empire more powerful than places like the Strip, where people weighed down by the heaviness of being went to be turned into pixels of light and became part of the Great Screen—a ubiquitous eye that blinked at the world—and those who dared meet its coltan glare were transfixed.

But Rosetta had no way of knowing this as she sat in the backseat, watching the spectacle roll by, her body spent from a night on the Strip. What she knew was that she had to get away from there. And after an acceptable amount of time only she and Nephthys seemed to understand, she asked, "You seen Lulu?"

"Uh-huh," said Nephthys. "Seen her around from time to time."

"She look all right?" What Rosetta meant was that she wanted to know if her little sister had yet changed from hunter to prey, and if the chaos of what used to be her home, where her mother was consumed by the attention of men, and where her siblings circled Anacostia like some lost flock of pigeons, had gotten better or worse.

"S'pose so," said Nephthys.

"Oh," said Rosetta.

They rode on in silence, listening to the white girl in the trunk, until they reached the bridge that would carry them over to the southeast side. A coral-pink sky was rising over the river, and it was then that the long night of debauchery and spectacle weighed heavily on Rosetta and she suddenly wanted to sleep.

But Nephthys had something else in mind. When they stopped at a red light, she said: "Read fuh me." She held up the *Afro Man* newspaper.

Rosetta knew that Nephthys did not mean for her to read the ongoing commentary about the Hanafi siege that happened three months before, where twelve black Muslims took control of three office buildings, held 150 hostages, shot and killed a twenty-four-year-old reporter and a security guard, and were responsible for the bullet that barely missed Councilman Marion Barry's heart. Nor did she mean for her to read about Benin adopting its constitution or the coup attempt in Angola. Rosetta knew that Nephthys wanted her to read the Lottery, Amber Kinwell's unmistakable proclamations of death. People were afraid of her but they still wanted to know what she dreamed, for there was much to know and much to fear in 1977. *What did she see?* Maybe she would tell of a fatally sick child with a name that began with the letter M? A fire in one of the public housing buildings? God no, please don't let her tell about a police raid rounding up black boys. We got any crimes of passion? What about accidents on the job? Who would be shot? Stabbed? Who would be found in one of the rivers this time? Or in an alley? Anacostia was interested in anything that could show them what to brace for.

Tiredly, Rosetta took the newspaper from the Car Lady's

hand. And since Rosetta no longer believed in God or the Devil (her world had taught her that people could act as either at any moment), she was not averse to those who claimed to conjure something entirely different. So she turned to the Lottery and read:

1. Police raid. Green house with the big philodendron on the porch. Body in the closet.
2. Pink pacifier and bottle. Box buried in the yard. Frederick Douglass house. Study cottage in the back.
3. Red, white, and blue beads on the ends of braided hair. Train tracks. Washington Bullets T-shirt. Kingman Lake.
4. Wires on fire. Apartment on Dotson Street. No numbers on the doors. Windows nailed shut. Woman can't breathe.
5. A mother. Five children. A man named Wilson holds his arm and loses his heart.

Rosetta yawned. "That's the Lottery this month," she said. She put the newspaper down on the seat.

"No more?" asked Nephthys.

"That's all there is."

And since Nephthys was good at encryption and seeing things that others said weren't there, the omission of Dash confirmed Amber's dream about the boy.

They rode on. Nephthys turned onto V Street by the old Big Chair, its four thousand pounds of mahogany rotting under the weight of time.

"Right here, please," said Rosetta.

Nephthys slowed the car. She always picked up Rosetta and dropped her off in different places, for the girl had seemed to pick up the traits of a woodland creature on constant alert for threats from the forest.

"Here is good," Rosetta said, and she reached down to squeeze her feet into the red stilettos once again and winced. "Thanks for the candy."

"Thanks fuh the readin'," Nephthys said. She looked at Rosetta in the rearview mirror. They would see each other again, when the call of one and the answer of one would lead them to each other.

Rosetta shoved the little bag of candy into her purse and put her hand on the door handle. "Bye," she said, and she got out of the car and disappeared into the Algonquian mist.

HARBOR

Nephthys docked where her heart guided her so that souls might board, and together they sought passage through the unseen perdition of pain . . .

Nephthys sat in the parked Plymouth outside the entrance of Greater Southeast Community Hospital, waiting. She was drawn there sometimes without the direction of the fog, for its halls were filled with the souls of the lost. She sat watching the ambulances roar in and roar out, thinking about the bottle of liquor she couldn't find earlier that morning. She was sure she'd left it on top of the refrigerator in its brown paper bag the day before, and now it was gone. And as she watched the hospital bustle, she thought about the nurse's letter too, still lying in the debris of her living room floor, calling to her without her ever touching it. What could she do about the words on that piece of paper? She didn't know. She stared into the dark hospital entrance glass, listening to the hiss of the automatic doors, waiting for who was destined to ride in the car.

And in accordance with signs omens bones, out walked Nurse Higgins, a tough and stout-looking woman. Her white uniform fit snugly over her full-figured frame; she wore it like a nun's habit whether she was on duty at the elementary school or not. She was coming from an emergency check of her blood pressure, which seemed to be rising with each passing year since the death of her son. Every time she thought about him, she was struck by the dark irony with which creatures of passage live, since she'd spent a lifetime healing the children of others but was powerless to help her own boy. And in the end her son escaped St. Elizabeths and jumped from the top of a radio tower, at last freeing the people in his head from each other.

Nephthys watched the nurse clutch her purse and little white bag of medication to her bosom as she squinted in the bright sun. And since she was never surprised by constellations, circumstances, and events, she waited for the woman to notice her.

When Nurse Higgins saw the car, she stopped in her tracks. But she nodded at Nephthys as if resigning to the inevitability of the car waiting for her at last, and she walked over and got into the backseat.

Nephthys let the nurse get settled, then looked at her in the rearview mirror, thinking of the history (debt?) she had with her. For she hadn't been able to give safe passage to her son, and she placed him on the list in her mind of souls she'd lost on the path. It happened sometimes in the places and spaces through which she traveled, when the body went in one direction and the mind another. And now with this letter about Dash, it seemed that the nurse was implying that her great-nephew was in some sort of mental distress. In spite of barely knowing the boy, there were reasons why this bothered Nephthys more and more.

Many years before Dash brought that ominous letter to her door, Nephthys was driving slowly down the street when she spotted Gary, Nurse Higgins's twenty-year-old son. The fog had told her about his wandering heart many times before, and she'd given him rides to the usual places (McDonald's, Morton's Department Store, Peoples Drug Store, the National Arboretum) that she knew he wanted to go. She slowed the car to a full stop and waited for him to notice that she was there.

Gary Higgins was perched on the Big Chair, a nineteen-and-a-half-foot Duncan Phyfe dining room chair on the corner of V Street, his legs dangling between the spindles. From that vantage point, he surveyed the topography of Anacostia and the wild happenings east of the river, for the Big Chair was a kind of lighthouse, an eye fixed on the happenings of that isle of blood and desire.

Sometimes in the doldrums of his surveillance, Gary thought about the grinning man, Mercy Ratchet. And ever since he was a little boy, he'd been trying to decide if that perfect row of teeth was real. If the touching was real. He thought about telling his mother about the smile and the touching, for she worked at the same elementary school as Mercy Ratchet, but he didn't see the point. Because there were many things that he'd tried to tell her that she did not believe, like the existence of Slim Willy, Baby Cakes, King Catfish, and Slide Dog (his friends since early toddlerhood).

And she didn't believe him when he told her about the talking shadows either. They spoke to him about the histories and oracles of man. They talked of "the order of cause and effect": the apocalyptic spread of immunodeficiency viruses and blood diseases and opioid dependencies; hurricanes and tsunamis swallowing cities whole; radioactive oceans and toxic crops and mutations of plant and animal; believers who took cyanide to get to heaven and believers who took arsenic to get to spaceships and believers who burned in flames; skyscrapers crashing to the ground and countries leveled into the sand; people with bodies under their homes and glee in their hearts; children murdering other children in sunny classrooms; and weapons exploding the earth one hundred times over. Gary didn't think the shadows would lie to him. But aside from his friends, he had his doubts about the things he experienced sometimes. Like the smile and the touching. Which was why, even now, he wondered about the realness of that shining row of teeth, that pockmarked face, and those glasses of lemonade.

Gary's legs started to cramp on the hard edges of the Big Chair and he pushed those thoughts aside. There were other urgent matters now, more burning things that required his attention. And when he saw the Plymouth, he climbed down from the Big Chair and ran over to the car. He jumped in the backseat and shoved a five-dollar bill at Nephthys, shaking. He looked around nervously and smoothed the once clean shirt his mother had left out for him three days before. He had to be ready now. More than ready. Because the police, Gary had learned from the red rabbits who sometimes surfaced from their subterranean lairs in the sewers to warn him, were mounting a new attack, an onslaught more powerful than the one before. The red rabbits said the police were a ubiquitous, radioactive force, dispatched at any moment. *Watch out for the Isotope Army*, they said. *Watch out for the xenon, cesium, and barium troops.* Sometimes the rabbits gathered at the bottom of the Big Chair to warn him. *They're coming*, they told him. *You need to go.*

"We need to go," Gary said. He shoved the five-dollar bill at Nephthys again and slammed down the door peg to lock it. "They're coming."

"Put that money back in your pocket. Where to, chile?"

"Gotta get there quick." The red rabbits knew and they never lied.

"Where to, chile?"

"Hurry!"

"Then tell me first."

In spite of the dire situation that weighed heavily on his mind, Gary tried to calm himself. "The Safeway. Quick. The Safeway. It's the only glass they can't bust through."

The white girl in the trunk pounded the trunk lid.

Nephthys drove to the Safeway as Gary asked. It didn't take long for it all to unfurl. For soon after Nephthys pulled in front of the grocery store, Gary threw the five-dollar bill at her and jumped from the backseat and charged into the Safeway, shouting about the coming of an Armageddon of radioactive xenon, cesium, and barium troops. She watched him run in and sipped from her flask. Then she heard the roaring sirens of a police cruiser.

The rest of it played out in the time-lapse rendering that happenings in Anacostia wrought: Gary climbing a ten-foot stock shelf at the front of the store to bang on the wall of glass and make sure that there were no fissures; children pointing and squealing as Gary shouted down from the top of the rack that they needed to get to the back of the store where it would be safe; Gary taking out a cigarette lighter to prepare the glass with a protective half-life-accelerating layer of the sun's fire to burn the isotopes away; the store manager running toward the fray. "Lock the automatic doors!" Gary shouted. "We can't afford to let one of 'em in here!"

Nephthys saw the police cruiser skid into the lot and two cops jump out, guns drawn. She knew why they were there, and she followed behind them just in time to see Gary holding the lighter in the air.

"Get these kids out of here!" Gary shouted. "Head to the back!" He took one look at the two isotopes approaching, held the lighter to the bottom of his torn shirt, and said: "If this means I need to be the fuel for this fire to start, then so be it. I'm willing to make the sacrifice."

One of the cops, his finger on the trigger, was moving closer to Gary when Nephthys stepped into his path. "Move!" he thundered.

In the seconds between seconds, Nephthys did not move, for she could smell the bloodlust in the air. And she knew—as all women of the ghetto do—that the lives of the males who cohabitate with them totter precariously between existence and extinction. Mammalian instincts took hold and she spoke quickly: "I was just comin' to get him, mistuh."

"Who are you?" asked the cop.

"He's my nephew."

"Well, your nephew is not going to make it."

"He's fine," Nephthys said. She looked at him without blinking.

The police officer stared back at her with icy eyes. "You need to move, lady."

"It ain't no trouble, mistuh. Like I say, I was just comin' to get him. Places confuse him sometimes, you know. He don't mean no harm." And here Nephthys turned to look up at Gary, saying, "Put that down, baby cootuh. It ain't wuh you thinkin'." She turned back to the cop, eyeing his drawn gun. She could hear more sirens approaching outside in the parking lot. "I take him and we can go, mistuh. It's just little clouds in his head. Happens sometimes. I take him fuh a nice ride to the National Arboretum and sweep them clouds away."

The police officer seemed momentarily mesmerized by the light water magic in her faraway voice, and he eased his finger from the trigger and softened and said, "Lady, you need to move aside."

Gary was looking down in horror. "Miss Nephthys! Get away from that thing! It's insoluble. Immunological destruction. And we don't have the marrow to replace what we lose!"

"I believe you, chile," said Nephthys evenly without taking her eyes off the police officer. "Come down from there and tell me about it in the car. We gonna go."

Gary shook his head vigorously. "No! No! It's too late for that now. If they had just locked the doors like I told them, we could have stopped it before it started happening! But now it's too late! Goddamn them, it's too late!"

Gary continued, describing the coming apocalypse in infinite detail and sequences of events as the red rabbits had warned him. And while he was describing the dome of electromagnetic energy that would corral them like animals in a slaughterhouse, other officers rushed in while the one whom Nephthys was trying to block ran around to the side of the stock rack and pushed it over, sending Gary flying through the air and crashing to the floor. The impact knocked the lighter from his hand.

"Now you've done it!" Gary shouted as he was handcuffed

and an ambulance pulled up to take him to St. Elizabeths. "It's all over now! The streets are gonna run red!"

An ambulance screamed into the Greater Southeast Community Hospital entrance and stopped. A car was following closely behind it, and it too stopped and the driver's-side door flew open and a woman jumped out, crying.

From the backseat of the Plymouth, Nurse Higgins looked at Nephthys in the rearview mirror, considering the years she'd seen her go in and out of Sonny's Bar. For she was yet conflicted by the feeling that Nephthys Kinwell had both doomed her son by taking him to the Safeway and saved his life by keeping him from being shot by the police. "How you been?"

Nephthys was watching the woman race over to the ambulance as they pulled someone out on a stretcher. She looked away. "Been fine. You?"

"Still livin'."

The white girl in the trunk sighed and thumbed a spare hubcap.

"Where to?"

Nurse Higgins hesitated. She didn't know where she wanted to go, now that she was in the car. "Just around for a while, if you don't mind. A drive. Something to ease my mind."

"A drive, huh?" Nephthys said, as if to herself. The uncertainty of a destination always made her uneasy, for it brought on the unbearable inertia of one. She put her foot on the gas pedal, revving the engine softly, and pulled off.

They meandered in the Plymouth down one road to another, until at last they reached the end of the quadrant and entered Suitland Parkway, the imaginable forest flanking them on both sides. And in that way that women of age start on something from the edges, the two women inched closer and closer to what they really wanted to discuss, asking small-talk questions about things they knew all too well and nodding at things with which they actually disagreed.

They neared the cemetery where Nephthys often took Professor Evanston to visit his wife's grave, and she turned into the quiet groves on impulse. It was as good a destination as any.

Nurse Higgins made no protest and looked out at the rolling hills of graves, wondering when she might be among them.

Nephthys pulled into an overlook and turned off the engine.

A thick silence filled the car and slowly suffocated the *click click click* of the engine cooling and contracting, and then there was nothing.

The white girl in the trunk was somber and still, for each visit to a cemetery was a reminder that her body had never been found.

Nephthys took a sip from her flask and stared into the green expanse. An enormous tree stood in all its ancient wildness amid the symmetrical lines of graves in the manicured grass, its ashen trunk twisted and knotted, its bark riven with deep gashes and scars. The tree stood like some otherworldly being that had long borne witness to the events of one era to the next, each great ring of growth and death filled with the blood spilled from happenings folded into the pages of time. Many years later, the tree would again drink deep of the abominations of men and the blood of hordes from the kingdoms of the land, and be fortified by the desires of empires risen and fallen.

But Nephthys had no way of knowing this as she looked at the thick leaves and sat quietly in the Plymouth with Nurse Higgins. What she knew was that one happening was always linked to another. "Talked to Dash the other day."

The nurse took a pill from the little white bag and swallowed it dry. "Did he give you my letter?"

"He did."

"Well, we know that boys will be boys, wherever they are. But they'll be boys over nothing. And with the principal on my back about the stuff these young'uns get into, I had to tell you my mind about Dash. And I just didn't want to say anything to Amber about it."

The two women went silent now for different reasons.

"I've seen what happens to children who don't have any people," Nurse Higgins finally continued. "It's a terrible thing. They get into trouble, fights and such. They do strange things. Because the Lord knows that there are things children suffer. And a lot of times you can't even tell what's eatin' 'em." And here she thought of the puzzling and bizarre things her son did and said when he was a boy, how she cried about him through the years, for he did not seem to hear her over the wild and incredulous voices in his head.

Nephthys was listening to the nurse, thinking about Dash. She could still hear the words that chilled her. *I think Mama had a dream about me . . .* She took a sip from her flask and looked at the nurse in the rearview mirror. "Hard to tell a lot of things."

Nurse Higgins sighed. "God knows, it is. Take this girl a while back at the school. Her name was Annie Porter. She was doing weird things. Biting off the tips of pencils and eating erasers until she was sick to her stomach. Jumping up and down whenever anybody came near her. I kept trying to get to what was bothering her. Talked to her mother and she said she didn't know, but the girl was carrying her dead father's picture around. Then the girl just stopped talking. I mean she went mute, poor thing. And one day I found her in the bathroom rubbing herself with a bar of soap." The nurse paused, and she closed her eyes and opened them again. "I was beginning to wonder if . . . I don't know . . . if somebody was . . . messin' with her."

"Oh?" said Nephthys, troubled. "Be a wicked, wicked world if that was so."

"Wicked indeed," said Nurse Higgins, falling silent. Because whenever she thought of Annie Porter in that bathroom, she had to think about the time she caught her son rubbing himself with a bar of soap in his bed. And she remembered the awful thought that crept into her mind that day—although it was only for a moment—and how she chased it away. "Well, back to what I been trying to say about Dash. Lord, my mind wanders sometimes. We know kids play at things all the time, and playin' is natural. But it's a strange thing to be talking to a make-believe somebody like it's real. And I thought you should know about it. See about him."

Nephthys nodded. But she didn't know what knowing and seeing about him could do. And now what she'd been drinking had pushed her own blood pressure to Mt. Everest heights, and she looked out at the graveyard rows, sweating.

The nurse watched Nephthys wipe her brow. "And children can be cruel. They like to tease, you know what I mean?" And here she paused again, unsure of how to bring up what she really wanted to ask, for she'd overheard Lulu taunting Dash about his father being in the war, saying that he was crazy and lived in Amber's garden.

"Where's his father?"

"Wuh?'

"Dash's father. Hope you don't mind me asking."

"Don't know."

The nurse shook her head. In the dealings with the children in her charge, the whereabouts of fathers was a question she found herself asking more and more as the decades wore on. Because she felt that no one knew better than she about the things that could happen. And when she thought of Gary's talk about Slim Willy, Baby Cakes, King Catfish, and Slide Dog, she wondered once more if her husband could have helped Gary, had he lived to see what was happening to their boy. And there were times when she thought about the odd thing her son used to say as a young child: *I am not a beast.* Such a bizarre proclamation for a little boy. She could never get him to tell her what he meant, and she tried to understand what the pang of guilt she felt about never getting to the bottom of that could mean or not mean. So she couldn't put any of those things in the letter to Nephthys, and could only remind her that things could happen to a boy.

The nurse looked out over the rolling meadow, thinking of

the radio tower from which her son had jumped. “Well, I wanted you to know about this thing with Dash and see about him. Because it’s a worrisome thing, Nephthys. It’s odd and troubling, that River Man.”

It was getting on toward dark, long after Nephthys took Nurse Higgins home, and she was ending her work of ferrying people from one quadrant to another. She parked under a leaning maple tree near her apartment building and sat.

The white girl in the trunk lay motionless. For there were times when the heaviness of Nephthys Kinwell’s thoughts filled the car like a thick and noxious gas, and there was nothing to do but wait for it to subside.

Nephthys stared at the dashboard clock, its hour and minute hands depicting a point in time. All that day she’d pushed away what was in the back of her mind, and every time she thought about the wall mirror and the missing bottles she only wanted to drink more. Her half finger throbbed and she touched its hardened flesh and sank deeper into the leather of the Plymouth. The River Man. Why did she feel so strange when she heard that name?

Circlin' round de ring shout lap
No beginnin' and no end . . .

But she never reacted when he sang. He listened to her labored breathing through the haze of liquor, and her commitment to self-destruction pained him. That was why he moved her bottles of alcohol. She sat them on the little end table next to her chair and he moved them to places he thought she wouldn't think to look: on the broiler tray of the unused oven; beneath the piles of debris in her closet; behind the piping under the bathroom sink. He knocked the flask from her hands and watched her pick it up again, and he hid other bottles only to discover that she had found them. He watched her get in and out of the Plymouth and go into Sonny's Bar. Countless times he'd even stepped into the wall mirror glass, looking at her as she stared into the reflection, hoping she would see him. But now the mirorr was broken. He tried harder to speak to her in the symbiotic language of twins, but she did not seem to hear him through the rancor of her despair.

In the early dawn, Osiris moved through the old steel of the Plymouth Belvedere and into the passenger seat next to Nephthys. He knew that she was waiting for the fog, and he watched her put the key in the ignition as he had a thousand times before. He looked on as Nephthys took sips from her flask, and once more he worried about her ruination.

Osiris heard the white girl in the trunk flip a rubber mat over and back again, and he moved into the zone of her internment.

She acknowledged him with the dignity of one ghost to another. *I was here. This is mine.*

Osiris nodded. She said this every time.

The white girl in the trunk sighed. *There's nothing you can do.*

Meanin'?

She looked through the trunk at Nephthys sitting at the

REQUIEM FOR THE LIVING

Osiris had traveled many waters since he was murdered and dumped into the Anacostia River. Each time he thought about Nephthys, he felt the interstellar cold of his solitude. And he knew—as all ghosts do—that the dead worry about their loved ones even after they are gone. So it was no surprise that Osiris visited her on each anniversary of his death, the only time of year he thought his sister might sense him through the brume of her melancholy. Each time he wandered the floors of her apartment building and through the sights and sounds of the lives of others, until he came to her door and moved through it and found her slumped in her chair.

He whispered her name and shouted her name but she did not respond. Sometimes he tried to influence the things around her to get her attention: banging on the walls until the plaster cracked, stopping the refrigerator motor, pressing against her front door so that it was difficult to open. He often moved the many objects that littered her living room floor from one place to another. And to his surprise, he even found a remnant of indigo cloth that their mother had made in her closet, and he put it in other places where he thought Nephthys might find it and remember what they once had and who they once were. And he sang a Gullah riff from that faraway long-ago place they once shared, hoping she would realize that he was there:

Indigo swirlin' round de vat
No beginnin' and no end

steering wheel. She'd learned many things about her in the years of haunting (accompanying?) her in the Plymouth. *She drinks too much, as you know. I've seen it before with my own father, and this sort of drinking never ends well.* And here she tried to reconcile the hate love shame she felt whenever she thought about her father, and once more she mourned the unspeakable reasons that girls could not go home. She collected her thoughts and looked at Osiris. *She can't cope with what's happened to you. And she feels guilty about separating from your daughter. And now she's worried about the boy.*

Osiris rubbed his half finger. *Go on.*

She stroked the worn-out carpet lining of the trunk where her gold necklace had been. *It's a mournful thing about your sister. Hopeless, really. Because she tries to save them. People, I mean. Even though she can't. Save them, I mean. Everyone carries their own affliction and none can carry it for them.* And here she thought of Rosetta's scurrying, Professor Evanston's misery, Gary's urgency, and the guilt of the colonel's wife. There were so many others, countless passengers, each with burdens that kept them frozen even as they moved from one place to the next. And there were times when she turned away from her own sorrows and looked at them with a pang of pity, for a joyless life was no life at all. And each time one of them got into the backseat of the Plymouth, her heartstrings played a requiem for the living.

The white girl in the trunk sighed again and rolled over. *Some can never be saved.*

Meanin'?

But she did not respond, for she was once more overcome with the grief of her own ending.

Osiris moved back to the passenger seat and stared at his sister. *It's me, Nephie. Nephie?*

Go on now, Osiris, said the white girl in the trunk. *She can't see you, goddamnit. But I was here. This is mine.*

* * *

She wiped the black slag from the sides of her face and waited for Osiris to leave. It had been many years since the day of her death, but no matter how much time passed it frightened and saddened her just the same. For those twenty-four years of a living life were gone and she could never get them back, stolen as they were by someone whom she thought loved her. In her living life she had been dating a man whom others said was important, who ruled in critical spaces and worked with others who reigned in the kingdoms of the land. But it seemed that she'd gone too far when she told him about her dream of traveling with him through the quadrants in his car instead of a dirty cab in the middle of the night, how she was ready to live an unending vacation with him, and that she was going to tell his wife about their affair and her pregnancy.

She rolled over in the trunk and started to cry when she thought about the rest: the two men who grabbed her (they were waiting in her Georgetown flat when she got home that night). No one ever saw them pull her body from the trunk. Nor did they see when one of them dropped his end and her head hit the littered shore and he picked her body up, slippery with the black slag that years of dumped industrial-furnace residue along the banks had wrought. And when they carried her body to the edge of the Anacostia River and threw it in, no one heard one of them say, "She gonna see new places yet." And the seed of the important man's child was no more.

Many years later, there would be other young women in the back rooms of organizations and behind the frosted glass of boardrooms and under the desks of powerful men and in the gold-trimmed offices of the Acropolis. And they would discover that their efforts often led to more ways to lose than to win. But the white girl in the trunk had no way of knowing this as she stared into the oil spots on the carpet lining, fingering through it for her missing necklace as she had a thousand times before. What she knew—as all who find themselves in Anacostia do—

was that dreams come true even when people don't want them to. She sobbed and curled up tight next to the spare tire. For she could never go back to her Allegheny home in the Kingdom of Pennsylvania, a wasteland of plundered coal deposits and dying hemlock forests, a place she ran to the capital to escape. And she couldn't stay in that river either, dark and cold as it was. So there was no other place for her to be, no other space she felt she could belong but in the trunk of Nephthys Kinwell's car.

ARK

Nephthys sailed the unrelenting gales and swells, collecting souls who waited to board her ferry, for there was no passage for them through that unforgiving nighttide without it . . .

Nephthys divided time, whether minutes, months, or decades, into sections of which she alone knew the meaning, for her wandering heart drove her forward according to its own design. And as she sat in the Plymouth, tracing the places and spaces of the quadrants in her mind, the fog emerged from the dawn and drifted into the car as it had so many times before, and she knew who needed passage. *The professor*, she thought, turning the key in the ignition. *It's the professor today*.

Dr. Gordon Evanston, retired professor of literature at Howard University, was waiting patiently for Nephthys to arrive. His gray sideburns flanked his face like tiny sentinels and he looked out at the world through deep-brown eyes that shifted intensity from one moment to the next. He wore the same jackets—linen in summer and tweed in winter—that he'd been wearing for thirty-five years. He lived in the oasis of Fort Dupont, a collection of small castles surrounded by a moat of disenfranchisement. His redbrick colonial sat in the center of a quaint cul-de-sac with similarly lovely homes, so that his neighbors to the left and right knew his every move and the long intervals of his solitude.

After years of teaching literature at Howard University, Professor Evanston had achieved the Olympian feat of tenure, only to retire in disgust. His colleagues were relieved to see him go, tired of bracing for his comments about the farce of black critical thought within earshot of board members, and his unending appetite for the campaign against what he called "black lethargy." Things finally came to a head in the heat of an argument he had with the university's president over the content of his syllabus, and he called him a "fearful potentate."

The professor sat waiting in his parlor, an octagonal monument to scholarship and culture with floor-to-ceiling bookshelves. The shelves to the left held his enormous jazz album collection, which he organized according to mood and tone with the precision of a locksmith. The shelves to the right were reserved for what he called his books of literature and light. He sat at his mahogany desk in the center of the parlor, hand carved by his sharecropping grandfather on a Greensboro porch in the Kingdom of North Carolina. On the desk sat an ancient Smith Corona typewriter he hadn't touched in years, and next to it was a cedar box that held his unfinished novel manuscript, *Progeny of the Sun*. Although a man of letters, he found that he no longer had any use for verse or glyph as the years ticked by; no cause for what was written down or way to describe the wanderings of his heart. For the death of his wife had burned everything, and he could think only of what flowers to bring to her grave and what condition the cemetery grounds would be in when he arrived. Would he need his galoshes or would his Florsheim loafers do?

He looked through the antique lace curtains that his wife had hung on the windows two decades before, and saw Nephthys pull into the cul-de-sac. He stood up quickly and put his wallet in his pocket. For he was ready, as ready as he'd been at three o'clock that morning.

Nephthys was sitting patiently in the car outside the professor's house, waiting for him. From the corner of her eyes she could see the drapes of the neighbors in a few of the houses being drawn slowly apart and then snatched together again when she looked up. She heard a door open somewhere and then another one slam shut. A woman came out on her porch to water potted flowers already drowning from the overnight rains. She looked at Nephthys sitting in the car and went back into her home. Then one of the front doors opened and out came the professor.

Dr. Evanston got into the Plymouth ceremoniously and with slow deliberation, as if entering a confessional booth.

Nephthys was just as solemn as her passenger, and she let the gravity of the ride they were about to take settle over them.

"Morning, Ms. Kinwell."

Nephthys took a sip from her flask. "Mornin', Dr. Evanston. How you been?"

The professor looked around at the interior of the Plymouth and out at his own car, a cream-colored 1971 Oldsmobile Cutlass Supreme, sitting in his driveway. "Been fine." He didn't mind riding to his wife's grave in the charmed hearse. But the Cutlass was unbearable. He could still smell his wife's perfume in the buttery leather. The imprint of her body in the passenger seat tortured him each time he got behind the wheel and looked to his right. And everywhere inside of the vehicle was her infinite fastidiousness: the pressed handkerchiefs she placed in the glove compartment in case he forgot one; the pink hand lotion (Rose Milk) she kept in a cloth clutch under the armrest; the bottle of Windex she stashed under the seat to keep the dashboard and windows clean.

The professor handed Nephthys some money. "Good to see you again. Same place."

Nephthys nodded and pulled off.

They weaved along in the Plymouth, humoring each other with the contemplations of small life: shiny new fire trucks at stations; years-old potholes that had yet to be filled; the wedding procession that held them at the light a full five minutes (what a beautiful Lincoln Continental!); the store where the best roast beef and ham could be bought; the new stereo systems on display at Woolworth; the disappearance of the daffodil patches over the years (where did all the flowers go?). They rode on, passing a gas station with long lines of cars waiting at the pumps and people cursing what was being called "the energy crisis."

They passed by the abandoned Riley Furniture Shop, and Nephthys looked at the boarded-up facade and the crumbling bricks, thinking of her brother, unaware that the key to the mystery of his demise was riding in the backseat of her car. And in accordance with the dark irony with which creatures of passage live, the professor looked at the old shop too, thinking of his son and the broken music box, unaware of the significance of seemingly insignificant moments, and how one life can intersect with the death of another. So it was no surprise that together they went along their way—Nephthys and the professor—with the small talk between them defined by a relationship complicit in the private contemplation and unending sensation of losing the other half of one's soul.

They arrived at the border of the Kingdom of Maryland, crossed over, and headed to the cemetery.

Nephthys drove to the exact spot where Mrs. Gordon Evanston was laid to rest and stopped the car, and in that quiet there was only the sound of the wind, the caw of some fowl in the acreage, and the white girl in the trunk turning over and sighing.

Finally, the professor took out a single white rose from inside his jacket pocket and put his hand on the door handle, bracing. "I guess it's time," he said, looking at the grave site just over a grassy mound.

"Guess it is," said Nephthys.

But the professor did not move. As many times as he'd been to his wife's grave, he could never prepare himself for that first glimpse of her name on the granite. He fidgeted in the backseat. "Care to join?"

Nephthys glanced at the professor in the rearview mirror. She had her own reasons for staying in the car each time they visited the cemetery. But she recognized a certain look of despair in his eyes, and she understood his plight of being one of what was once two without having to be told. "Sure," she said.

Together the silver-haired pair got out of the car and walked to the grave. A soft wind caressed them as they stood.

The professor stared at the mauve-colored granite, the perfectly shaped letters that spelled his wife's name, the finality of the date of birth and the date of death. And in his mind, he read the words as he had a thousand times before: *In Loving Memory*. They were three small words, as infinitesimal as three small stars in the uncountable billions of a galaxy. But they were his words, his stars.

Nephthys was peering across the cemetery meadow at the many graves, each one marked with the symbols that named the holder of an unknowable, disappeared life. She wondered what signs omens bones these souls had reckoned or missed. And slowly, thoughts of Gola crept into her mind. Because she was buried not far from where Nephthys was standing, laid to rest as the attending doctor at the hospital had wished. Nephthys looked over at the area where she knew the grave was, thinking of that terrible day: the news of the hit and run; the doctor coming down the hallway with an infant in his arms; the look on her brother's face. And she could never get Osiris to come out to the cemetery to visit Gola's grave, convinced as he was that she was not there.

In accordance with constellations, circumstances, and events, the attending doctor on the day Gola Kinwell's lifeless body was brought into the hospital happened to be a cedar-colored man who hailed from the iron-willed Republic of Haiti. He was a descendant of a long line of practitioners of vodun brought to that island on slave ships. The ancestors of his family were West African devotees for whom signs omens bones were the language of God, and the scattered epistles that drifted to them through time were the meaning of the message entire.

But the attending doctor had no way of knowing this as he held the infant girl. What he knew was that despite his Roman Catholic rearing, the word *ombre* drifted into his mind when he cut the infant out from Gola Kinwell's body and saw the mark between her eyes.

He brought the baby down the hospital corridor himself, where Osiris sat shell-shocked in a chair, Nephthys crying next to him. "Sorry for your loss."

Osiris looked at the doctor, uncomprehending, as if he were speaking in some other language. "Wuh?"

"Your wife."

"Wuh?" asked Osiris.

The doctor looked from one twin to the other and back at the newborn. "I am so very sorry for the loss of your wife. But she left a beautiful baby girl in the world." He planned to talk to them later about handling Gola's burial himself, in answer to an urge to give thanks for a message from the Great Mystery. "A child of the shadows," he declared softly. "Ombre."

But in accordance with the dark irony with which creatures of passage live, neither twin had heard the doctor right, lost as they were in woe. So that one word was taken for another in their grief, and they named the infant Amber without ever understanding the complexities of her name.

Nephthys looked away from Gola's grave and back at the professor.

Dr. Evanston was placing a white rose down on the cold stone and stood in silence for a long time. And after a while, he said: "I guess we'll head back." It was a weightless airless statement, filled with the uncertainty of his days, the inevitability of his nights, and the helplessness he felt when he stared at his wife's empty side of the bed. And sometimes in the isolation of his dark colonial home in Fort Dupont, he thought he heard sounds coming from his son's bedroom—sometimes laughter and sometimes cries—and he awoke as if from a dream within a dream and felt the wetness of tears on his pillow. And standing at his wife's grave now, he did not dare think of a deeper fright; that the loss of their son confirmed that there would be no echo of his wife's existence or his own, since the person meant to keep them alive in memory was gone. He looked across the meadow at the Plymouth and back at the headstone, wondering where his salvation might be. Because part of him wanted to stay and lie down next to his wife, and another part wanted to leave. But he did not know what he was being saved from, or where he was going, once he got into the backseat of Nephthys Kinwell's car.

BARGE

Nephthys sailed on, numbed by the amaranthine mist and damp that soaked deep into her being, and she wished for a place to dry but none could be found . . .

It was near sundown and Nephthys had been driving all day and sipping from her flask since she started in the dawn light. She felt the fatigue now that she was back in Anacostia, and she coasted slowly along the curb until the car stopped. Her half finger throbbed and she looked at its dark tip and held it tight. Thoughts of all the people she'd ferried that day circled her mind like schools of fish. The white girl in the trunk was quiet too, sad that there were no more riders of the day to pity or to make aware of her lost existence, and in the seclusion of the trunk she was plagued once more by the memory of her last day on earth.

Nephthys turned off the car and listened to the engine contract as eventide approached. She had two rules that governed her when she carried people from one destination to the next: (1) leave before sunrise; (2) return before sunset. The early-morning fog that allowed her to do what she did with the Plymouth was long gone. And now that her day was at an end and the flask that lived always in her pocket was empty, she could at last bring what she really wanted to do from the back of her mind to the front. Go to Sonny's Bar. For she knew—as all drinkers do—that there was no opiate more powerful than one that smoothed the sharp edges of terrible memories and sculpted the guilt and disappointments of a life into lesser monstrosities. So there was no need to say the words *I am an alcoholic*. Instead, she could focus on the magical liquid that flooded her mind and overtook her body and allowed her to splash indefinitely in a suspension of unreality.

She got out of the car and walked down Sycamore Lane, named for the old-growth trees that no longer lined it. She reached the entrance to Sonny's Bar and went into the murky interior, moving forward slowly, touching the tops of the high-backed chairs along the way like a blind woman in familiar territory. There was a greasy film that covered the floor even after it was freshly mopped. Diner seats lined the counter, each of them gashed from concealed knives and pocket razors. These were the weapons of choice for the husband or wife of an adulterer. Or fading beauties and old lions exploding with indignation. She took her usual place on a stool at the bar counter, a cluttered barge of glasses and peanut bowls and ashtrays, where from its deck the other patrons nodded shallow salutations.

The bartender, a burly man named Captain, came over and put a glass on the counter in front of her and filled it with what he knew she wanted.

Nephthys drank some down right away. She felt the first wave wash over her and pull her out to sea. She finished off the rest of the drink and began the drift. But just as she was floating away, an old love song started playing, one of her brother's favorites. He used to say it reminded him of Gola. And she didn't mind when Osiris married Gola and brought her home, a pretty woman with tide-pool eyes and a ferocious appetite for fish and crabs. Her aquatic affinities had filled their lives once more with the joyful feel of the Sea Island waterways they missed. And Gola made her brother happy, the only thing she wanted her twin to be.

The song played on and Nephthys took another drink, thinking of the boatman. She once had that kind of love too. But in accordance with the dark irony with which creatures of passage live, she'd learned that loving a wandering heart was the most difficult kind of love there was. For the boatman hailed from the everglade swamps of the Kingdom of Florida, a descendant of a long line of watermen who were navigators of lakes, rivers, and seas. There was the bygone cousin who'd unshackled himself from a slave ship off the Guinea coast, and with his comrades killed the watchmen on deck and held the rest of the crew captive, sailing the Atlantic back to the Sierra Leone River of his birth. There was the lost half brother in the Kingdom of Alabama, who stole a shrimp boat and sailed the Gulf of Mexico, crossing the Tropic of Cancer out to the Caribbean Sea, where he joined a band of Haitian sailors looking for schools of diamond-crusted isopods. But Nephthys had no way of knowing this. What she knew was that with each departure the boatman took a bit of her with him. And one day he did not come back.

She stared into her glass. All that was behind her now—Osiris and Gola and the boatman were gone. She was alone and she would never have any children of her own, and what little family she had seemed beyond her reach, bound by things she could not control. *I think Mama had a dream about me* . . . Nephthys tried to get back to the drift but the words pulled her in like the tide. All that seemed to be left were death and dreams . . . and perhaps love. Wasn't there love? Maybe that was what she'd felt when she realized that it was Dash standing in the doorway, the thing that was resuscitated when he called her "Auntie." Was that why she'd looked for Amber in the hallway even though she knew she wasn't there? She didn't know. But what bothered her more than all she'd heard about the boy was the dream that he was going to die; her brother's grandson, the last of the Kinwells. She couldn't just stand aside again, could she?

A bar patron accidentally knocked over a pitcher of water. The spill spread across the bar top and down onto the empty stool beside her, and the nurse's question echoed through her thoughts: *Where's his father?* She stared at the red vinyl and someone slowly reappeared in her mind, a man of war who once sat in the stool next to her ten years ago. It seemed that he was the only person ever to get close to Amber, the only one able to reach her in her realm. But he'd left long before Dash was born. She never found out why. Did the man even know he had a son alive and breathing in the world?

Nephthys looked into her empty glass. She knew that death could not be stopped. But now she wondered if Amber could be stopped. And since she was good at encryption and seeing things that others said weren't there, an idea began to form like the faint brushstrokes of a painting, deepening into view. And she recalled a tall leathery man with stilt-like legs, who granted the wishes of others to relieve the pain of losing what he could never find. He'd served one purpose on the day she first got the Plymouth and now she wondered if he might serve another. Crazy. It was a crazy idea. But in her mind, it grew.

Nephthys motioned to the bartender to refill her glass and he came over.

"Been here fuh years, huh, Captain?"

He poured her drink and sighed. "Eternity and a day, baby doll."

"Need to find someone."

"Yeah? Well, that's what everyone says in here. Someone to love or someone to cut."

Nephthys shook her head. "Nothin' that way. Find Out. I'm lookin' fuh his help in findin' somebody."

The bartender raised his bushy eyebrows. "Yeah? Well, if you want to locate something or someone for sure, Find Out is the one. That is, if you can find him down there in that scrap heap where he lives. Earl's. It's abandoned now, you know. Nobody there but squatters. He been in that maze of junk for years."

A flash of Find Out leading Nephthys through the tunnels of

the scrapyard to the Plymouth lit up her memory and faded. She rubbed her half finger, marveling. After all this time, he was still there.

Captain whistled. "That Find Out is something else. I'll tell you that. But nowadays you gotta bring his remedies. Like a toll. He won't do what he does without his medicine. Even though he don't need that stuff, I heard. Been able to do what he does ever since what happened to his woman, they say. She just up and disappeared one day. Drove him over the edge looking for her. He never did find her, though. Didn't find nothing but that smoke." Captain stared into the ashtray on the counter. "It'll make a man pause, that thing he does. That goddamned blue smoke is something else."

Nephthys emptied her glass in one long draw and set it down as if it were something fragile and expensive. "Medicine, huh?"

Captain winked. "You know, his shortcut to paradise. He's been taking the trip for years. You know what I mean, right?"

"Uh-huh."

"And who you want him to find gotta be living and breathing, I heard. Ain't no finding somebody who is dead."

Nephthys blinked. She hadn't thought about the possibility of who she was looking for being dead. She stood up slowly to depart and waited for the walls to stop tilting. "Thank you fuh the notice, Captain."

He shrugged. "That's what they say about Find Out, anyway. It'll make a man pause, I tell you. But if you see him down there in that scrapyard, ask him to find old Captain a pot of gold."

Nephthys knew well enough where to get heroin. All she had to do was wait in the stairwell of her apartment building, a small market for almost anything. She stood on the second-floor landing and soon heard male voices approaching from above.

A young man came down and saw her there in the shadows. "What you need?" he asked.

"A little smack," said Nephthys.

When the young man looked closer and realized who his buyer was, his eyes widened. For Nephthys was the one who'd let him have as many lollipops as he wanted when he was little, who'd never refused his early-Saturday-morning requests, who'd given him the orange jawbreakers he liked. "Tell me you not on the stuff now, Ms. Nephthys."

"No, chile. Stop talkin' crazy. Fuh someone else."

"Oh." The young man reached into his pocket and pulled out a small plastic bag and held it out in his hand and put it back in his pocket. "That do it?"

Nephthys could barely see what he showed her, and she had no understanding of the quantity or quality of the bag's contents. She shrugged. "Reckon so. How much?"

The young man looked down and shook his head. "Nah. Don't even worry about it, Ms. Nephthys. As many times as you opened the door at the crack of dawn and gave me candy sweets all them years when I was running around these hallways, you ain't got to give me nothing." He handed her the bag, and after a pause he said, "Whoever you getting this for needs to come get it from me theyself. Not you, all right?"

Nephthys took the bag and put it in her pocket along with her flask. "All right. Thank you, chile."

The young man peered at Nephthys, unable to say anything more. He was beginning to feel ashamed of something he couldn't quite grasp. But his mind was already shifting to the sounds rising from the level beneath them, new business. He tipped his cap. "Remember, Ms. Nephthys. Tell 'em to come to me on they own next time."

Nephthys watched the young man walk down the stairwell and out of sight as she'd watched him when he was a boy. She took the bag from her pocket and looked at the substance once more and put it back. *'Ceitful medicine*, she thought, shaking her head, and she made her way out of the building and headed to Earl's Scrapyard.

PASSAGE III

RESIGNING LIFE TO ANOTHER

FALLEN

With the medicine in her pocket, Nephthys approached Earl's Scrapyard, a woeful grave for things used according to their intended design and for other purposes alike. It was alive with the silence and sounds of the fallen, and the legions of angry spirits from the Nacotchtank villages and the slave plantations who still haunted the land on which the scrapyard was built. She parked the car and walked toward the ruins. Crushed steel and shattered glass glittered in the dying light. The clutter of discarded barbecue chicken sandwiches pulled from the backs of restaurants and rusty cans filled with rainwater circled abandoned vehicles. She stepped over polluted puddles and the excrement of mangy dogs, walking through the squalor until she heard voices.

And slowly, as Nephthys moved through that federation of misery, she came upon two men arguing next to a burned-out Ford. Both were shouting and flailing their arms and kicking up dust with their feet. In the long shadows of the nearby bonfire, one undead was diminutive in stature and the other towered above him, and they looked like mismatched warriors in preparation for battle. Each took turns making wild gestures, flips, and spins in a display of agility and threat, moving about the other as if in capoeira combat. Nephthys stood by, listening to the fray.

"Look, man, what you saying don't make no damned sense!" shouted the scrawny one. "You ain't got nothing in there, fool!"

The other one pounded a stack of scrap metal with his fist and cut his hand, barely noticing. He pointed at the disintegrating Ford. "Motherfucka, I *did* have one in there! And I had it in the glove compartment and I know your sticky-fingered ass took it!"

His opponent paced, looking around for a weapon. "I'm about to let you know something."

"I been knowing everything. And you a damn lie!"

"I ain't got your fucking cigarette! And you better quit that shit before I break them giraffe legs of yours with a baseball bat!"

The tall one circled the other like a vulture. "Oh yeah? Niggah, I got your bat."

The two foes would have entered a fight to the death that very moment, if they hadn't noticed Nephthys standing there watching them. Together their eyes raced over her hungrily, determining in quantum seconds whether she was someone who would turn them over to the police, give them a blow job, or provide them with means for their next hit.

"Hello, Find Out," Nephthys said.

Find Out's long neck, which had been strained and erect in outrage, wilted suddenly like the stem of a dehydrated plant, and his eyes died down to a low gleam. He looked at Nephthys without seeming to recognize her. "Yeah, that's me. What you want?"

"Need to find someone."

Find Out shook his head. Despite all he could do and what others praised him for, his power had been spawned by the loss of his wife, and it was this cruel irony that drove him from one fix to another. He stood among the scrap heaps and the dogs on many nights, staring into the bonfires, watching her beautiful face fade into the pyre, asking himself the question he'd asked a thousand times before: *Where is she?* And it was a long time since he'd engaged in the trade of blue smoke, since with its cobalt cues he'd found everything except what he most sought. He looked into the bonfire and turned away. "Lady, I ain't done that in a thousand Sundays."

"Captain say you might help me. Brought a little medicine

too." Nephthys fingered what was in her pocket. How could so small a thing hold such great dominion?

Find Out's lips began to twitch, his mind quickly unscrambling the hidden promise in her words. Because more than eating or sleeping or bathing, every second of his life was spent consuming or thinking about new ways to consume one thing: heroin. Many years later, there would be a magical chalklike substance that eclipsed the one that he believed was keeping him alive, and it would black out the sun and light up the moon and plunge the quadrants into a lasting night, where mothers sucked the life from babes and babes raised their hands to hit their mothers. And the kingdoms of the land would be bathed in a lethal opioid brew of powders and pills and pipes and dips, where the zombie-eyed were both doctor and patient. And criminal producers and sanctioned producers and shepherds of treatment and destruction would play their parts in each decade, all complicit in the endgame of gain.

But standing in the badlands of Earl's Scrapyard, Find Out had no way of knowing this. What he knew was that the closer he looked at the woman in the firelight, the more he remembered. The Car Lady. 1967 Plymouth Belvedere. Sky blue. White girl in the trunk.

"How you been?"

"Been fine," said Nephthys. "But I need to find someone. And I got medicine."

Find Out wiped away the sweat dripping into his eye. "Yeah? Where is it?"

The other man began to fear that he would miss his chance to share and he smiled nervously. "Hey, man. Hey, Find Out. Why don't you check with Lockjaw Jimmy about that cigarette? Yeah. Yeah . . . come to think of it, I saw him messing round that old Ford when we was grubbing on them sardines with Goobie."

"Shut up," said Find Out without taking his eyes off Nephthys. "I think I can work something out."

Nephthys glanced around and heard other sounds, other voices. The place was becoming more animated as dusk darkened into night. “Not here. Sonny’s Bar.”

Find Out nodded and began walking swiftly away from the bonfire, motioning for Nephthys to follow him. In the timetable of his affliction, it had been a long time since his last hit and he felt like his blood was boiling. Now he was sweating through his clothes, and his eyes and nose were running, his stomach a roiling vat of acids.

The scrawny one hollered for fifty yards as Find Out and Nephthys walked away. “Hey! Come on, man! Don’t do me like that. If the shoe was on the other foot, I’d be looking out for you! Come on! Share and share alike! We got to hang tight in this messed-up world! All right, you stingy bastard! Go with that bitch! You’ll be back. And when you are, don’t ask me for shit! Find Out! Hey . . .”

TRANSIT OF SHADOWS

Nephthys carried the living as she carried the dead in her vessel, its bow aimed at points known and unknowable, its stern the keeper of the jinxes in its wake . . .

Nephthys sat in the car and waited for Find Out to get in. He was standing where he'd been standing since they got back to the Plymouth. Although he seemed to be in a hurry to get to what she was offering when they'd first left the scrapyard, now he seemed to be hesitating, and he'd been staring at the closed trunk for a long time. She was breaking one of her two rules now that it was dark, and she looked up at the moon. It was big and low in the sky. "God lantern," her brother liked to call it. Nephthys smiled to herself. Osiris used to tease her about being the firstborn, how he led her forward by the hand. "Cyan't get lost dat a-way," he'd said.

Indigo swirlin' round de vat . . .

She thought she heard the nearby river gurgling and her smile quickly faded. Were the missing pieces of her brother still drifting in the current somewhere? The clumps of his hair and scalp? The torn-off part of his leg? That was why she'd spread the rest of him in other places than the Anacostia River where his body had been found, better spaces. The cherry blossom–flecked currents of the Tidal Basin, the shallow majesty of the Lincoln Memorial Reflecting Pool, the slushy inflow of the McMillan Reservoir, the black tranquility of the Georgetown canal, the roiling deep of the Potomac River.

No beginnin' and no end . . .

Nephthys felt her legs falling asleep and she shifted in the seat behind the wheel, for the unbearable inertia of one was setting in once more. It was time to get moving. She looked at Find Out's long shadow in the rearview mirror and blew the horn.

Find Out wiped the snot running from his nose with the back of his hand and got in the backseat.

The white girl in the trunk was somber and still, and she acknowledged him with her silence.

"Ain't been inside this car since that night."

"She still back there," Nephthys said, turning the key in the ignition.

Find Out looked at the bonfires in the distance. "I know. I been knowing everything." The cracks in his mind deepened and frightful thoughts of the unknown escaped. He wondered if his wife was in a trunk somewhere too, shipped away from him and disposed of. He felt a sharp stomach cramp and winced.

"The Plymouth ain't been no trouble neither," said Nephthys, listening to the engine purr.

"I know," said Find Out, scratching at the tracks in his arms. And as he fidgeted in the backseat, he was struck again by how it was that he knew the whereabouts of a ghost but not his wife. "Listen, we ain't got to ride nowhere. We can do it here."

"Not here," Nephthys said, pulling off. The moon had moved higher in the sky. "Sonny's Bar. It ain't safe here."

Find Out listened to the white girl in the trunk drum a half-empty motor-oil bottle. "I know. I been knowing everything."

Find Out had looked everywhere for his wife on that terrible day when she did not come home from her job at the laundromat. He retraced his routes, then rushed home in case he might have missed her while he was out searching. The hours clicked on and the midnight air drew him out of their rented house and onto the streets once more. His fears mounted and his mind ran wild with the stories he'd heard about women going missing. That there were brothels run by people dedicated to the blood sport of transforming ordinary women into dope fiends and then putting them on the streets to turn tricks. That there was something called the "Traveling Circus" that moved from place to place and week to week, and tickets were sold in the basements of speakeasies and the freight elevators of government buildings.

There were secret circles of rich men in nearby fiefdoms, he'd heard, who wanted a "Bessie," a pretty dark woman to keep in beautiful secluded homes in the Allegheny Mountains or along the Chesapeake Bay or in the thick woods of the Kingdom of Virginia. And there, each man could do whatever he wanted to his purchased Bessie indefinitely. *I'll find her*, he'd told himself as he looked in the countless places and spaces of the quadrants.

But later on, Find Out remembered only the route to the laundromat where his wife once worked and forgot everything else (eating, bathing, sleeping), because the only thing that mattered was the search. He had the police add her name and picture to the infinite list of the missing, those fated to haunt the memories and fears of their loved ones. And he stopped every person he saw, waving a picture of his wife taken on the day they were married by the justice of the peace, asking, "Have you seen her?" Days turned into weeks months years, and time became an inert substance that he no longer reckoned.

The drunks and the junkies, whom Find Out would later join, pitied him when he came around to ask if any of them had seen his wife as he'd asked them a thousand times before. They looked at him with tender eyes. For they, too, had women long lost to them and family that they were now ghosts to, and each time he came to ask they answered him softly, saying, "Naw, man. But you'll find her someday."

One sunset turned into another and Find Out filled his body with heroin in an existential plea to God for relief, moving aimlessly through the streets and the years. And one sweltering late afternoon, he sat on the banks of the Anacostia River with his feet soaking in the dirty current and his mind bucking and thrashing, until his last hope of finding his wife set with the closing rays of the sun on the water. It was at that exact moment that his soul disengaged from his body in a vaporous cloud. And then a blue smoke formed from the reaches of where his soul had been just moments before. The blue smoke snaked around and caressed him, a cobalt trail of wish and longing that only he could see. And that was when the whole business began: the blue smoke that led Find Out to all things lost and all things found.

When Nephthys and Find Out arrived together at Sonny's Bar, Captain stood behind the counter with a look of disbelief. But he put his hand towel aside, understanding the importance of the task at hand without having to be told, and ushered them both to a small room hidden in the back of the bar. The green velvet curtains that marked it were revered by the bar patrons down through the decades, for behind them all sorts of happenings took place. In the days of Prohibition when whites used the bar, the room had been an important meeting place for bootleggers. There was trade and extortion. Interrogation and murder. Now loan sharks took prey there to make a point. Contraband was dumped out on the table from black handbags and inner jacket pockets for examination and distribution. But on this night, it was an alchemist's den.

Find Out took a chair and sat down hastily at the lone table, motioning for Nephthys to sit directly across from him. And like any practitioner of the mystic arts, he first needed to set his stage. Because his tools of the trade were not crystal balls, magic cards, trick knives, or a rainbow of handkerchiefs. His instruments were a spoon, a dirty needle, a lighter, and a rubber hot-water bottle tube, which he pulled from the dark world of his pants pockets.

Captain brought a glass of water, set it on the table, and left the room quickly.

Find Out stared at Nephthys, now that he was prepared. "Got that medicine?"

Nephthys reached into her pocket and pulled out the little bag.

"Come with it then. Can't answer no wishes without it."

Nephthys stared into the wasteland of his eyes, hesitating. "Been ten years now. Might be crazy and a waste of time." But more than that, it might not work. Who was she to try to find someone who she herself did not really know?

Find Out was growing impatient, his eyes watering and forming little pools in the corners like quicksilver. "I been knowing everything. Ain't got no time for no games."

"Ain't no playin' with me neither. Just wonderin' 'bout my niece and this man. Thinkin' 'bout my foolishness."

Find Out shook his head violently. "Look, I'm a goddamn tracker. That's what I do. Track what's lost. Don't matter where or how much time. 'Cuz I been knowing everything." Except one thing, he remembered, and he seized with pain. But the hit would erase it all. His medicine would wipe everything away. There would only be the blue smoke and the wish, and he wouldn't have to feel anything until the wish was fulfilled. "Hand it over."

Nephthys gave him the bag and watched him work.

Quickly, deftly, Find Out busied himself with the heroin. He examined it briefly, which was a joke because there was no way to tell whether he had some bad shit or not. And there was no way he could stop himself from taking it, even if it was. He began the special task of cooking up the stuff in the spoon, then tying the rubber tube around his arm. "Tie it tight. Tie it tight. Tie it tight, goddamnit," he chanted, his hands shaking. Because if it wasn't tight, it was an eternity to find a vein that was not collapsed or hiding from the needle.

Find Out injected himself and began what he called the "rise." He went up and over lost dreams in the first second. He soared above the disgrace and shame that years of being a junkie produced in the next four seconds, rocketing at the speed of light over crap games and street fights. He drifted above the churches and shops and bus terminals and alleys and train stations in which he had hoped to find his wife. He floated by the empty dumpsters and barrels in which he had hunted for her. At the seventh second, he rose above his broken will and up to the unchecked stratosphere of his mind, an odyssey of kaleidoscopic spaces and pathways to other galaxies.

Find Out continued the rise to the ninth second, speaking in whispers. "Nothing. Ain't. Nothing. Else." He levitated to the next level of levels and traveled to the outposts of existence, where he shed what he was and became something else. And once there, creatures long extinct and creatures yet evolved came to sit with him and share in the ecstasy of increasing nonexistence. He continued elevating. At last Find Out reached his destination on the tenth second, and his eyes rolled back into his head.

Nephthys was watching in wonder and fear. She backed away from the table in a panic when Find Out started convulsing, and she almost went to get Captain. But now he seemed completely still and filled with serenity like that of a shaman. She moved a little closer to him and began: "Listen. Find me a certain man. Get him here to see about . . . the last of we." She told him the rest. Amber. The boy's father. A dream. Dash in danger.

In Find Out's adulterated state, each word Nephthys said moved in long-range rifts through his mind, and he understood the nuances and complexities of her wish without having to be told. Because now that the spell of longing had been cast, he felt the heroin dissipate and the wish take hold. The first spires of blue smoke drifted across the corneas of his eyes and through the green velvet curtains; it would lead him to what Nephthys desired. "I been knowing everything."

He said no more, and Nephthys watched Find Out rise up through the reaches of his flight from the seat. She wondered how he would find Dash's father. He could be anywhere. And would he come back? Was Dash reason enough? She wanted to know. Because she thought that the boy and the man meant something more together in the world than apart.

She was about to ask Find Out how she would know the man she was looking for had been found, but she did not. For he seemed to be in an unbreakable trance, and she wondered if he could still hear her voice or understand the language of men. She stood up, accepting the mystery of her small undertaking, resigned to leave Find Out to his voyage on her behalf. She moved back through the bar without stopping, not even for a drink, nodding to Captain on her way out.

Nephthys walked out to the night air and back to the Plymouth. Evening had settled over the streets like a cloak, and the vesper bell of Saints of Eternity chimed eerily in the distance. The night was laden with a viscous dew that soaked into her and through her. She reached the car and sat blinking in the dark, wondering if Find Out would have any success. Now she felt a new fear growing inside of her and she tried to understand what it could mean or not mean, and what it had to do with Find Out getting this man. Because she'd already lost her brother and his daughter. Now there was only this boy, the last of them all, a piece of what was left of the Kinwells drifting in the world. And this man who had helped make him was out there somewhere too. Weren't missing pieces worth trying to find? She looked into the black dashboard as if the answer might be there. Her half finger throbbed and she sank deeper into the seat feeling old, older than her place in the lines and circles of existence. The dampness bored into her, the kind of wet that felt like it soaked into the soul.

The white girl in the trunk turned over and sighed.

Nephthys nodded as if in agreement. “Tired too. Sometimes I wonder if we ridin’ through this world like you ridin’ in that trunk.”

RAFT

Nephthys held tight to the implements of navigation, her heart her only buoy on the surface of the Great Deep, the fog her only compass . . .

Nephthys took a sip from her flask and brought out the little container of Vaseline from the glove compartment of the Plymouth. She opened it and dabbed a bit on her lips. Then she rolled down the window and waited as she had a thousand times before. And after a while, as always, the fog drifted into the car, and she had that feeling once more; what made the thing she did with the Plymouth possible. The fog swirled around the interior of the car and circled her head. *Rosetta,* she thought. *It's Rosetta today.*

Rosetta sat in the dawn light on a park bench in Hains Point by the Washington Channel, eating a stale honey bun pulled from the bottom of her purse. She'd had a long night in a motel room with a Lockheed lobbyist from the Kingdom of California. He liked to choke and now her neck was sore. She stared into the current, listening to the water slosh. Early-morning joggers, new National Defense University recruits from Fort McNair, raced by her like a flock of low-flying birds. The pain in her feet overcame her concern with needing to be ready to jump up and run at any moment, and she took off her pumps and put them on the bench beside her. She'd picked up the senses of a nocturnal creature and was keenly aware that sunrise was just around the corner.

This meant that she would soon need safe harbor, a place to hide and get some rest. She was thinking this when she turned to make sure no one was behind her, and she saw the Plymouth enter the lot across the field. She watched Nephthys park the car, feeling no surprise, only relief that she did not have to think about her next move. She grabbed her pumps, threw what was left of her honey bun on the ground for the squirrels, and ran barefoot to the Plymouth.

Nephthys sat waiting, and when Rosetta slid into the backseat and settled into the leather, she turned around and looked at the girl. "How you been?"

Rosetta tossed the tufts of her wig. "Been fine."

Nephthys turned back and took out a little brown bag of candy from the glove compartment. She handed it to her passenger.

"Thank you," Rosetta said. Then after some silence, "Seen my little sister Lulu?"

Nephthys took a sip from her flask and put it back. "Not recently. But she probably ain't never too far."

Rosetta looked out at the Washington Channel and let what that could mean or not mean settle into the dark water.

"Across the bridge?" asked Nephthys.

Rosetta was soothed by the lapping sounds of the nearby current and the ease of being in the car. Her pimp would be looking for her by now. She opened the little bag of candy, took out a Charleston Chew, and for the first time since her parapsychological driver-passenger relationship with Nephthys began, she said, "I don't know."

Nephthys looked into the rearview mirror at Rosetta in the dim light. She'd always wanted to drive her someplace safe, maybe child welfare services or a shelter or a social worker's office, or . . . somewhere. Not necessarily the police station, where the outcome was a game of chance, but a place where she could stop what she was doing. Yet there never seemed to be an occasion when Rosetta didn't have a destination in mind. She was always adamant that she be taken somewhere in the quadrants.

So it was no surprise that Nephthys paused at the girl saying that she didn't know, and she took the opportunity to finally ask the question pervading her mind whenever Rosetta was with her in her car: "How 'bout home?"

The white girl in the trunk groaned.

Rosetta's stomach soured and she sank deeper into the seat at the word *home*. For all thoughts of that place came down to one moment: the day she'd tried to find a way through her corrupted world to say his name.

"Mercy," Rosetta said on the last day she was at home. It had taken a few years for her to say his name out loud at last; the small but mighty effort of a young girl trying to find the words for what had happened to her. But that canyon-deep word went ignored by her mother, who thought it meant something else. Because her mother only fussed about how she was lazy, how all she wanted to do was shake her ass and run her mouth. How she would be pregnant at fifteen, if she didn't watch out.

"Don't you be asking me for no mercy, Rosetta, especially when you ain't paying no bills."

"Ma . . . Mama. I mean—"

"Be quiet, girl."

So the happenings of the winterberries in the snow and the syrup in the milk went undisclosed that day, and were folded into the creases of other happenings in the shed. And later that night, before she ran away across the bridge, Rosetta sat her little sister down on the bed.

"Lulu, you be the hunter, not the prey."

"What you mean?"

"Hunt. You hear me? Don't you never be the one hunted."

Rosetta left her little sister and ran away that night, calcifying the bedrock of that first layer of filth that Mercy Ratchet had spread over her, and on which yet more layers would form and harden into an unbreakable patina.

* * *

From the backseat of the Plymouth, Rosetta looked through the windshield and saw an orange glimmer forming over the Washington Channel and quickly looked away. "Take me to that barbershop, Ms. Nephthys. You know, the one across from St. Elizabeths." She unwrapped another Charleston Chew and put it in her mouth.

Nephthys was still waiting for an answer to her question. "How 'bout home, chile?"

The white girl in the trunk scratched at the soiled carpet.

Rosetta shook her head.

Nephthys sighed and pulled off and they rode in silence. And when she neared the dark-windowed barbershop, she coasted to a stop and turned off the car.

"Okay, thanks," said Rosetta.

Nephthys looked into the black windows. "It ain't open yet."

Rosetta shoved the bag of candy in her purse and pushed the door open, scooting out of the car. "Yeah, I know. That's why I'm here."

"Wuh?"

Rosetta bent down and leaned into the open passenger-side window. Her eyes spoke once more of how the worse that could happen to her had already happened and how she knew all there was to know about the rise and fall of women down through the ages and didn't need anything else explained. "I can't go home," she said. Then she turned and looked into a narrow alleyway and back at Nephthys. And in a way that seemed to reverse the notion of who was lost, she smiled thinly at Nephthys and said casually, and not really in the form of a question: "Can you?" And she turned away and headed through the alleyway that led around to the back of the barbershop and was gone.

Nephthys sat in Rosetta's wake and took out her flask. The girl's parting question (judgment?) stung, and she sat drinking until the orange-glow sunrise dissipated. No, she didn't feel like she could go to that place she once called home. Amber was down there somewhere, still floating in the substance that filled the house, she supposed. Drifting through what drove her on. And like Rosetta, she couldn't do a damned thing about it. Because the truth was that she and her brother had never felt like they were raising Amber after her mother's death. Rather, they merely watched her grow.

Nephthys recalled the calm gaze with which Amber stared at her as she changed her diaper when she was a baby. She never cried when she was hungry and seemed to wait expectantly for her bottle to be filled. By the age of three, she selected what she wanted from the garden, seemingly understanding what was ripe for eating and what was ready to harvest and what had spoiled. She would not eat or sleep without the sound of moving water: the patter of heavy rain; the splash of clothes being scrubbed and wrung; the trickle and drip of the faucets; the boil of broth in a pot. She smiled before the onset of sudden showers and was cheerful in the ceaseless mist of the valley.

But that was before the dreams started, Nephthys thought, looking into the alley where Rosetta entered and disappeared. That was before the river, her brother, and the shark. And once more she tried to understand why Amber couldn't see what happened to her brother clearly. Why the senseless tale, the talking shark? And with all the foreknowledge and private necromancy that her relationship with death seemed to allow, why couldn't she see enough to stop it from happening?

"Scuse me."

Nephthys jumped, for she was so engrossed in her thoughts that she'd lost her island sense that someone was nearby. She turned and saw the young man who had given her the little bag for Find Out standing on the sidewalk.

"How you been?" she asked.

"Been fine," said the young man. "I was coming by and I saw your car."

In the early-morning light, Nephthys looked at the young man carefully. Gone was the usual swagger he exhibited. And since she was good with encryption and seeing things that others said weren't there, she said: "Need a ride fuh someone?"

The young man nodded, relieved that he did not have to ask, since his trade had made him used to being the one whom people came to for something and not the other way around. Besides, ever since he'd given Nephthys some of his supply, he couldn't shake a sobering feeling. It was the same nameless sensation that lurked now, and he stared down at the ground as if he would find it there. And he was struggling with news he'd received that morning to pick up his grandmother from Greater Southeast Community Hospital. The cancer that the doctors at the clinic kept missing was now killing her. He didn't want her to suffer the indignity of the bus. And calling a cab was useless. He looked at Nephthys apprehensively. "It's my grandmother. They say they can't do nothing else for her. She gotta go in hospice."

"Sorry to hear," said Nephthys.

The young man looked across the street at the brand-new red Pontiac Firebird he had acquired through the spoils of his profits. It had been the car of one of his rivals, and a deal gone bad ended with the stabbing of his adversary and the car in his possession. He turned away from the Firebird and looked at Nephthys with nervous eyes. And after a long pause he said, "I can't pick her up in that."

"She waitin' on you now, right?"

The young man looked down at the ground once more. "Yes, ma'am. She is."

"Well, come on. Let's go, chile."

"Course I got money to pay you and I can—"

"Ain't no trouble. Get in."

The young man did as he was told in that moment, as he had when adults addressed him in apartment hallways as a boy.

Nephthys waited for him to settle into the seat and handed

him an orange jawbreaker candy ball, remembering that it was his favorite.

The young man took the candy, thankful to put it in his mouth so that it would be difficult to speak, for he had no words for the fear of losing his grandmother.

As they glided down the street in the Plymouth, Nephthys glanced at the Pontiac Firebird, then looked through the rear-view mirror at the young man slumped in the backseat. He would leave the car parked where it was and enter it no more, she supposed. After all, he'd long been driving ill-gotten cars of desire around Anacostia like the other children who appeared and disappeared. And now he was riding in the Plymouth instead of his Firebird, perhaps feeling less victorious, now that he'd learned that dreams come true even when people don't want them to.

PREY

Osiris looked into the Anacostia River, thinking about the spaces through which he traveled. The fires of the Hours and the crack and sizzle of souls. The vast waste of the Gray and the empty pan of blue. The endless spirals and latitudes of the deep. And he thought of the Conundrum of Three, where the mind sought the memory of a body long gone, and the body withdrew from the mind and the spirit, and the spirit chased the echo of the other two. Was he thus trapped? Sometimes his mind slipped into that remote day with Gola on the dock. *You're right, you know. The reason you're here . . .*

The phrase gripped him like a spell, and he looked down at the glowing tip of his half finger. When he looked up again the boy was there, and once more he wondered if he had conjured the child or if it was the other way around.

They greeted each other with the usual salutation: a quiet stare and affirming silence.

Dash kicked a tin can and looked at the innumerable layers of the River Man's shimmering cloak waving in the sour breeze coming off the water. It was getting harder to remember the first time he saw the River Man or how many times he'd met him there, and sometimes it seemed like he'd always known him and other times not at all. He looked at the half finger. "You think dreams are real?"

Osiris smiled and scowled and smiled again. It was a good question, one that he himself began to contemplate. More and more, his living life felt like he'd imagined it and his altered state the only thing certain. *Dreams bein' real? Seems so.*

"My mother dreamed something about me. About death and me."

Osiris stared into the boy's face, so much like how he remembered his daughter. He had been to Amber's realm many times, this grown-up child of his that he could not seem to reach, for the treasure of seeing her. There were nights when he watched her picking in the garden that Gola had started and marveled at how much she looked like her mother. There were days when he stood outside the kitchen window, watching her. Or he stood in the trees near Gola's patch of lilies, hoping Amber would notice him there. But she seemed to have no sight of him. He looked intently at the boy; once more he was filled with the worry that the dead have for the living. *Death?*

Dash shrugged. "A death dream. I don't know . . . but I know it's about me."

Osiris was about to ask the boy more when he thought he saw the glimmer of goldenrod eyes in the bracken along the banks. But when he looked closer, it was gone. He thought (hoped?) that it was just the glint of some discarded toy or pieces of broken glass reflecting the sun. But he stared yet. Because if what he saw were eyes, he'd seen them before. During the Hours. In the Gray. And perhaps . . . on the wharf.

"What's the matter?" asked Dash.

Osiris stared, silent.

Confused, Dash looked. He didn't see anything. "What is it?"

The River Man turned away from the bracken and back at the boy. *Nothin' . . . Ain't nothin' . . .*

"Oh," said Dash, nodding. But he wondered why the River Man's face seemed to say something else. It was like when he opened the utility-closet door (if it ever existed) and the man inside looked like that janitor at first, but as he stood trying to understand what he was seeing, the man looked like someone else. He picked up a rock and skipped it across the water. "Can someone change his face?"

Osiris was staring into the bracken again where he thought the glimmer had been. *Meanin' like a smile to a frown?*

"No, like from one person into another person."

That day on the dock flashed in his mind and Osiris pushed the thought away. And after a while he said: *It be hard to tell wuh we can see and not see. Even in dreams.*

Dash picked up another rock and skipped it across the water. Again, he tried to find the words to talk about what *doing it* was but was unable to do so. And every time he saw the janitor in the hallways at the school (now he seemed to always be smiling), he wondered how a face could look so different from one moment to the next. *Maybe that was someone else with Annie Porter,* he thought. And again, he wondered if he'd imagined the whole thing. Because now that door was gone.

Mercy Ratchet was watching Dash from a thicket of tall reeds on the paper-littered banks. He'd been following him around, learning his habits and the places he frequented, and whether or not his mother knew when he left the house. He did not believe in the powers of the infamous Amber Kinwell. After all, she was a woman, and he'd learned from observing his own mother that magic women did not exist. He watched Dash talking to himself, shrugging his shoulders and shaking his head as if conversing with someone. But no one was there. *A disturbed boy,* he thought, and he recalled the nurse's son, Gary, with his four "friends" named Slim Willy, Baby Cakes, King Catfish, and Slide Dog. After a while, Gary seemed to think that he too was just another friend among the others that no one believed existed. That single belief made everything he did to the boy possible.

"Yes," Mercy hissed, watching Dash talk to the air. Maybe he could use that. Because he'd learned to focus on the details. Like that time when he crossed paths with a neighborhood apothecary, a teenager later shot in a drug raid, who mentioned to Mercy that if he really wanted to have some fun with a woman, he should try putting quaaludes in her drink. "You know, man. Disco biscuits," he'd said. Mercy didn't have a woman—didn't want a woman—but that was the first time he thought about it. Using something hidden. He remembered spending hours at the library reading about it in medical books. $C_{16}H_{14}N_2O$. Methaqualone. It seemed to help hide what was in clear view. The perfect covenant of secrets.

Mercy continued watching the boy, thinking of the others, the chosen ones. He was not entirely proud of his need to adulterate the purity of his intentions with the addition of a substance over the years. But after that unpleasant business with Hazel Eyes, he learned that he had to take precautions. And after figuring out a dosage that worked, he found that it made the chosen ones pliable. Open. More understanding of the garden. Which was why he liked to slip them $C_{16}H_{14}N_2O$. Sometimes it was in lemonade. Later on, he put it in other drinks made out of yet other things for those chosen. Punch or soda. Rosetta's sweet milk. It was working well with Annie Porter too, in the sweet tea he'd given her, part of the secret picnic he'd arranged in the utility closet, where he'd assured her that he was not a beast. And once more he couldn't believe that he forgot to lock the door.

I could do something now, Mercy thought as he watched Dash engaged in his mystic dialogue at the river. *Something quick.* He peered around in the reeds in which he was hiding and looked up and down the empty banks. It was secluded. Yet he hesitated still, a strange feeling that had come over him growing stronger. He watched the boy. "I could do something," he whispered, looking around and behind him and back again. But he held his place. Because for some reason, he felt like he was being watched.

From the bracken at the river, the wolf observed Mercy Ratchet in his surveillance of the boy. He'd seen a lot in his travels from one plane of existence to the next and across time and space and meaning, and had taken on many forms. He'd had adventures being both male and female too, and found interesting differences between them. For it seemed that males walked paths deliberate that led to a single ending, while females walked paths ad infinitum, so that a journey's finish was always the start. But most of all, he'd learned in his wayfaring that it was balance that powered the Great Pendulum, and he made hunting sport of the inevitable swing one way or the other. A good hunt held no thrill for the wolf without a worthy target. Which was why he liked to track those of abiding exile, those beasts that dwelled on the edges of existence and howled to the Void. Like Mercy Ratchet.

The wolf rolled over and scratched his back in the grass and positioned himself again. He thought about what was beginning to unfold, the pathway that was opening with the one down there in the valley, the one with the watery heart. What better hunter was there than a mother on behalf of her young? *Besides,* he thought, as he peered at Mercy Ratchet hiding in the tall reeds, *if she looks hard enough with those eyes of hers, she might even see me this time.*

HUNT

The wolf heard the flit and rustle of a target thousands of miles away and smelled the scent of a single mark among the pheromones of millions. He knew the quest of fellow ferreters from one place to the next and acknowledged their growls and grunts in the dark. And he sensed those living too deep in the isolated wilderness of pursuit, where they lost track of their prey in the haze of big-game cravings and walked in the circles of their predicament. So it was no surprise that the wolf came to Amber in the bedroom of her thoughts and stood in the doorframe, waiting once more for her to realize that he was there.

In the forward-backward stillness of the meeting, Amber opened her eyes and looked at him. "Who are you?"

The wolf shimmered in his fine black coat, slick with the elemental oils of the spaces through which he'd passed. *You know.*

Amber shook her head. "I'm dreaming. This is a dream."

About what?

"Hunting him."

Hunting who?

"The faceless man after my boy."

Do you think you can catch him?

"Why are you here?"

Why do you think I'm here?

"Because you can help me catch him."

If you want me to.

"Who are you?"

Don't you know?

"I've never seen you before."

It's only because you're not looking.

There were nights when Amber was startled awake. Not only by unrelenting panic about Dash, but by a pressing urge to remember what seemed to be a singular recurring dream. She lay blinking in the bed, trying to recall what it was. It was like she'd woken up in her bedroom and then left it to go into another, where she went back to sleep in another bed and awoke again and went to yet another room. But she could not remember leaving the room in which she'd first awakened, nor what the room she next entered looked like. Yet she had a sense that something had transpired—something was there—and it crawled around in her mind until she went back to sleep.

GARDEN OF MOONLIGHT

The blue cloudcap cleared as the evening deepened. The feral garden pulsed under the unblinking glare of the moon, the mating songs of the crickets in their legions ruling the night. The soil throbbed with the energy of its own ecosystem, and all things planted in its dark granules sprouted and shot up from the ground in an ultraviolet explosion of leaf and bulb and bounty, no matter the seed or the season. Fat cobs of early corn held a lavender luster in the lunar light, and they dropped from their stalks and plunged to the ground. Enormous basil and rosemary and oregano leaves waved in the night breeze. The stars flashed on the black surface of water buckets, and one silver canopy of vegetation cast great shadows on another.

Amber sat at the base of a bell pepper plant, night picking. Her basket held three soccer ball–sized peppers, and many more had fallen off their stems and rolled into a wild growth of peppermint and disappeared. She stood up to survey what she wanted to harvest next and saw Dash sitting on a mound of asparagus they'd stacked like firewood the week before. He was getting bigger now, and she could no longer ignore that he was starting to look more like him. When Dash was a small child, she could act like he was conceived in her mind and somehow appeared in her arms. But more and more, when she caught him chewing the gum she forbade, or when he tilted his head and gazed at her just so, she saw the boy's father in his eyes, looking at her.

"We got a while before you have to start getting ready for bed. Wanna do some picking?"

"Sure."

"Some of the eggplant is probably about ready."

Dash nodded. He enjoyed night picking. Like deboning the fish, he could be close to his mother in a way that felt untainted by the haunts of her dreams. He took an empty sack from the basket. He knew the geography of the garden from an early age, where to watch his step and how to navigate the vegetation and the mazes of growth. He found the patch of eggplant easily, glimmering like great oblong pearls. He plucked six of them and put them in his sack. The moon glowered bright above him, and he stared into the blacklight of the garden. Shapes jumped at him in fluorescent relief against walls of black. And it was in the polarity of that galactic light, where one thing forced the projection or obscurity of another, that the odd comment Lulu had made that day was backlit in Dash's mind: *Your daddy was that crazy niggah from the war who used to be in your mama's garden . . .*

The words jumped from his mind and ran wild through the herbage. And once more he thought of the pictures in the unit chapters of his schoolbook (mother, father, little girl, little boy, golden retriever) and wondered who his father was and why his mother never talked about him. He gathered up the eggplants and slowly headed back to where she was picking.

"Mama?"

"Yes?"

"Was my father in this garden?"

Amber let the spade she was holding fall from her hands, for it was part of what she'd been using to try to bury the man deeper in the ground on each of Dash's birthdays. But like everything else planted there, it now sprang into the mercury-laden eve. "Yes," she said finally.

"Was he in a war?"

"Where did you hear that?"

"Was he in a war?"

"Yes."

"What war?"

"It doesn't matter. They're all the same."

Dash looked at his mother in the alkaline light, and suddenly it felt as if the whole of his ten years had come down to a single question. "Where is he?"

Amber sank into the soil, feeling fragile and worn like some artifact unearthed at last. She said nothing, her silence her answer, and it circled the garden and settled at the center of the blank space between them.

They sat together in the tabernacle of that silence—mother and son—each looking through the other, each feeling older than in the moments before. For it seemed that under the cold stare of the great moon orb, all things known darkened and faded from sight and all things hidden glittered in its gaze.

WATER'S EDGE

Nephthys steered through serpentine currents that played tricks on her navigation, turning one pathway into another, and in the miasma of doubt she questioned the way forward and the way back . . .

Nephthys coasted slowly down the street toward Veronica Wilson's home. But the closer she came to it, a peculiar feeling became stronger. Because the fog had told her just a while earlier that she should go and pick up Veronica Wilson, but unlike most other passengers, she got no sense at all of where she would be taking her. She pulled up to a hundred-year-old Uniontown house with a falling-down porch and stopped.

Veronica Wilson stood on her porch waiting for Nephthys Kinwell in the darkness of dawn while her family was still sleeping, risking the happenings that places like Anacostia sometimes wrought at that hour. The maternal side of her family hailed from the Kingdom of Tennessee on the bluffs of Memphis, named after the ancient capital of Egypt by one of the city's wealthy founders. And in the lines and circles of existence, her great-grandmother was a descendant of the Cherokee who had once dominated that southern region. The British had been observing her great-grandmother's people with interest. They led the construction of a fort there, within which plans to remove the Cherokee were devised, and Captain Raymond Demere of the British Army scribed who he thought her great-grandmother's people were in the letters of his time:

The savages are an odd kind of people; as there is no Law nor Subjection amongst them, they can't be compelled to do anything nor oblige them to embrace any party except they please. The very lowest of them thinks himself as great and as high as any of the rest. Every one of them must be courted for his friendship with some kind of a feeling, and made much of; so what is called great and leading men amongst them are commonly old and middle-aged people, who know how to give a talk in favor of whom they have a fancy for; and the same may influence the minds of the young fellows for a time; but everyone is his own master.

But Veronica Wilson had no way of knowing this when she came outside to stand in the dark. What she knew was that she was in full mastery of her will alone on the porch, waiting. Because she had an important question, and who better to take her to the one with the answer than Nephthys Kinwell? And if the things she heard people say about the Car Lady were true—her knowing when someone needed a ride without being told—she would be along soon. So it was no surprise that when she saw the unmistakable Plymouth pull up to the house, she stepped gingerly down the steps and got in the car.

"Good morning, Ms. Kinwell. How you been?"

Nephthys shrugged. "Fine, I guess." The peculiar feeling was even stronger now, and she took a sip from her flask to steady her stomach. "You?"

"Hanging in there, you know."

"Yes indeed," said Nephthys, feeling queasy. She was beginning to wonder if she should go home for a while, maybe try to use the bathroom. And she still had no sense of the nature of the ride for the woman in her car. "Where to, chile?"

Veronica hesitated, but there were other matters at stake. "Amber."

Nephthys looked at Veronica in the rearview mirror without blinking. "Say again?"

"Amber Kinwell, your—"

"Know who she is," interrupted Nephthys, harsher than she'd intended. Now she understood the peculiar feeling she had and there was nothing she could do about it, since she could never bring herself to refuse anyone passage. She listened to the engine purr, wondering why Veronica wanted to visit Amber. But since she was good at encryption and seeing things that others said weren't there, she realized slowly that it must have something to do with the Lottery.

Veronica sat rigid. Because the Lottery had been on her mind for days ever since she'd read the latest installment, and she had to know what it meant.

1. Police raid. Green house with the big philodendron on the porch. Body in the closet.
2. Pink pacifier and bottle. Box buried in the yard. Frederick Douglass house. Study cottage in the back.
3. Red, white, and blue beads on the ends of braided hair. Train tracks. Washington Bullets T-shirt. Kingman Lake.
4. Wires on fire. Apartment on Dotson Street. No numbers on the doors. Windows nailed shut. Woman can't breathe.
5. A mother. Five children. A man named Wilson holds his arm and loses his heart.

And every time Veronica's husband said his jaw was tight or that he felt dizzy or rubbed his chest at the dinner table, she thought about the Lottery more. He seemed more tired and irritable than usual, and he was short of breath lately, and she often caught him holding his arm. "It's just a little pain and numbness sometimes," he'd said. She wanted him to see a doctor, maybe go over to the hospital or see someone at the clinic. But he reminded her that they didn't have insurance, and that the money he made needed to go into the mouths of their children and not into the pocket of some cheat who would only give him aspirin. He didn't need anybody checking him. It would all be fine. "So don't ask me about it again. I'm all right," he'd said, massaging his arm and wiping the sweat from his brow.

All this had driven Veronica up and out of the house before he and the children awoke, what came in the dark be damned. Because when she was a little girl, she thought that her life would consist of three steps: get married, raise a family, and go to heaven. She did the first. But the second had been so difficult, taken so much to sustain, that she wondered if she would have the strength for step three and walk through God's gate if she ever got the chance. She thought of all the small indignities that ate at her soul, all the scraps of a life hanging by threads: the shoes the children needed; how the stove sometimes quit on her; the holes in the linen and the bugs in the flour. And burning in her mind was what she'd read in the Lottery.

The white girl in the trunk rolled over and sighed.

"Please," said Veronica. "It's important. It's the Lottery."

Nephthys glanced at her in the rearview mirror and swallowed hard. "Something 'bout you?"

Veronica looked up into the darkened window where her husband was still sleeping. "No."

Nephthys felt her stomach turning and she put her foot on the gas pedal, revving the engine softly. "Can take you to the edge, but you got to walk the way down."

At the top of the hill, Nephthys watched Veronica get out of the car and walk to the edge, where she paused for a moment before she began her descent and disappeared. But long after she was gone, Nephthys sat in the car, unsure whether to stay or drive away.

The white girl in the trunk understood such times when Nephthys was weary of the heaviness of being, and she acknowledged this with her silence.

Nephthys got out of the car and walked to the edge. The hilltop was as far as she'd been in years, and now that she was once again at the edge, she had to think about why. She had to think about her brother, the river, and the shark.

Patches in the cloudcap cleared and she glimpsed the two-story house. Even in the faint light, she recognized that unmistakable color clinging to the exterior. Because it was the beginning of things—not the end—that had first inspired her and Osiris to pick periwinkle-blue paint for the house all those years ago. For the hue reminded them of the moment when their mother dipped white cloth into vats of indigo; that alchemy of air water light when the ultraviolet magic began.

Now the painted exterior was faded and the once-sturdy porch was warped and it had all been taken over by a tide of angst and ire. She squinted, trying to get a closer look, but she couldn't see much else. Veronica was long gone, she supposed, sunk into a water world meant to capsize anyone who entered. The cloudcap thickened, and now everything beyond the edge was obscured, as if stirred into the brew of some strange sea.

Indigo swirlin' round de vat . . .

Nephthys closed her eyes and opened them again. How was it that this passenger in her car had found the strength (courage?) to walk down the hill to the house of her past and she could not? She felt the inertia of one drive her on once more, and she stepped away from the edge.

WOMENFOLK

In the early-morning dark, Amber woke up in tangled sheets and a soaked nightgown, dazed and weary. Her sleeping patterns were worsening; either she couldn't sleep or couldn't seem to wake up. Again, she had the sensation that she'd awoken in her bedroom and then moved into another room and gotten into that bed and gone to sleep.

But the images about Dash rose before her like a malevolent sun. The dark forest. The faceless man lurking in the trees. That dead cardinal falling to the ground. Dash lying still in a creek. How could she stop this from happening? And she felt the fear of that very first death dream about her father. Because she couldn't stop that one from coming true, nor any of the rest that followed. Why would this dream be any different? Such thoughts drove her up and out of the bed, and she went to Dash's room and peeked inside. He was sleeping peacefully. She closed the door and drifted downstairs and through the phytoplankton-filled hallway and out to the porch.

The hill stood in the darkness of the valley, a hulking wall of black. Numb, she sat down on the step. The cloudcap was thinning and she looked up at the moon. The planetoid beamed down, casting the valley in silver. And in that argent gleam, the question Dash had asked her in the garden shone brazen once more: *Where is he?* She looked away, erasing the question from her mind. The cloudcap thickened again and the shadows returned. And just as she was about to close her eyes and try to calm her thoughts, she saw a woman appear.

* * *

Veronica Wilson had made her way down from the top of the hill. She thought it odd that the Car Lady seemed reluctant to take her there; not stepping one foot out of the car, not going with her to see her own people, even if it was at an unholy hour. But she couldn't worry about that now. There were greater concerns. She walked on in the dark, determined, looking around anxiously. She gripped her purse and tried to speed her approach, cursing the mud for slowing her down. *What a thing to do*, she thought. But she had to know. The thick mist made it difficult to see, fraying her nerves, and she braced for animals that might pounce on her from somewhere in the murk. She jumped at every crow caw, each owl hoot. Then the house appeared out of the mist and she saw a figure sitting on the porch step in the gloom. She stopped in her tracks. *It must be her*, she thought. Goose bumps spread over her skin. But she reminded herself why she was there and looked around once more, gathering her courage.

She stepped closer and stopped. "Good morning, Ms. Kinwell, early as it is."

Amber was too exhausted to be surprised by an unexpected visitor and gazed at the woman. The mist thinned. And slowly, she recognized her from one of her death dreams and she understood why she was there without having to be told. "Morning to you."

"My name is Veronica Wilson." She was careful not to look into those eyes, even in the dimness.

Amber stood up. "Uh-huh. You can call me Amber."

Veronica was startled by such nonchalance. "I know it's early. Your aunt brought me over."

Amber froze. She looked up at the hill but the cloudcap obscured the top of it from view. *Was she there?*

"Sorry to be bothering you."

Amber looked away from the hill. "It's all right. Come."

Veronica mounted the porch and stomped her feet, trying to

scrape away the slabs of mud stuck to the bottom of her shoes.

Amber opened the front door and gestured for her visitor to follow.

Veronica hesitated. All the terrible things she'd heard about the Death Dreamer, the one who lived at the bottom of the hill, flooded her mind. Broken mirrors. Fingernails in wax. Blood-filled bowls and bones hanging from the ceiling. Was she entering some cursed place where none returned? But she'd come too far to turn back now. She trailed Amber into the house. Immediately, the deep-blue look of everything inside stunned her. And as she followed the woman down the hallway that led to the kitchen, it seemed that it was more and more difficult to breathe, and she felt like a weight was pressing down on her chest. As they walked through the house, she looked wide-eyed into the living room and dining room, at the sofa coverlets that seemed to float and the algae-laden objects. *Where is she taking me?* she wondered.

At last they reached the kitchen in the back, and Amber pointed at the table. "Please, have a seat." She went about pouring water into two glasses.

The visitor did as she was told and sat down. She felt short of breath and drank the whole glass. The water seemed to ease her breathing to something more comfortable and she was surprised.

Amber refilled her glass.

"Thank you," Veronica said. In the flicker of the overhead light, she stared at patterns in the nightgown Amber was wearing, avoiding her face. "I'm here about the Lottery."

Amber nodded.

Veronica shifted her eyes down to the table. "I don't normally read it, you know. Not that I wouldn't read it—I just don't usually have time to read—but I happened to look at it while I was waiting on the clothes to dry at the laundromat." She fidgeted with the buckle on her purse. "And I guess . . . well, it seemed like . . ."

"You read something you recognize."

Veronica swallowed hard. She drank more of the water and set the glass down. "Yes. There was something about a man. And his heart." In fact, she'd read it over and over: "*A mother. Five children. A man named Wilson holds his arm and loses his heart.*"

Amber nodded again.

"Well, I just wanted to know what you mean by that."

Amber refilled her guest's glass and sighed. "Only what I can see."

Veronica shifted in her chair, trying not to meet Amber's eyes. "Well, you said you saw . . . This all just seems so crazy to me. Because I don't know who you could have been talking about in that Lottery. After all, people with the same name live all over, right?" She opened her purse as if to get something from it and closed it again. "But I couldn't help thinking about the one Wilson that I know. The one Marcus Wilson. My husband. And I started to wonder if . . . Is it true?"

The house creaked, and the two women sat listening to its structure contract.

Amber thought about Dash sleeping peacefully upstairs and her own secret fear. "You think it's true, Veronica. Isn't that why you're here?"

Veronica was staring at the mold rings on the kitchen walls, and the fear inside deepened. Because she'd learned that a house with no men is a frightful thing. She'd seen it in the eyes of other women. Young pregnant girls standing alone at bus stops and behind the malice-laced gaze of spinsters. Widows in church pews and ladies walking into funeral homes. Females after prison visits. And if the lights were turned off in beauty parlors, the eyes of some of the women in the chairs glowed in the dark with it. "But what can I do?"

Inside, Amber felt her pain and the terror for Dash struck through her like lightning. "I don't know."

Veronica was shocked at Amber's response. Earlier that morning, she'd gathered the strength to do things she would never have done before, only to be disappointed. She wanted to be given hope, to be told that she was mistaken. And if it was all true, why couldn't Amber fix it? Put a root on the prediction. A reverse spell. Something. Now she looked at Amber directly, no longer caring about the glare of ruination. "What?"

"I don't know," said Amber softly, and she peered beyond Veronica at the window above the sink and out to the mystery that seemed to linger in the trees, yet something else beyond her cognition. "All I know is what I can see."

Now Veronica felt her breathing grow shallow, like she was slowly drowning, and she thought she had to get out of that house right away or she would never leave. She stood up abruptly. "Thank you for your time, but I should be going." The resolve she'd inherited from her distant relative hardened once more and she gave Amber a defiant look. "I don't know much either. But let me tell you something I do know. My life is still mine. My husband is still here and he's going to stay if I have anything to do with it, no matter what your dream says."

Amber stood on the porch, listening to the planks buckle. She couldn't be angry at Veronica Wilson's parting words, driven as she was by the fear of a truth that they both shared. But what also drove the woman to her door, she supposed, was love for a man who would hold his arm and lose his heart.

She heard the *thump thump* sound of something ripe falling off a stem somewhere in the garden. And the question she'd buried out there in the soil sprang up once more: *Where is he?* She let the question fall back into the space where it had been buried. Because in her heart there was a vault where she kept a satin pouch of the memory of Dash's father hidden; the man she cherished (loved?), for he was the only one who had saved her from the tyranny of her dreams. She looked over the deserted valley, and in its emptiness felt all the more alone. *It doesn't matter where he is anymore,* she thought. The echo of that fleeting life with him existed only in the crypts of her mind now. And like all phantoms, he was there and then gone.

It started when she'd asked him a single question. After that, he seemed to turn into someone else. It was a simple question, Amber thought, yet one he wouldn't answer. But he seemed different. He would sit on the bed and then jump up to go to another room, and just as quickly he would come back, only to rush off somewhere else. She often found him in the garden, where he held the look of a startled steer. She tried to find out what was wrong as the days wore on, but that only seemed to make matters worse, so that he drifted through the house more and talked less and would no longer look her in the eyes. And one morning she awoke to find only his lingering scent of wintergreen and crushed leaves and firewood. The death dreams came back that very night, a merciless confirmation that he was gone.

Then she discovered her pregnancy. She was in the garden trying to pull up a collard plant when she vomited into its wide, leafy bowl. An ancient understanding suddenly became clear, and she knew what it meant without having to be told. She sat down in the soil and called to him from the deep-blue depths of her heart, but there was no response.

Later on, there was the loudness of his absence on the day that she went into labor, when she waited in the unlabeled section for indigent care. She sat blinking in the hospital fluorescent lights, watching the medical interns walk by her from one hour to the next. She tried to distract herself from the labor pains by listening to them talk, and she overheard them marveling about how the young mothers could eat french fries and drink Rock Creek soda through their pregnancies and still deliver healthy babies.

"These black girls are breeders," one of them said in a lowered voice.

"I know," murmured another, snickering. "And the daddies make a dash for it."

It was a familiar joke, it seemed, made lightly and often by the interns, and each one laughed at the wit of the other over coffee and cigarettes, and they looked at Amber without seeing that she was there.

When the baby was born, she was overcome with a glacial resolve and she spelled the name out slowly so that there would be no mistake: *D-A-S-H.* But in accordance with the dark irony with which creatures of passage live, Amber would not understand the duplicity of the name. For not only did it describe what the child's father did as he disappeared into the territories; it also foretold the happenings of a singular day in the imaginable forest of Suitland Parkway ten years later, when the boy was going to have to run.

PASSAGE IV

SURRENDERING ONE'S LIFE

RUNNING MAN

Red, Dash's father, had been running through the kingdoms of the land since the day he was discharged from the army, thinking only of the lightness of his duffel bag and filling it to fullness with the nothingness he needed. His DD214 papers read, *General Discharge Under Honorable Conditions,* and he wondered what had been honorable. On the other hand, he knew the conditions all too well. He'd been camping with various species along the Mississippi River. He waded across the Flint River of Albany in the Kingdom of Georgia and fed on roasted opossum given to him by a wild woman living in a hillside shack. He hiked north along the Appalachian Trail and up to the eastern panhandle of the Kingdom of West Virginia to Harpers Ferry, where the Shenandoah and Potomac Rivers converged. His days in the wilds of the territories made him more at ease with the shelter of nature. He was a better hunter since his days in the army, now that he was no longer required to hunt humans. And years of living with other species had sharpened his ability to discern the sounds of men from all others.

Red had wandered into Prince George's fiefdom in the Kingdom of Maryland, not far from the District of Columbia line in the southeast quadrant. He drifted into the paltry remains of a thick antebellum forest protected by the National Park Service, where Suitland Parkway parted the last remaining woods with the precision of the arrows that Nacotchtank warriors had once launched there. And in accordance with signs omens bones, the woods defied all topographical logic and limitations of scale, so that the landscape of the imaginable forest shape-shifted and took on the depth and richness of the mind entering it.

Red had pitched his tent in the solitude of a small clearing near a creek where the forest became what he wanted it to be. It felt safer there, a refuge from what he might see elsewhere. Or who. Nature offered both space and proximity, so that when he saw the one who was always there on the other side of the creek where he often bathed, or sitting at the foot of a silver maple tree, or from behind a cluster of hollyhocks, he could see her clearly (in order to better escape her) and without the obstructions of crowded places, where one thing might be mistaken for another. At night the imaginable forest shaped a resting spot that reminded him of a place where he once watched the northern lights, when he stood on the edge of Quartz Lake in the Kingdom of Alaska. And among the viridescent and crimson flashes beaming down to the forest floor where he was lying in his sleeping bag, he felt solar and ephemeral.

He stayed in this one place longer than he'd planned, spending his time in the imaginable forest, until one day he ventured across the district line into the realm of Anacostia and stopped at Sonny's Bar.

Sonny's Bar was a place that provided a deep well of nothingness from which to draw, and the people who gathered there floated from one escaped reality to the next. Red, too, had been sitting at the counter all day, drinking and eating peanuts, rinsing his face in the men's room. It was his habit to unwrap one piece of gum after another and put it in his mouth. And now and then when he looked up from his drink, he saw the one who was always there. The hours clicked on, and Red looked around the bar at the great vortex of distraction. Voices filled the air like actors in a playhouse . . .

"What I should have done was tell him to pull himself together," a woman was saying. "You know what I mean? I can do bad by my damned self and I already know how to lose. Oh yeah, I got that down to a science, and I sure don't need nobody's help to do bad." The woman took a long drag from her cigarette. "But shit, I ain't bitter. That fool did me a favor."

Other women grunted in agreement.

A toothless woman said, "Honey, you should have left him alone. Ain't no man right in the head no way, and time only makes 'em crazier."

Another haggard lady sucked her teeth, throwing a rotten peanut to the floor. "I always say if I got to live with a fool, I'd rather die alone a genius."

The women burst into laughter and went on with their cajoling, showing each other their open wounds and scars, remnants of companionship etched in deep scratches on their confidence. Assaults on the dignity of their womanhood were swept away and worries were tucked under the floorboards of their minds. The son not seen in six months. The pending eviction. The unemployment lines. Loved ones in prison. Grandchildren needing new shoes. And they were ashamed to admit that they once offered devotion to the men who they now debased. That like the younger versions of themselves who sassed and annoyed them now, they once dabbed perfume on their necks and curled their hair.

The voices of the men filled the air with the acid rain of the disappointments and indignities they both suffered and inflicted. They spoke of children they found it more and more difficult to talk to and women who seemed to listen to them less and less. They damned the stagnation of circumstance and chance, and they looked at each other with the burnished eyes of infantrymen who had seen and done and heard too much. And love and hate had the same design in the theater of their lives.

"So the motherfucker fired me right there on the spot, man," one of them was saying. "And it was for some shit I ain't have nothing to do with neither. They got amnesia when you remind 'em what *does* make sense. But they can't remember shit about you warning them about them raggedy-ass machines. Talkin' 'bout budgets. I'm telling you it ain't right. It ain't right at all."

Other men grunted in agreement.

"And my old lady didn't do nothin' but tho' salt in the wound. Talkin' 'bout the rent. Like I don't know we got bills. What the fuck does the woman want me to do? Rob a bank?"

The men went on, affirming the outrage, cataloging and taking inventory of the infinite ways in which the game they were compelled to play was rigged. How each harsh word from the women was a lash on the back. That they'd withstood so much to see the women smile in spite of what it meant to live in the kingdoms of the land: the union representative who said there was nothing he could do; the car that wouldn't last until a water pump could be purchased; the twelve-hour days and the docked paychecks; the emasculation and the jive. They could have withstood it all and more, if they had that smile to look forward to. But in the end, it was the she-tongue that broke them.

Red turned back to his drink.

Nephthys came into the bar and sat down on the stool next to him. The bartender, Captain, filled her glass with what he knew she wanted. She settled into the gloom and the riffs of Marvin Gaye playing softly in the background, and after a while she turned and said: "Where from, mistuh?"

Red looked into the woman's streaked eyes. "Everywhere. Nowhere. It don't really matter."

Nephthys nodded and swirled a piece of ice around in her mouth until it dissolved. "So wuh Anacostia got goin' fuh you then, huh? Family? Chilrun?"

"Kids? Nah. One of me is enough." Again, Red looked across the bar and saw *her* there. He took his gum out of his mouth and sipped his drink and put it back. "I'm the last of me and there won't be no trace."

Nephthys drank more of her drink, the open-water feeling washing over her. "Last of a man, huh? Well, so be it. We got drink at least."

"Yup. Hate to know what this terrible world would be without it."

The colors of the bar had changed from the dim shades of brown and gray to soft yellows and mossy greens, and Nephthys smiled. "Wash 'way scorn and 'buke Satan."

Red pounded the counter, laughing. "You ain't never lied!" Now he looked at the woman more closely. She seemed old enough to be his mother. He could see that once she might have been very attractive, but years of drinking had set her body in a sort of brine, so that she appeared much older than she probably was and her breasts sagged and were long bereft of the promise of milk. But he'd dealt with older women before and appreciated their directness and seeming disdain for pretense. "So what might be your name, young gal?"

"Nephthys."

"Say what?"

She leaned closer, her eyes as big as saucers. "I said *NEFF-THIS*."

"Well, there you go. Nephthys it is." Red noticed her hand deformity too, but he planned to make no inquiry about it, since he'd learned that asking a woman about particulars implied significant interest, and he was firmly committed to not being significantly interested in anything.

"Well? Got a name?" she asked.

Red looked at the one who was always there and back at Nephthys. "They call me Red."

Nephthys smiled. "Red, huh? Hot man, right? Well, well, well!"

Red was warmed by her cheer and nonchalance. For asking seriously about his given name could lead to wanting to know why he was called Red and send her down a road with him that he could only travel alone. He took the gum he had in his mouth and put it in the ashtray and brought out a new piece from a pocket, unfolding the little silver wrapper gingerly.

Nephthys raised her glass in salute. "Water of life, swonguh man."

Red liked the faraway sound of her voice, how it sighed and faded at the end of each word like the Key West sunsets he saw melt into the sea. "Yup." He picked up his army duffel bag from the floor and fished out another pack of gum.

Nephthys looked at the bag. "Fightin' man, huh?"

"Not for a while."

"Wuh it be like? That war?"

Red winked at Nephthys, silent. For in accordance with the dark irony with which creatures of passage live, he had only ever wanted to get away from the happenings he'd experienced in the Kingdom of Illinois as a boy and take up the promise of buying real citizenship with a gun and the flag, not realizing that the military would bring him to places that stayed with him from sunrise to sunset, from one waking moment and thought to the next, and there would be no relief except in the act of fleeing. And it was not so much the names he was called when he first returned from Vietnam (*green coon, army nigger, darky soldier*), it was that none of those names matched the one he felt he'd earned that day in the jungle.

"I say, wuh it be like?" Nephthys asked again.

Red looked from his drink to Nephthys and smiled. "Darling, it ain't really *like* nothing and there ain't nothing to say. Besides, talking leads to remembering and remembering leads to dealing. And honey, I'm done dealing with anything."

Nephthys chuckled. "Testify! Nice enough to deal with nothing here."

"Yup. Any place is a nice place, sugar. But nice places got things that keep 'em from being nice enough to stay."

"Right so," said Nephthys. She rose unsteadily. "Getting late.

Gotta go." She swayed on her feet, nodded at Captain, and smiled at Red. "Welcome to Anacostia, place of dreams."

It was near closing time at Sonny's Bar and Captain had been watching the newcomer. He wiped the counter and refilled Red's glass. "Quite the lady friend you got there."

"Who?"

"Your drinkin' buddy, Nephthys."

"Yup."

"She's something else, you know. Well, truth be told, them Kinwells are all something else."

The others at the counter who were listening looked on with knowing eyes.

"Yeah?"

"She's a twin, you know. Had a brother named Osiris, but one day they fished him out of the Anacostia River."

Red took a long draw from his glass and set it down. "Damn."

"Indeed they did," said Captain.

A man with a deep scar on his cheek motioned for Captain to refill his glass. "Well, he should have known better, if he thought bein' too nice to that white woman was safe."

"Well, don't nobody know what really happened," said a woman wearing a matted wig. "Wasn't no secret that the Rileys hated still being here after most of 'em left. But they couldn't leave, even after the riots. Guess they didn't have no money. I said good morning to 'em once and they looked at me like I had an elephant sitting on my head. Seemed like they cared more for them damned dogs and cats they had than people. Lovin' 'em like children."

"Kill a nigger, save a pet," said the man with the scar.

"'Cuz black people are different but white people are the same," quipped the wigged woman.

"Well, they're both dead now," said Captain. "Riley took sick. From cancer, I heard. And they found the wife laid up in that house on Alabama Avenue that should have been condemned."

"The smell was worse than the cats," said the toothless woman at the counter. "That was what let 'em know she was laying in there."

Captain turned to Red. "But somebody killed your new drinkin' buddy's twin and she been in here at my counter ever since."

"Scary as can be," said the wigged woman.

Captain looked from her to Red. "There's that thing she does with her Plymouth. Bet she ain't mention that."

Red shrugged. "Ain't cared about cars in a long time."

"She can take you anywhere you want to go in that Plymouth, maybe even before you know where you want to go. It's haunted."

Red smiled. "Quit jiving, man."

"Ain't jiving. Them Kinwells is something else, you know. Especially the niece."

"Niece?"

The patrons who had joined the conversation stared into their glasses, silent.

Captain refilled Red's glass and gave him a look. "Guess you wouldn't know about her neither. Not yet, anyway. Your drinking buddy's niece. The Death Dreamer."

"What?"

"Amber Kinwell. She dreams about death. How people are going to die."

Red put the gum he was chewing into the ashtray and took out another piece. "You don't say."

Someone at the counter grunted.

"The Lottery," said Captain. "Witchcraft and voodoo stuff. She even got the store owners buying those monstrous vegetables and fruits out of that bewitched garden of hers. How she makes her money, I suppose. Selling that black-conjure produce. Biggest things you ever seen. Some kind of magic in the soil there and things only grow in moonlight, never in the sun. They say if you eat 'em you feel like you can live forever. I never touched any of it and don't plan to ever touch any of it, so I wouldn't know."

"Spoils of the damned," said the scar-faced man.

Captain grinned. "Who knows? But being raised by an aunt like Nephthys Kinwell, what do you expect?"

"If you could call it raising," the toothless woman chimed. "That girl was born with the eye, on account of what happened to her mother, Gola. Nine whole months pregnant and just minding her business crossing the street. Hit and run. Killed her. The doctor that got the baby born insisted on paying for her burial." She took a drag from her cigarette and blew a stream of smoke like steam from a kettle. "Can you believe that? Buried by somebody else's people. The work of the Devil."

Captain shook his head. "Well, they say Satan is always working, ain't he?"

Red listened on, feigning interest, but *eye* hung in his mind.

"Anyway, I try to steer clear of Amber Kinwell. If she's seen how I'm leaving this earth, I don't wanna know nothing about it. And I damn sure don't want nobody reading the Lottery about me to see if she's right."

Red was about to tell Captain that he thought what he was saying was bullshit, when from the corner of his eye he saw *her* standing by the door. He stirred his drink around with his finger and looked up again. She was still there. He drank what was left in his glass.

"Well, it ain't the Rapture yet," the bartender was saying. He shook out his apron and looked at the others at the counter and back at Red. "But there are things that'll make a man pause in Anacostia. Like Amber Kinwell."

GONE

Red heard all kinds of talk about Amber Kinwell in the southeast quadrant. Voodoo Girl. Snakehead. Swamp Thing. He made sure never to ask Nephthys about her when they drank together at Sonny's Bar, since he did not want to admit to himself nor to her that the talk held his interest. Besides, her profound silence about her niece seemed to affirm the ominousness of what people said. There were wild stories about Amber's death dreams, and people talked in low voices of how her visions appeared in the obituaries and the evening news, and they vowed never ever to go near her. "You don't want her marking you," they said. But Red heard such talk and thought of Amber without fear, wondering if she might know the answer to a question that he'd asked himself a thousand times before: *Would* she *ever go away?*

It took time for him to figure out where Amber lived without asking around too much. He discovered that she dwelled in an outlandish place, a lone house at the bottom of a hill. He trekked down through the cloudcap, marveling at how different it was from anything he'd seen in the wilds of the territories. It was strange topography and seemed to have its own weather; a landlocked site with a house sinking into mud. He snuck about the valley like the deer that once wandered there and he crept around the garden, gawking at the miraculous growth of things the size of which he'd never seen in his travels through the kingdoms of the land.

But more than anything, he realized immediately that *she* was gone. Down in that place, he didn't see the one who was always there at all. He exulted in this absence, and he began to wonder if this dark woman and her dark realm had something to do with it. He looked around at the old trees, the garden, and the hill. Nothing. Finally, he trekked through the mud to the front door and knocked. As he stood waiting in front of the translucent glass, he tried to see into the deep-blue interior but could not make out anything. *Did the woman already know he was there?*

Amber appeared suddenly like some marine creature emerging from the murky deep and opened the door, having no fear of others since most feared her.

Startled, Red looked into her impossible eyes gazing back at him. He swallowed hard and said the first thing that came to mind: "Well, ain't you something to see."

And in that way that women of Anacostia come straight to the point, she looked at him without blinking and said, "There's no reason for you to be here."

Red smiled. "Baby, that's true. But there might be a reason for me to stay."

Living alone in her domain had made Amber as harsh and inhospitable as the marshes that once covered all of Anacostia; even mosquitoes did not bite her. She thought the man looked ridiculous on her porch, smiling. But she was not made of stone, and even as she glared at the absurdity of him standing there at her door (visiting?), she tried hard not to smile. For no one had ever talked to her so easily or looked her directly in the eyes. And he was not the newsman come to hear her death toll. He was someone else.

Red came around more and more. They talked on the porch about the harmless things that the little valley wrought; the movement pattern of the cloudcap and the shapes of the trees in the dark. The atmospheric conditions of her world did not seem to affect him at all. And little by little, she looked forward to seeing him and an excitement inside grew. Sometimes he helped move big wagons of bounty from one side of the garden to another and did small projects around the house. And later on, as he sat in the tub of hot water that she ran for him, she thought about how it was possible that he smelled of wintergreen and crushed leaves and firewood whether he was wet or dry, clean or dirty, and the expanse this made her feel inside.

But most of all, the death dreams stopped. She did not dream a single night that Red was there. And when she watched him hauling wheelbarrows of cherry tomatoes out of the garden, or quietly sitting on the porch chewing his gum, or staring at her from across the table, she wondered what the cessation of the death dreams in his presence could mean or not mean. She even told Mr. Johnson that she hadn't seen anything for him to record in the Lottery, which for a while was true. Because in accordance with the dark irony with which creatures of passage live, there was an invisible line between Amber and Red, and on each side lay the salvation of the other as long as neither one of them crossed it. And one evening, as they lay together in the bed watching the curtains wave in the drift, Amber said, "Why do you go by Red? I know it ain't your real name."

Red turned over on his side away from Amber, unable to think, unable to breathe. It was like something had detonated in his head. He tried clenching his eyes shut, but it felt like something was prying them open. His pupils dilated and his eyes pulled back wider and wider, unrestrained, unblinking. And there *she* was, standing next to the algae-filmed dresser drawer, staring at him. And Red looked with seeing and believing eyes and the memory of what drove him to run was reborn.

He was coming off a four-day barbiturate binge, lovely drugs that made Vietnam melt into a volcanic lava swirl where the unseen vortex of hell welled up from the abyss. He inched through the morass, a small beast among many: blood-siphoning leeches, old men clutching their rags, young women hiding in the mud, pythons and lizards. There were other things alive and dead in the jungle, and they lay under him thick and green and stinking, and as he slunk, he knew not what he was seeing nor what eyes were on him.

But he knew that something moved. And when he knew that it moved, he knew he was at the mercy of that which tracked and ambushed and killed again. That which questioned why he was in this foreign kingdom as he himself had asked. So when it moved he fired his rifle and it moved no more. He crouched and listened and crept closer. The foliage was like a heavy emerald curtain, and when he pulled it back with the end of his gun, he saw what it was. *How can it be so small?* he thought. *Such a small thing in this great pit.* He saw that it was holding something. He bent down and took the something from the little fingers and opened it up to find three things: a coin, a wooden bead, and a silk ribbon, which fell to the ground along with his broken heart.

He blinked in the sweltering heat, trying to rewind the happening like a tape so he could erase it. But it was there still, the little hand and what fell from it. And then he looked at the rest. A small body, immobile, turned to stone like some found instrument of idolatry on the jungle floor. The face wide-eyed, two hot balls of glass from a kiln made to see him only, looking at him and through him and out to that place where committed acts are judged and back again. And across the forehead was a streak of blood that trailed down and pooled in a color he'd never seen before, a color absent from the light spectrum, but which existed now only because he had made it.

And slowly, he registered that it was a child, a girl no older than five or six. And as he watched her not moving, he knew that she would never be like the children he saw other soldiers kill, because this one he himself had murdered. And he thought about the dead children never avenged in the cross-burning towns of the kingdoms of the South and the riot-plagued streets of the kingdoms of the North and how killing children on the other side of the world was not what he'd enlisted for.

He was holding his head as if doing so might keep it from falling off his shoulders, when two men from his platoon walked up behind him. They called him by a word that sounded like the birth name his father had given him. But as the seconds passed, he understood them less and less and looked at them without recognition, convinced that they were calling someone else.

"What the fuck you doing, man?" asked one of the soldiers.

"It's a little one," said the other. He spat and took something from his pocket and put it in his mouth and swallowed it.

The first man looked at the body and shook his head. "When Satan come, you gonna be first. Me, right after you."

"Won't be no 'ticular order," said the other soldier. He spat again. "He just earning a name. Like we done and doing. Earning."

"Guess you been in this shit too long. 'Cuz you was supposed to be finding the goddamn supply checkpoint but you over here turnin' the ground red with baby blood."

His platoon called him Red after that. And he began to see the girl he killed everywhere. He found it more and more difficult to concentrate, to follow the most basic of commands, to remember what simple items were called. He couldn't get anyone to understand that the girl he killed really was in the barracks sitting on his bed, and that she really did stand by the tray of meat loaf in the mess hall sometimes, glaring at him. Finally, the military psychologist on base recommended that he be released.

And when he left the jungles to return to the kingdoms of the land, he found that more was different and more was the same. But *she* was there. Always. So he kept the name without dispute or reprieve, red being the closest description of the color he'd made. It was a special tint that when mixed with the little hand and the glass eyes and the streak made him who he was; proof that good and evil were nameless formless things in constant change, with no regard for the lives of men.

* * *

With Amber's inquiry about his name, Red saw the one who was always there every day and everywhere in the valley. Behind the leafy folds of the cornstalks in the garden. Standing on the porch. Sitting on the bed. Amber was asking him what was wrong but there were no words to explain what could not be erased. And the harder she tried to get him to talk, the more frequent the sightings became. One day, it seemed like the one who was always there looked at Amber as if she too had sinned against her, then glared back at him with the unflinching eye of her indictment, and this only frightened him more. That was when he knew he couldn't stay.

Again, the imperative to flee gripped him and he left the little periwinkle-blue house at the bottom of the hill at the edge of the world. He stepped foot in Sonny's Bar no more. He exited Anacostia and returned to the imaginable forest of Suitland Parkway and fled deep into the Kingdom of Maryland and out to the wilds of the territories. He ran back to the hinterlands of his mind and tried to forget the solace of Amber's aquatic realm; her impossible eyes in which he thought he'd found a refuge.

But each time he saw the one who was always there, he felt the lightness in his head and the emptiness of his duffel bag. The opiate of extinction called to him from the depths of the Void once more, and he basked in the fullness of futility and wanted only all traces of himself to be gone. Which was just as well, since the nothingness occupied every bit of space he had, and there was no room for anything else—least of all the trace inside of Amber.

WILDERNESS OF THE HEART

Red spent many years trying to forget Amber Kinwell and the peaceful waters of her dominion. He left her without explaining or saying goodbye, for with her question about his name she'd tried to join him on a road he felt could only be walked alone. The nothingness called to him and he filled the spaces of his mind with it. He wandered the wilds, bragging about his escapades to the other drifters he encountered: the giant trout caught in Nova Scotia; the seven-foot bear shot in the Black Hills National Forest; the three-day walk with no water and only the dew of a cactus that kept him alive in Death Valley.

In his quest to find a place where *she* wasn't there, Red drifted on. He had as many women as he could stand in the kingdoms of the land and he moved from one fiefdom to the next. San Francisco. Philadelphia. St. Louis. He squatted in the Kingdom of Florida on secluded shores in Clearwater and Indian Rocks Beach, bathing in the ocean and sleeping on the sand. Someone broke his nose in the icy reaches of Flint, and he put a man in the hospital in the Kingdom of Missouri. He smoked peace pipes with chiefs in the Kingdom of Nevada and stood naked at the summit of Boundary Peak.

The gold and red clay of the southwestern territories soothed him as he gazed at the tumbleweed blowing across the Mojave Desert. He stayed in an abandoned ice-fishing shack on a lake in the Kingdom of Wisconsin and made pleasant conversation with the moose poking around its perimeter. He discovered that there was nothing like the profound cold and droning wetness of the northwestern territories. He spent weeks foraging through the forests of the Kingdom of Oregon, dazzled by the emerald shades of the pine, dogwood, and fir trees. He supposed that the mountain men living there didn't like him sharing in their free range, having spent generations clearing the native peoples of that space for the contemplation of their own madness. Because sometimes he heard rifle shots near his camp, a reminder that he was nigger brown, not bear brown or deer brown.

He kept moving. But *she* remained. Everywhere. Sitting on curbs and hillsides. In afternoon shadows and in the flashes of thunderstorms. And one day he came to the cliffs of Monterey in the Kingdom of California, where the black water of the western ocean crashed into white foam. He was thinking he might leap into the watery oblivion, where perhaps the one who was always there wouldn't follow. But he stopped at the edge to watch the humpback whales breaching, their great mounds of flesh moving through the water like beasts come to collect the sunken souls of men.

He drifted on for weeks months years, until he entered the foothills of the Appalachian Mountains. He came upon a small cave that had housed other men down through the millennia. He crawled in and clicked his lighter. On the cave walls he saw the ancient etchings of artisans down through the ages, who with their implements had recorded the rise and fall of man. He held the lighter up and searched the rest of the cave. A pair of smooth black rocks lay near his leg and he picked them up and held them in his palm. And he tried once more to forget Amber, who with obsidian eyes like the stones he held had made the one who was always there disappear. An owl hooted as if calling the hour, and Red looked into the black night framed by the rock, a great window of night. His eyes sought points of light and retreated when none were found. A wind gust blew and doused his lighter, and the night that the flame had kept at bay rushed in and all was dark. Red looked into the black and beyond it to the nightmare that had no beginning and no end, for there was no need for light or eyes to know that *she* was there.

BELOW

It was in the summer of his tenth year of running from the one who was always there that Red grew tired of the futility of fleeing and came upon an old abandoned mine. It was a place that marked hidden spaces, places the earth shielded from the insatiable greed of creatures of passage. So it was no surprise that in the subterranean sprawl beneath the eastern parts of the middle continent, in an infinite web of underground pathways that led to other pathways, tunnels that led to other tunnels, formations that led to other formations, there was a place of reckoning for the wandering heart. But in 1928, any one of the impoverished white Appalachian miners living on the lands stolen from the Cherokee and Creek would have said that the mine ruled the world. And there they begged the earth for coal with machine and pick and shovel, and they were told by company doctors that their ailment was not black lung, but some other malady. And in the choked dark of their deathbeds, they penned epitaphs to their children on the walls of their minds. *Dear Sally and James, mind your mother and know that I love you. Until we are all together again. God bless us and goodbye.* And they lived and died this way, through the poisoned air, underground rock avalanches, and deadly gushes from unknown water sources until the mine finally closed in 1937.

But Red had no way of knowing this as he stood before it. What he knew was that the pursuit of emptiness was useless if it was filled only with the girl he killed. And again, he pondered his own death. He looked at the desolate entrance of the mine and into its blackness and beyond that to the Void that called to him from its depths. *Maybe she won't follow me there*, he thought. He walked up to the opening, a gaping, toothless mouth, and climbed into a small cart suspended over the abyss. He took hold of the fraying cables and lowered himself down, the circle of light above his head shrinking as he descended. Deeper and deeper down the shaft of jagged rock he dropped. In the intensifying darkness, he strained to see and held out his hand. Nothing. It was like it was invisible, a part of the air and the pitch black all around him. The cable clinked and jerked every few yards. Minutes went by, he couldn't tell how many, until at last the cable stopped and he realized he was at the bottom.

The pitch black seemed to reach out and touch him, and Red recoiled as if dodging the claws of some beast. He climbed out of the cart and stumbled along like a blind man. All he could hear was the movement of his limbs and footfalls and the sound of his beating heart. But then it was like the instincts he'd had when he first learned to walk resurfaced, and he felt his way with his hands. He moved forward, holding out his arms until he felt an opening. "Deeper," he said to the dark. "Deep enough to disappear." He would see the firelight of the sun no more, nor look into the lamplight of the moon. He would vanish without a trace.

He stumbled on for minutes hours days, until he bumped into what felt like an opening to something else. He squeezed through and tried to stand up, hitting his head on a rock shelf. The sharp pain dropped him to his knees. He felt around. The narrow passage didn't seem to be more than four feet in height, a flattened crawl space. He scaled it on his belly like a snake on a downward slope. He crawled on, until the ground beneath him dropped and he tumbled down a pathway. He lay there, spitting out the particles that got into his mouth.

Then out of the black atmosphere, Red thought he saw a faint light. He stood up and stumbled toward it. *Deeper*, he thought. *Where no one will ever find me.* He lurched on, falling and getting up again, until he reached yet another crawl space. He peered inside and from within a yet more distant light shimmered. He moved down that narrow space foot by foot for minutes and hours, until it opened to an enormous cave filled with gigantic boulders.

And there, in the center of the vast jungle of stupefying angles of contorted rock, was a cluster of massive crystals piercing the darkness like a kaleidoscopic light show. They'd been forming in the peace and secrecy of time since before the supercontinent broke into its smaller pieces, and they reached high to the roofless cavern like a grand cathedral instrument. Red stood before them and they turned the color he'd created in the jungle, and out of that unnamed hue the girl he killed appeared.

"Aww . . ." Red groaned when he saw her, resigned to yet more torment.

The one who was always there looked at Red with fresh hatred. It was taking her longer and longer to find her murderer lately, and she did not understand why someone she'd haunted for so long was now so elusive. But she was with him again now. The sight of her killer set her rage alight once more. And she thought of that day that ended all others, when her mother only had time to stroke her cheek and hand her some keepsakes before the soldiers carried her off. Her father lay in a pool of blood at her feet. She ran and ran, and only when Red shot her did she stop. There were times when she thought (hoped?) that what had happened to her was just a nightmare. But each time she followed Red and he looked at her with seeing and believing eyes, she confirmed that she was indeed a ghost and was newly incensed by this truth.

Red stood rigid as the girl he killed glared at him. He would not try to fight what was to happen next, and he did not know whether to laugh or to cry.

The girl moved closer, wiping the blood dripping from her face. And in the language beyond all worlds, she said: *Look what you did to me.*

Red was silent.

Look what you did to me, she said again.

Red nodded. If this meant it was time to die, he was ready.

You took my life.

"And you have my heart."

And I'll take more, if there is more to take.

Red smiled a tired smile. "If you can take nothing, you can have that too."

Now the girl was silent, thinking of what she heard from the other spirits she'd encountered who spoke of things she'd been trying to ignore. Like how she would come to a point when there was nothing left to have and nothing left to take. That unless she accepted what had happened to her, she could never move on and would continue to be doomed to the Conundrum of Three, where the mind sought the memory of a body long gone, and the body withdrew from the mind and the spirit, and the spirit chased the echo of the other two. *Don't you want to see your family again?* they had asked.

The girl glared at Red. *Look what you did to me.*

Red nodded again, for she was all he could ever see. Everywhere and always. And he knew—as all the guilty do—that if what he was about to say were uttered ten million times or more, it would never be enough. But he said it anyway: "I am sorry."

The girl heard the words but she did not feel them, fearful as she was that the other spirits were right, and now there was nothing left but the nothingness to take. She wiped the tears that had mixed with the blood on her face and said, more to herself: *This is what happened to me.*

Red sat down on the earthen floor, as if doing so might help the process of decomposing into it begin. "And I am nothing."

She looked at him, sniffling. *But you left something.*

Red went down on his back as he listened to the girl talk, resigned to live out eternity there with her.

And it's not fair, she said, wiping snot from her nose. *I saw him in her when he first started to grow.*

Red blinked in the color he'd made. "What?"

Look what you did to me. It's not fair that he is here and I am not.

"Who?"

Now the girl was looking into the shimmer of the crystals, distracted. The anger was beginning to subside, and she felt older than the rock formations surrounding them. She stared into the color and sighed. *Don't you know?*

Red sat up. "What?"

But by then the girl he killed would say no more, because at last she heard her mother calling her in for dinner. And she saw her father waving to her from their rice paddy field. And she nodded at Red and disappeared.

CARGO

Find Out had not needed a hit since the wish took hold in the back of Sonny's Bar, and it energized him and fortified him and drove him on. He hitched his way through the territories, from Tuskegee to Knoxville, then rode on the back of a crowded truck of farm laborers to Newport. The hot sun beat down on his head and he was rolled and jostled with the others in the truck all the way to Morristown. They passed a sign pointing northeast to Tazewell in the Kingdom of Tennessee. And when they neared a road sign in the Hancock fiefdom in the Kingdom of West Virginia, Find Out saw the blue smoke again. He jumped off the back of the vehicle and began walking, following the cobalt wisps to an old fire station. There was a run-down diner next to it. A flickering yellow sign in the greasy window read, *Best Suds and Dogs*. He walked in and looked around. Plumes of blue smoke curled above a booth by the door; he went over to it and sat down.

A pudgy waitress behind the counter stopped and stared at Find Out, as did three truckers sitting at the bar. A young boy was throwing a baseball up in the air, and when he saw Find Out, he let the ball hit the ground. Other patrons seemed to look at him in a kind of trance, part disbelief and part disgust.

Although the wish kept him from fiending, Find Out forgot how he must look. And smell. Black skin in the rural South aside, he hadn't bathed. He was wearing filthy jeans and one of his shirt sleeves was torn, exposing the tracks on his arms.

The truckers were watching him, and after a while they turned away.

* * *

The pudgy waitress behind the counter slowly came over with a coffee carafe in her hand, her eyes filled with echoes of the Confederacy and Jim Crow laws, and she stood over Find Out, studying him. "Coffee, mister?"

Find Out looked at her with the extraterrestrial eyes of a visitor to earth, for he'd almost forgotten what coffee was. "That'd be fine, thank you."

The waitress turned over the coffee mug sitting on the table and poured him a cup, eyeing him. "Meeting someone here?"

Find Out was watching the steam from the coffee rise and dissipate into the blue smoke that was circling the hanging lamp above his head. He'd found many last things and put them in his tin can, but it had been a long time since he'd found a person. The last time had been when he unearthed the Nacotchtank man, the sole survivor of his tribe, who'd called to him from the depths of Luray Caverns in the Kingdom of Virginia, where he'd been hiding for over a century. And at the man's request, Find Out told him of the things that had transpired since the genocide and in his years of exile in the belly of the calcite caves. That the Blue Plains sewage treatment plant and the Bolling Air Force Base military installations now blanketed the water and the land of his people in everlasting filth and the fog of war. And that mention of the Nacotchtanks having ever existed could be found only in the brief pages of carelessly written books, among the cracked artifacts showcased at the national museums, and in the comedy of absurd mascots and sports monikers.

The blue smoke loomed and ebbed and Find Out looked at the waitress. "Yeah, in a way."

"Oh." She looked into his bug-eyed gaze and quickly away. "Well, just a while back, there was a fella come by here."

Find Out watched skeins of the blue smoke drift around the booth lamp and toward the front door. "Yeah?" he said, feigning surprise.

The waitress looked at the truckers and back at Find Out. "Reckon you'll find who you searching for. And soon." She snatched the bill out of her apron pocket, slammed it on the table, and hurried away.

Find Out wanted the coffee. Not to drink, but to take in its domestic fragrance, a reminder of that distant time when he had a home, when he had his wife, the one who'd made his life. She was gone now, like the steam that rose from the cup and disappeared, her whereabouts unknown. And once more the dark irony with which creatures of passage were compelled to live washed over him, and he fumbled around for his lighter and lit a cigarette, his hands shaking. But he steadied his nerves with Nephthys Kinwell's wish and pushed his memories away, watching the white cigarette smoke float up and mix with the blue.

One of the truckers pushed back from the counter and rubbed his potbelly. "Well, Cody, I'ma be gettin' on up the road."

"Yeah, you gotta make this one count," said another man.

"Damn right. This run'll pay me double. My old lady can shut her trap about that new kitchenette she's been wanting me to get her."

The other one laughed. "How's the old ball and chain anyway?"

"Heavy and holding."

"Ha! Hang in there, buddy."

"Will do."

"Where you off to?"

"Sneedville," said the big-bellied man. "Gotta stop off in Sneedville first to weigh my load."

The blue smoke thickened. *Sneedville,* thought Find Out. That was where Red had gone after coming to this diner.

He watched the truckers slap each other on the back and polish off the last of their drinks.

"Gotta take a whiz in the can," said the one heading to Sneedville. "Catch you next week."

* * *

When the man came out of the bathroom, he laughed over a few nasty jokes with the waitress and settled his tab. He went out to his truck, climbed in, and hung a new air freshener on the rear-view mirror. He tooted his horn and pulled out of the diner parking lot, bound for Sneedville in his open-top eighteen-wheeler with a full load of potatoes. And secret cargo.

SMOKE AND TRACE

Red's voyage back to the inner harbor of his soul was a long one, for the years he'd spent moving through spaces still made it difficult to face his unease with staying in one place. After the girl he killed disappeared, the color he'd made drained away from the crystals, and he thought about the things she said. He sat blinking in that mineralized light for minutes hours days, without the need for food or water, listening to the wind pass through the hollows into yet deeper pathways. He felt like he'd been asleep for years at one point and awake forever in another, and there below he was mineralized and fortified and steeped in a thousand centuries. And as he fossilized in the igneous rock layers, he thought about the sun, the moon, and the stars, and began to wonder if such things ever existed or if he had just imagined them. That was when he began to hear the Great Hum, the sing-low sound of the subterranean world whispering in his ear, for the earth held many secrets, and like a woman held them forever. So it was no surprise that he heard in the Great Hum that his hermitage was to come to an end; it was not his place to stay below since it was still his time to be above. And that was when he understood that he should leave.

Red left the mine and resurfaced. He looked around at terrain and sky, uncertain of what filled the nothingness now that *she* was not there. He did not see the girl he killed again, but he thought of her often. He moved through the hamlets of the land, traveling many winding two-lane roads where the terrain turned from hilly pasture to majestic peaks. And sometimes, when he looked into the stray beams of moonlight that shot through the dense mountain forests in the velveteen dark, he thought of that obsidian-eyed woman he'd buried in the morass of his memories, how she looked as she gardened in the night beams. Amber. Was she still in her water realm dreaming of death? He looked up at the stars as if the answer might be in one of the flickers. "It doesn't matter now," he said to the pines. All that was left was trying to understand how to *be*, now that the one who was always there was gone. He traveled on, feeling more and more as if he needed something to do, something that had a beginning and an end. He stopped to take work in a lumberyard deep in the mountains of the Kingdom of Pennsylvania. He rose each morning to wield chain saw and ax, comforted by the start and finish of each task.

And in accordance with constellations, circumstances, and events, as he was sitting on a mound of scrap wood on his break one day, a tall stranger climbed up and sat down next to him.

"Been looking for you," said the man, his eyes bulging from the sockets of his bony head.

Red looked at the man. He was a sprawling mess to behold and worse to smell, with his hangdog look of leathery skin and ragged clothes. But Red had seen all kinds of people in the kingdoms of the land, and he knew that he, too, had been a sight at times before. "Me?"

"Yeah."

"You sure?"

"Yeah."

"Why?"

"It's what I do."

"Humph . . . Well, you found me. What's happening, man?"

"Everything. Everything been happening."

"What's happening?"

"Everything. In Anacostia."

Red looked at the stranger's intense glare and into the tree line behind him. All the other spaces he'd traveled had melded together in his head and were collectively one land, one place through which he had been moving. And even though there were times when he thought about Amber, he thought of her only in that watery realm, apart from some larger place. "Anacostia?" he responded, as if saying it himself might help him remember its existence.

Find Out was watching the blue smoke circle the mound on which they were sitting. "Yeah," he said. His years of tracking had taught him to come straight to the point. "There's trouble. Amber got a child, a boy. But she had one of them death dreams about him. Come see about it. Amber and the boy. Your boy. And that's why I'm here. To do what I do. To find you." His words poured out like a burst of rain in a thunderstorm and just as suddenly stopped.

Red looked on, feeling dizzy. The noise of the lumberyard fell away, and he tried to swallow but couldn't. Because something the girl he killed had said to him resurfaced in his mind, words he thought nonsensical before but that now came together in the symmetry of that moment: *But you left something*... And he tried to balance the equation of years spent erasing himself with news that he'd left a part of himself in someone else. Amber. Amber and a boy. His boy. He looked at Find Out, speechless.

Now that the tracking was done, the pacifying effects were wearing off and Find Out felt the beginnings of his body crying out for the substance that was killing him. A rash was spreading quickly across his chest and he began to itch. "Everything. Everything been happening."

The tree line seemed to move closer still, and Red felt sick. The reason he left rose in his mind, as fresh as on that day he'd bolted; the question Amber asked that he'd been unwilling to answer. "What's his name?"

Find Out was watching the blue smoke dissipate. "Huh?"

"What's his name?"

"Dash. His name is Dash."

She named him something else, Red thought, relieved. B
now he remembered the rest. The Lottery drifted back, how
always matched the news and the obituaries. And the strange
said that Amber had a death dream about the boy.

"His name is Dash," repeated Find Out.

Now Red looked at the man from Anacostia who was sitting
with him out in the middle of nowhere. How was that possible?
"Who are you? How did you find me?"

Find Out fidgeted with the itching, scratching his chest and drawing blood. He saw the last of the blue smoke fading, and now he was feeling more and more flustered. "It don't matter."

"How?"

"Huh?"

"How did you find me?"

"Who?"

"Me."

The blue smoke was gone and Find Out looked around as if he was only now seeing where he was. "Nephthys. She asked me to."

Red searched his memory. Sonny's Bar. Amber's aunt. "Nephthys? How the hell did she—"

"Look, man, I gotta get out of here." The image of his wife's face in the blazes of the bonfires was beginning to reappear in his mind, and he felt the panic inside rising, for now he had no way to numb himself to the agony of being unable to find her. "I gotta go. Need to get me something for this . . . chest thing. Gotta get me something. Go somewhere."

Red felt a shiver as a new feeling came over him: fear for someone else. "Is he all right?"

Find Out was rocking. "Who?"

"The boy."

"Reckon so. But not for long. You get back there."

The shriek of the workman buzzer filled the lumberyard, startling them both.

"You get back there," said Find Out, agitated. "I gotta go somewhere. Sure as hell ain't here."

Red stared at the stranger, feeling pity, for he reminded him of his own barbiturate hazes. There were some things that no drug could blot out.

Find Out scratched harder, his hands shaking. "Gotta get outta here."

Red looked at the man's shirt, now streaked with blood.

"Need to go somewhere . . ."

Red looked into the pines and back at the stranger. "I know a place."

VANISHING

At the river's edge, Osiris watched the sunlight dance on the currents. More and more, he had a troubling feeling that he was slowly vanishing, and this filled him with an inexplicable fear. For it seemed like it was getting harder to come to the river when he wanted to. To cope, sometimes he tried to remember what existing as an organism of the biosphere felt like, and he indulged in the sensation of cellular energy and electromagnetic waves moving through him. He shook away the carbon atoms that settled on the thick ropes of his anthropomorphic hair and watched them bond and diffuse and settle again. He looked at his half finger. Its smoldering glow at the tip somehow remained. Why?

His invisibility to his daughter remained too, and it saddened him that Amber never once saw him standing in her mother's favorite lily patch when she was by the kitchen window. Or when he followed her around the garden when she was night picking. Nor did Nephthys acknowledge his presence when he moved her bottles around or sang to her in the Plymouth or tried to reach her in the interstellar cold of his solitude.

He was thinking about this when he looked up and saw that Dash was there, and once more he wondered if he had conjured the boy or if it was the other way around. But he was glad to see him.

They skipped rocks in pleasant silence. Every now and then some interesting object or cluster of debris from upstream would appear and they'd stop to watch it float by.

And once more Dash prepared to ask, as children often do, the same question he'd asked before. Because what he saw was slowly vanishing from view in his mind, his belief fading that there had ever been a utility closet where there was now a white wall. "If you're not sure you saw something, does it mean that you just imagined it?"

Osiris thought about what had happened to him at the bottom of the river, the Gray and the deep, and it all seemed dimmer in his mind than before. And he thought about what he did to the Rileys, the memory now more distant, and he wondered if they were somewhere else now forgetting what they did to him. *Could be.*

"And it doesn't matter if it was good or bad?"

I 'member good matterin' more, said Osiris. But when he thought of how marvelous it felt to do the things he did in the Twelve Hours of Night, the rapture of killing Riley and his friends, the glee of terrorizing Amy, and the thrill he'd felt when he set the policeman on fire, he couldn't be sure. Because even after all of that, he'd wanted to burn more. Until he came across the wolf. Was that bad? And then he thought of that dawn with Gola on the dock. How they broke the sound barrier and bent space and time, and in their ecstasy made $\pi - \pi = 1$, and each the other became. Until she was gone. Was that good? He couldn't be sure. The things that happened in his living death seemed more and more like dreams, things he'd just imagined.

He looked at Dash, wondering if he was imagining him too. *Could be,* he said. *Might could be.*

SIGNS OMENS BONES

Nephthys listened to the frightened calls of creatures of passage, their fearsome tales of happenings in the darkest of dark, unaware that she held the light of the path in her hand . . .

Nephthys sat on the front stoop outside her building, taking in the early-Sunday-morning breeze. Hopscotch chalk faded from showers in the night, and the morning sunlight shimmered on little puddles. She didn't come out to sit very often, but she was tired, too exhausted to ferry souls from one quadrant to the next. Children played nearby, and a toddler perched on her knee licking a lollipop. The irony of such times was never lost on Nephthys: a barren-wombed woman and failed aunt surrounded by children. She suckled her unease by taking sips from her flask. The little ones rejoiced in the candy that Nephthys was giving them, and each took turns going up to her so she would reach into her crumpled paper bag and hand out more.

The quiet of the early-morning hours cloaked the chaos that had laced the place the night before. While the children ran the hallways and played on the stoop, adults in the building were still sleeping off the revelry that helped them try to escape the trials and traps of the capital over the week. Nephthys was gazing into the black windows of the abandoned houses across the street, when an expensive-looking black car with tinted windows pulled up in front of the stoop and stopped. The children scattered.

It was the colonel's wife. She had been driving aimlessly around Anacostia since leaving St. Elizabeths earlier that morning, too numb to heed fears stoked about the southeast quadrant on the six o'clock evening news. She spotted the parked sky-blue Plymouth in her wanderings, unmistakable among the other cars on the street. The wonder of how she'd found her way to Nephthys sitting on the front stoop was not lost on her, and she took it as just one more mind-bending thing about that day. She rolled down the window and gazed at Nephthys with glassy, protruding eyes that gave her the look of a lifelike porcelain doll. "He's dead," she announced, as if a crowd had gathered in front of the apartment building to hear what she had to say. "He's dead and he killed himself and today is his thirtieth birthday." Then, after a pause empty of all hope and understanding, she said, "He left me a note. Addressed to me in an envelope on stationery." She stared down at the faded hopscotch outline on the cracked sidewalk. "He's dead," she said again, louder.

Nephthys looked at the colonel's wife for a long time without saying anything, for when she thought about the things she heard went on in St. Elizabeths, she was not sure if this was good or bad. "It was his choice."

"Was it?" asked the colonel's wife. And here she remembered her son's ravings about the long conversations he'd had with Death and the five ways that creatures of passage die: moving through spaces; staying in one place; resigning life to another; surrendering one's life; and entering the Void. And she recalled the years of wishing her son could end this life and start another, and she was filled with that feeling that all who find themselves in Anacostia have when dreams come true even when they don't want them to.

The truth was that the son of Mr. and Mrs. Colonel Piper Abramson had long entered the Void since the time he strangled his girlfriend, and he had willingly resided in it, a labyrinth within the labyrinths of St. Elizabeths. It was filled with those amorous of the bloodletting of the world, the people of the alley and the corner and the pole, proselytes of the bottle and the needle and the pill, the legions of the missing, and all souls lost. And each beheld the other in that everlasting orbit of the Void, rapturous in the fullness of horror, comforted only by the increase in their numbers. So it was no surprise that even after the colonel's son ended his living life and continued roaming the wasted reaches, he recalled how it was that his hatred for his girlfriend and her cheerful family grew the more time he spent with them. For their smiles and chatter with each other made the subzero cold of his own parents in their loveless marriage more chilling and the wind blowing through the big empty rooms of his life all the stronger. He was sickened by the vacuous banter of his mother and her guests in the parlor and the sight of his father at his desk, deliberating ceaselessly over the classified happenings in which he played a part. And one day he had the clear thought that happiness—this thing he witnessed in the lives of others—could be sampled like a glass of wine, which is what he poured his girlfriend's blood into before he drank it.

The colonel's wife took two pills from her purse and swallowed them down hard. "And do you know what the note said, Neph?" She waited as if she might get a response.

Nephthys was silent.

"Nothing. It was just blank. It read *Dear Mother* on the sealed envelope, and when I opened it and took out the paper it was completely blank." She looked into the black windows of the empty houses on the other side of the street and beyond them across the bridge to the Ebbitt Hotel and out to the southern rings of the Acropolis, where her husband was sitting at his desk refusing to come view the body. "Well, you won't see me anymore," she said. Her face had morphed again and she had the frightened look of a bush animal. She took more pills from her purse and swallowed them. "And I want you to know something, Neph. You and that death-dealing niece of yours. The Lottery is blank too. There's nothing there and there's nothing we can do. Because we'll never know." And she rolled up the window and drove away, steering erratically down the street until out of sight.

ADRIFT

Nephthys sailed the abiding sea with the souls in her charge, her eyes on the surface for a chance sign of the remnants of her brother, for there was yet no answer to the Great Mystery . . .

Nephthys felt uneasy after the colonel's wife left, and she thought about what her words could mean or not mean. *The Lottery is blank too . . .* Maybe there was nothing to see because nothing could be done. About the past or the future. Like her transaction with Find Out. She'd tried to do something but maybe nothing was all there was. In the end, what would it matter if Red came back? What would that change for Amber or Dash? She didn't know.

The children had long disappeared into the hallways of the apartment building, and she raised herself from the stoop and went back to her unit. At the door she turned the key in the lock and shoved hard. Once inside, she went to her sunken chair to get the bottle she'd left in the cradle of the cushion earlier that morning. But it was not there. It was gone. Moved, like the others. It was happening more and more, it seemed. Unnerved, she went to the kitchen to retrieve the flask that she'd filled the night before, and was relieved to find it next to the rattrap in the utensil drawer, just as she'd left it. She put it in her pocket and looked at her chair. She didn't want to sit in it, not right now, and she grabbed her car keys and headed out.

It was already a late start for ferrying souls, the fog long gone, but Nephthys headed to the parked Plymouth anyway, for that was better than listening to the echoes of her thoughts in her apartment. Better than thinking about the missing bottles. *Gonna buy more later*, she thought as she neared the Plymouth. Although there was no need to ever lock the car since no one dared enter it alone, she was surprised to find a young woman sitting in the backseat when she arrived. Her hair was in neat cornrows and she wore a Mickey Mouse T-shirt with a pink pull-on sweater, and even in the heat she sat with all the windows rolled up, her arms folded tightly as if in midwinter. Nephthys almost didn't recognize her without the Farrah Fawcett wig.

Rosetta waited in the Plymouth, listening to the white girl in the trunk rap softly on a rubber floor mat. Earlier that morning she'd gone to the clinic of her own volition, sensing that something was different. Her menstrual cycle had stopped. She had fevers and chills that came and went. She didn't feel debilitated but didn't feel well either. So she went to the clinic to make sure she wasn't pregnant. The overworked clinician seemed to examine her with the mild indifference and cynicism that underfunded social services engendered. Tests were run quickly. She was informed that she wasn't pregnant and sent on her way with a bottle of antibiotics and a pamphlet warning against reproduction. Many years later, there would be antigen and antibody and protein tests designed to detect what was already swimming in Rosetta's blood, and the streets and villages of the world would run red, and there would be new pathogens and superbugs to ravage the earth and a leprosy to end all others would be spawned. But Rosetta had no way of knowing this as she stared at Nephthys through the windshield. What she knew was that the sickness she felt had started on that distant day in the snow when she was a young girl, when she went out to look for winterberries and found something else.

Now as she sat in the Plymouth, she could think of only one place to go. It was not home, a word that denoted a place that held no meaning to her beyond its label. Like mother or brother or sister. Like hunter or prey. Lulu would find out one way or the other, she supposed, for there was nothing she could show her that Anacostia would not compel her to learn. So Rosetta wanted to go somewhere that led to someplace else, where she no longer had to be who she was.

Nephthys got in the car and started the engine and rolled down the driver's-side window. She waited for the usual minutes to expire, and after a while said, "Where to, chile?"

Rosetta shivered and pulled at her sweater as if the gesture would help her answer the question. "Saints of Eternity."

Nephthys took a sip from her flask and reached into the glove compartment. She took out a little bag of penny candy and handed it to Rosetta. But the young woman didn't take it.

They drove on. Anacostia was alive with the happenings of the day. An ambulance roared behind them and Nephthys pulled over and waited for it to pass.

"It was blood in the snow," said Rosetta.

"Wuh you speakin', chile?"

"Not winterberries.

"Berries?"

"Not cherries."

Nephthys looked at Rosetta through the rearview mirror, and once more she wanted to take her someplace safe, but she did not know where that safe place could be. The ambulance screamed by and she drove on.

"That's what it was all along. Little drops of my blood in the snow."

"Baby cootuh, wuh you sayin'?"

"Little . . ."

"Rosetta?"

"Drops . . ."

They arrived at the Saints of Eternity parking lot.

Nephthys stopped the car and turned to Rosetta. "Maybe sit fuh a while, chile. Somethin' ain't right with you."

Rosetta rested her head on the window and looked at the church, wondering if it was the gateway to that special someplace else that she'd heard others proclaim it to be. And although the streets had taught her all about the rise and fall of women, still she wondered about one thing, now that she was sure something more was wrong, no matter what they said at the clinic.

"Ms. Nephthys?"

"Yes, chile?"

"Tell me about time."

"Wuh?"

"Time."

"Meanin'?"

"Does it repeat?"

Nephthys sighed. "Wuh folks do repeats. Seem like time ain't got to pay us no mind."

"Then we only have to do this once?"

"Wuh, chile?"

"Do this time."

"S'pose so. It's like we come this-a-way and pass on through to someplace else. But don't nobody really know, baby cootuh."

Rosetta pulled at her sweater. "Well, I hope so."

"Wuh?"

"Hope it's someplace else. I can't do this again." She was silent then, tired as she was from trying to make sense of what felt like a great and terrible puzzle. After a while she said, "But thank you for the rides." And she got out of the car and headed across the grass and disappeared.

Nephthys watched Rosetta walk into the church, a lost soul she feared was now lost forever. The sanctum bell chimed, and she sat listening to the engine, staring into the remnants of a timberland in the distance. And in accordance with the dark irony with which creatures of passage live, she looked into the foliage of the imaginable forest, never realizing the form it was about to take, consumed as she was with shaping the small things that she thought she could shape. "Gotta do," she said, rubbing her half finger. "Gotta move." And she put her foot on the gas pedal and drove away.

ENCOUNTERS

It was midmorning. School was out but Dash thought of the summer months like a threatening storm. Without the schedule of coming and going, he would be bottled in the house with his mother. There would be no summer camp or amusement park trips, no Bible school or faraway relative to visit during those water-treading months. Only his mother's impossible eyes telling him that something was wrong. That look was like a presence that moved in and took over the house. And even though he'd grown up with her messages of death, his child logic told him that dying was something that happened only to others. Were her dreams the same as his imagination? Maybe she looked at him that way because of what she only imagined, not what was real. Like the man and Annie Porter. Like the utility closet and the white wall. *So it doesn't really matter if something just imagined is good or bad,* Dash thought. That made sense. And the River Man agreed in a way, hadn't he? And here he tried to ignore what seemed like a long time since the last time he'd seen the River Man, for lately he'd gone to the river to find that he was not there.

But he had other concerns now: escape. He slipped out of his room and went to his mother's door and listened. Nothing. Just the familiar heavy sound of her exhausted slumber. He crept down the steps and out to the porch, into the mud, and went up the hill. When he reached the top, he looked down through the mist at the house once more. He was out, breathing freely, and nothing could change that now. He turned around. The June day spread before him in that cheerful hopeful sunny-yellow that was so different from the blue depths of his mother's realm. He spotted a dollar stuck in the slab where the sidewalk began and picked it up, marveling at his luck. Now he could get something at the corner store. He began walking, filled with the thrill of possibilities. Then he remembered the Juneteenth celebration he'd heard the other children talking about at the end of the school year. The big cookout on the church grounds at Saints of Eternity. Games and fun. Free food and lots of soda. He wanted to go for the simple fact that his mother had never allowed him to go before. "Nothing but silence and stares," she said.

But she's asleep now, Dash thought, making his way down the street. As he walked, he noticed a woman standing over a man seated in a lawn chair, braiding cornrows into his hair. Dash saw her whisper something in the man's ear, and as he neared, they both looked away.

He moved on and came to the end of the street. An old man reading a newspaper on his porch looked up and waved. "Every day is a good day, boy," he said.

Dash nodded and walked by.

"Like I used to tell him when he come around way back, tryin' to see 'bout that gal down the bottom of the hill."

Dash stopped. "Huh?"

The old man laughed. "Spit you out, didn't he? Lookin' just like him, big as you gettin'."

Dash stared at the old man, baffled.

"Remember now. Every day is a good day, boy." The old man shuffled his paper and went back to reading.

Dash walked on, puzzled, and he placed this on the list of strange things the elderly said that he did not understand. He came to a side street and neared the school, which stood lifeless and empty, all the windows and doors shuttered like those of an abandoned prison. He felt a shiver and sped his stride, trying once more to forget the bits and pieces, the riddle of live or Memorex. And how there could be a wall where he thought there was once a door. He reached another side street and crossed a small square of parched and trash-littered grass where a homeless man slept on a bench, roasting in the sun. Squirrels skittered about and pigeons fought over old popcorn and scraps of Slim Jim.

He walked on and approached the corner store. It was a narrow hovel, the door propped open with a stack of old phone books. He entered, stepping onto checkered floor tiles dirty with shoe smudges. Shelves were stacked high to the ceiling with products that looked like they might tumble at any moment. The Asian shopkeeper stood behind a wall of bulletproof glass, and in the center was a small revolving mechanism that allowed the exchange of things like that of a prison-cell tray slot.

And standing at the counter was Nephthys, purchasing a giant pickle.

Dash froze in the doorway, unsure if he should leave before she saw him.

"You wan someting?" asked the shopkeeper, glaring through the bulletproof glass.

Nephthys had just returned from Saints of Eternity where she'd left Rosetta, and the mystery of what went on in the lives of children still lingered with her. She looked at Dash standing in the doorway, thinking about Nurse Higgins's letter of warning and her wild undertaking with Find Out in the back of Sonny's Bar. Would it work? She didn't know. "How you been?"

"You wan someting, you pay," said the shopkeeper.

Nephthys looked at the man without blinking, and he turned away and picked up a broom and started sweeping. She turned back to Dash. "How you been, chile?"

"Fine."

"Look like you made it out of school all right."

"Yes, ma'am."

"And wuh you doin' now?"

"Getting a snack."

"Yeah? Wuh you gonna get?"

"Something good. I got a dollar."

"Whole dollar, huh? Keep that dollar and pick a treat." Nephthys motioned for him to come closer.

Dash wondered what the encounter could mean or not mean, now that he was talking to his great-aunt for the second time in his life. He stepped forward and took out a soda from the cooler and a bag of pumpkin seeds and sat them on the counter. "Thank you."

"Welcome, chile." Nephthys put some money and the two items in the tray.

The shopkeeper twirled the mechanism around. He rang up the items on his cash register and made change and spun it all back to Nephthys without a word.

Nephthys looked out the door to the street with the futility she'd looked out to the hallway of her apartment the first time the boy visited. "Where your mama?"

"Sleep."

"Oh." *Was that true?*

A woman rushed in dragging two small children, each in one of her hands.

"You wan someting?" asked the shopkeeper.

The woman ignored him, addressing Nephthys. "Excuse me, I saw your car and I saw you come in here and I really need a ride downtown right away. Please."

One of the children said, "Mommy, Grandma told us not to go with the Car Lady. Not ever."

"Quiet!" the woman hissed.

Nephthys looked at the woman and nodded. "Where to, chile?"

"The courthouse. I gotta be there on time." One of the children started crying and she handed the girl an apple from her purse without taking her eyes off of Nephthys. "I can't be late."

"But Grandma said—"

"Girl, I will whip your tail if you don't close your mouth while grown folks is talking."

Dash saw his opportunity to depart. Time away from the house was precious and he wanted to get to the cookout. His mother would sleep for a while but not forever. And he wanted to get away before Nephthys could ask him any more questions. "Well, thank you. I gotta go now," he said, snatching the soda from the tray and moving quickly toward the door.

"Wait," said Nephthys. "Forgot your seeds." She grabbed the bag and tossed it to him.

But Dash missed catching the bag and let it fall, distracted as he was by a familiar gesture. Because in the instant of that motion of tossing the bag, Nephthys reminded him of someone tossing a rock. Slowly, he reached down to the filthy floor and picked it up. "Thank you."

"You no get another one," said the shopkeeper. "That one already pay."

Dash stared at his great-aunt's half finger and into her face and back again.

"Look like you seen a ghost, chile. Wuh be the trouble? Don't want it no more?"

"It's just that you look like someone."

"You already pay. You keep."

"Wuh? Lookin' like somebody, huh? Well, who?"

"Okay, boy, you go. Already pay."

"Someone at the river." He stared at her with the complicity of Nurse Higgins's letter.

"I gotta be at the courthouse. I can't be late."

Nephthys was struck by the look. But before she could say anything more, Dash ran out of the store and was gone.

Nephthys sped to the courthouse with the woman and her two children in the backseat of the car. More than the look on Dash's face, what he said stayed with her the rest of the day. *Someone at the river . . .* At each stoplight and every turn, she was troubled by that strange feeling, the one she had when she couldn't find her bottles and when she saw the broken pieces of the living room mirror on the floor. The constant movement seemed to be helping less too, and her half finger throbbed more. And again, that faraway riff played in her mind. *No beginnin' and no end . . .*

PASSAGE V

ENTERING THE VOID

POUNCE

Dash was enjoying the thrill of having escaped his mother's waterlogged realm, for there at the Juneteenth picnic he was just a ten-year-old kid and not the son of a witch. He played with the other children, all of them too busy with fun to worry about the dark magic of Amber Kinwell. He raced around the picnic tables with them, ignoring admonishments to steer clear of the food. And in the thrill of that golden Sunday, so many leagues away from his mother's realm, he was beginning to believe that anything was possible.

Even a snow cone. He looked around for the source of the icy treats dripping from the hands of other children, traced it to a table filled with bottles of colored syrup, and ran over to it. He was so excited and having such a wonderful time that he didn't even notice that the man serving the snow cones was Mercy Ratchet, and without glancing up from the rainbow of syrup bottles he was examining he asked, "Do you have any lemon?"

Mercy looked at Dash standing before him at the snow cone table and smiled. *Sometimes opportunity is like this,* he thought. A moment in time when everything comes together in some undeniable symmetry. Like that fish-fry Sunday in the church basement when the garden unfolded before him. Like Gary and his friends, the winterberries in the snow, and Annie Porter alone in the hallway when she came out of the bathroom. Now Dash was asking for lemon, opening a secret kind of door all by himself. And what Mercy could do to get Dash to step over the threshold and come inside slowly crept into his mind. *I've let it alone for a while, haven't I?* he thought. *I've been good and kept good intentions.* But a chance worth having was a chance worth taking.

Mercy blinked and made grand gestures with his hands like a circus ringmaster about to make some great announcement. "Do I have any lemon? Why, of course I got lemon! A snow cone wouldn't be a snow cone without it." He looked at the boy, smiling, and he turned around and made the snow cone and topped it with the crushed dose he had with him always. And he did so without anyone noticing as he had plenty of times before.

"Here you go," Mercy said. He gave the lemon snow cone to the boy and watched him walk away.

Dash left quickly, for he did not want to give himself too much time to think about Mercy Ratchet's smiling face when he looked up from the syrup bottles. He headed toward the other children and watched them play kickball as he enjoyed his treat, until a kind of lightness overtook him that he'd never felt before. He finished the rest of the snow cone so it would not melt in the heat. Now he tried to concentrate on the new dodgeball game that had just started but was unable to do so. He listened to the children squeal with delight from competing teams. They sounded so close, as if they were inside his head, but then they sounded far away. He felt restless, like he was riding on a roller coaster or a speeding train. And then he felt as if he were riding on the deck of a slow-moving ship. Or on the back of a tortoise.

Fifteen minutes. Mercy knew from all the times before that it took about fifteen minutes for the effects to start. For the game to begin. And since he was the one who was always moving about with tasks on behalf of the church and all things related to the important business of tending to the flock, no one noticed him packing up the syrup bottles and closing down the snow cone table. He looked around at the festivities. Someone had brought a coconut cake and now many of the children were lined up to get a slice. The men were talking excitedly around the barbecue pit.

Mercy scanned the grounds and spotted Dash sitting at an empty picnic table and headed over to him. He walked up to the boy casually and sat down in that way that countryfolk prepare to whittle the day away with pleasant talk. "Lemon snow cones are the best, ain't they?"

Dash nodded without looking up. Lemon. Lemons were yellow. Was that the flavor he had? It seemed so long ago now, all that yellow. Now he looked up and saw the man who was talking to him. It was like he had four faces that fused and separated and fused again in his mind; the smiling man in that other dimension and the smiling man in the school hallways and the smiling man at the snow cone stand and the smiling man before him now.

Mercy looked around and back at the boy. "You know, it just so happens that I've got some of the best lemon syrup you'll ever taste in your life. Homemade. From scratch. Not that fake stuff in the bottles over there. I was going to save it for the grown folks when the barbecue was ready. But . . ." and here he looked around as if he had been keeping the biggest secret known to one man, "well, it's just over there in the generator shack for the church." He pointed at the woods where the imaginable forest lay in wait to become what he wanted it to be. "There's a great big refrigerator in there, you know. That's where we keep it. Made from the best lemons on earth, my friend. Yellow like the sun. More sugar than you can shake a stick at. Something special." Mercy looked around again. "I'll let you have as much as you want, if you help me carry it back."

Dash stared into Mercy Ratchet's face and into that wild wide smile that now seemed to change his face yet again and made him look different from the images of the other four men in his head. He felt buoyant. Oceanic. And the sound of the man's voice bounced around his head like sonar.

"Could use your help too. It's heavy," Mercy was saying. "Big boy like you should be able to lend a hand."

The confusion Dash felt was fading, replaced by a soft blankness.

"And it's just as well," said Mercy, taking the boy's hand. "I'm going to need some more ice anyway. You can help me bring that back too. How about that?"

Dash nodded in the echo chamber of his mind. There were rings of color now, and he watched them appear and disappear.

Mercy looked around and into the woods. He hadn't been in there for a long time. Not since Hazel Eyes. "It's out in the storage shed the church keeps," he said. "The kitchen refrigerator was too packed for what I made. Won't take long to go out there and get that special lemon I was telling you about. We'll be back before you know it." He peered carefully at the boy. "Ready?"

"Okay," said Dash. And curiously, the more he thought about the idea of getting the special lemon syrup, the more he wanted it.

They walked together, past the children running around the picnic tables. They walked past the old men playing checkers and chess, and the gossipers sucking their teeth about hussies and thugs over bowls of potato salad and mounds of wax paper–covered chicken. And they walked past the 1927 church cornerstone and crossed the field into the woods.

The wolf sat under the last remaining weeping willow tree, watching Mercy and Dash head to the edge of the church grounds and disappear into the trees. He was always struck by the wandering of strays, how their naivete in hiding actually carried them farther out into the open. Like when he saw Rosetta out in the snow picking winterberries that cold season, and the day he saw Annie Porter walking to school without telling her mother about the man who seemed so nice to her, and all the other occasions he'd witnessed strays. He'd seen Dash too, sneaking to the river.

The wolf watched the people at the picnic, busy with distraction. And he thought of the things that men accepted or denied, and the things that happened to one generation in the absence of another. But most of all, he'd always wondered, down through the ages and in different realms, how these creatures of passage could be so careless. How could they see and not see something so precious as their young?

STRAY

Many hours after Dash snuck out of the house, Amber awoke from her insomnia-plagued slumber to discover that he was gone. He was not in his room. He was nowhere to be found in the house. She looked through the cornstalks in the garden and hunted the valley. *Where is he?* The dream crept into her mind once more. Death, that companion with her always, was now fingering her boy. Such cruel eyes that let her see. And the dream would come true, she feared, as true as the others before it, and she went racing up the hill.

The rest unfolded like a horror film in which someone else was the star. And with each step, each hyperventilated breath, flashes of the dream blinded all thoughts in her head. A dark forest. A dead cardinal. Dash running. Dash motionless in a creek. And that faceless face in the darkness. She checked the closest corner store and three others that were out of the way. She saw that the schoolyard was chained off and vacant. In growing desperation, she began approaching people randomly at bus stops and on the stoops of their porches and standing on the corner. Each balked with the shock of her speaking to them directly and rushed off without a response.

She doubled back to the street that led to her realm and saw an old man now sitting on his porch, reading a newspaper. *How did she miss him? He wasn't there before.* She went to the foot of his porch. "Have you seen my boy?"

The old man looked up from his paper. "Every day is a good day."

"I'm searching for my son."

"Lookin' just like him now, big as he gettin'."

Amber's mind was racing as she scanned up and down the street. "What?"

"Every day is a good day."

"Have you seen my boy?"

The old man nodded and shuffled his newspaper. "Yup."

"When?"

"A while back."

"And? Please tell me anything you know. It's urgent."

"Today Juneteenth, ain't it? Heard they havin' somethin' for the children over at Saints of Eternity. Probably went there."

"The church?"

"Yup. Lookin' just like him now, ain't he?"

"What?"

"Tell me it ain't so," said the old man. He laughed and fell into a violent cough and went back to reading his newspaper.

Amber entered the celebration at the church grounds like a storm cloud.

The sight of the Death Dreamer, a legend up close and in the flesh, stunned the people. Amber Kinwell. The Death Witch. African Doom. Talisman. Devil's Maid. Hex Maker. Faith Breaker. They feared her even more, now that she was before them.

Amber looked wildly from one person to the next, all of them averting their eyes. She looked around. "Dash!" As the minutes passed her hysteria grew, and she talked in random phrases about a dream, a man in the woods, and a creek. "Dash!" she called. Then she broke down and started to cry.

The sound of Amber's primal sobs cutting through the silence snapped the people out of their trance. Although it was known that children in Anacostia appear and disappear from one day to the next, each looked at the other with the same question in their eyes that they had so many times before: *What can we do?*

After a long silence, a woman said, "I thought I saw your boy playing with the other kids." She searched through the spectators for her daughter. "Lulu? Where you at? Girl, come up here if you know something."

Lulu was standing in the back with her stomach in her throat. Before all the excitement, she was planning to start up where Roy Johnson left off when she saw Dash getting a snow cone, but she was overcome with an urgent need to use the bathroom. She squeezed through the people and pushed into the clearing. "Yes, Mama," she said, sweating. She looked sheepishly at the bottom of Amber's dress, digging the toe of her shoe into the ground.

The woman glared at Lulu as she'd glared at Rosetta. "Well?"

"I . . . he . . . I saw him getting a snow cone." Lulu pointed to the stand, now vacant.

"There's a man," Amber said, her voice trembling.

Nurse Higgins was staring at the empty stand, feeling queasy. Because she remembered seeing the children lined up to get snow cones from Mercy Ratchet just a while ago, but now there was nothing there. "Was Dash with anyone?"

Lulu shrugged and looked around at the other children gathered nearby as if they might rescue her.

"We was playing kickball," said one of them.

"But maybe he left," said another.

"Could be in the bathroom," said one of the teenagers.

"I just came from there," said a man. "I ain't see nobody."

A potbellied man in charge of the barbecue pit broke through the tension with a business-is-business voice. "Look, the lady says her boy is missing." He gestured at Lulu's mother. "How about you round up all the children? Name and count all of them and have them sit at the picnic tables. You teenagers get over there and help her and then we'll take a look. Sure he's around here someplace." He glanced at the empty snow cone stand. "Where did Mercy go? Maybe he's seen him."

* * *

The tower bell chimed the new hour and the imaginable forest stood beyond the church grounds, silent and waiting. Amber stood shaking as the people talked, lost as she was in her terror, the dream flashing forward and backward through her mind. Dash lying in a creek. Dash running through the trees. A dead cardinal falling to the ground. A faceless man. A forest . . . She looked at the crowd and through them and out to the tree-topped expanse. "A forest," she murmured, and tore off running toward it.

IMAGINABLE FOREST

The imaginable forest began on the fringes of the southeast quadrant where Saints of Eternity stood, just over the line that marked Prince George's fiefdom in the Kingdom of Maryland. Young Nacotchtank men had shot arrows through its trees and big herds of buffalo had trodden its grounds just six hundred years before. And down through the centuries, the timberland absorbed the noble and unholy designs of all men who entered, whether salivary lust, deluge of rage, or inspired teardrop, so that the forest shape-shifted according to will, fear, or desire.

Mercy jaunted farther into the woods with Dash, the terrain taking on a likeness to the boondocks of his thoughts with every step. Before sunrise that morning, he'd pulled out all the long tables and chairs and set up the huge Juneteenth barbecue pit where men now nursed meat over the fire. He'd set up the snow cone table too, as he did every year. And when the festivities began, he stood at the ice stand and watched the children as he'd watched them from the perimeter of the schoolyard and the ends of corridors. He'd been watching Lulu too, Rosetta's little sister, imagining that there would be flecks of vanilla bean in her eyes in a certain kind of light. But all of that was eclipsed by the opportunity at hand now, and he placed her on the list he kept at the edge of his mind.

As they walked, he chattered on about the lemon syrup and the lemonade he would make, about how good the barbecue was going to be when they got back. He was giddy with the lies he

was telling and each footfall thrilled him mor
was no storage shed, no shack with a big refrige
ice. There was no special lemon syrup or lemo
except in the playhouse of his mind. And there we
go back to the church grounds. He was taking the b
way traipse through his intentions, and he alone wo
on the other side with the souvenirs of his appetite.
watered with this secret knowledge and he spat on th
and the soil tasted the flavors of his plot.

They walked on.

The forest conformed to the blueprints of Mercy's
one elaborate route stretching into another, the second
ing slowly like minutes and the minutes like hours. Every
and then he looked at Dash like a venomous creature survei
bitten prey. Because he knew that what was in the snow c
had taken full hold now. Amused, he recalled a little rhyme h
learned in his childhood. Even after so many years, he remen
bered it easily, for it took on new meaning after the happenin
with the Beast.

"Want to hear a rhyme, Dash?"

Dash nodded, then shook his head.

Mercy smiled at the boy's confusion. "Feeling all right?" Without waiting for him to respond, he began a singsong chant:

Wee Willie Winkie runs through the town,
Upstairs and downstairs in his nightgown,
Tapping at the window and crying through the lock,
Are all the children in their beds?
It's past eight o'clock.

Mercy stepped over the long-decayed carcass of a fox and smiled. "Do you know that rhyme?"

Dash was silent, busy navigating large dips and trying not to fall, for it seemed like the ground was moving. The trees around

m looked like they were growing taller too, the foliage thicken-g with each step, the rocks bigger. The canopy obscured most f the sky, and sunbeams shot down in thin yellow tubes of light. He was feeling dizzy and sweating more and more. Time itself seemed to be disappearing, and he had the vague feeling that he was entering something more than the interior of the forest. His memory of the Juneteenth celebration gave way to the loudness of the woodland, all the louder for the echoing in his head, so that he heard the strident crunch of dried twigs under his feet and the tweets of invisible birds.

Mercy sighed. "Well, you wouldn't know that rhyme. It's very old. Special from another time." He watched Dash closely. It seemed like the boy was trying to concentrate. *It won't matter*, he thought, smiling. Because there would be no colors in the boy's eyes to discover and preserve. Only that intolerable trinity (one part innocent, one part believing, one part disbelieving) to destroy. "Hang in there, Dash. We're almost there." And just as he spoke, a small clearing suddenly appeared and they stepped into the center of it and stopped.

Dash was thankful to stand still. The air seemed thinner and he began to pant, trying to catch his breath.

Mercy spat on the ground and the forest ingested his odium, forming a labyrinth of dead ends and false entryways. He looked at Dash, his smile disappearing, for now was as good a time as any to launch a different part of the game. He gazed into the wilderness and breathed deep of its aroma, feeling bigger, stronger. *This is all for me*, he thought. A new garden. And that was why what happened next was all that mattered. "I know you saw it."

From high above, a tree branch cracked and a dead cardinal fell to the ground in a flash of red.

Dash watched the bird fall, his stomach dropping with it. And that was when he understood at last that the other dimension really did exist. That there was a girl who was there and then gone named Annie Porter, and this must have been the face

she saw too. That he in fact did enter a place behind that wall. "There *was* a door," he murmured. Sweat pushed through the pores of his body and dripped onto the forest floor, and the ancient grounds drank of his terror.

Mercy smirked, proud of his composure in the preceding weeks when he was following Dash. He was patient. Careful, even. He could have done something at the river. But when he had that strange feeling in the reeds, he waited. And here was his reward. "Well, of course there was a door," he said, peering at the boy. "But it's gone now. Like you."

Dash looked into the trees behind Mercy, which in that moment seemed to part a pathway, and he ran off into it.

Mercy watched Dash scurry away. He was excited by the onset of the game, and he wondered what this part of it would bring. There was no need to rush behind the boy, since now he was his clay. He stood singing the nursery rhyme, entertained. *That's a good head start,* he thought, and he gave chase.

Dash could hear Mercy singing behind him as he ran. But his legs felt heavier, and the harder he tried to move them, the more they seemed to resist. And as he darted, the forest grew bigger still. He dived belly-first under a fallen tree and jumped up running again. *Faster!* he shouted at his legs. But it was like he was wading waist-deep in some unseen liquid.

"Upstairs and downstairs in his nightgown . . ."

He tripped over a tree root, and in the seconds that it took to get back on his feet, it seemed that he could even hear Mercy's breathing and heartbeat. He thought he heard something else nearby, like running water, and in one moment it sounded like it was right beside him and far away in the next. It was hard to think. He lurched forward and slipped on a nest of tangled roots, hitting the ground hard. While he was trying to command his body to move again, he felt Mercy grab at his ankle.

"Tapping at the window and crying through the lock . . ."

Dash slipped from his grasp and scooted under a fallen trunk. *Up!* he shouted inside. He got to his feet and started running.

Mercy was laughing. *"Are all the children in their beds? . . ."*

Dash tripped again and fell into a leaf mound that had been piled on over the seasons like mortared stones. Now it seemed his body was becoming one with a quagmire of tar beneath him, and he was numb with fear. He closed his eyes and opened them again and Mercy was standing over him. His teeth seemed whiter and sharper in the wooded shade. And in his fright, Dash's mind drifted back to the safe waters of home, the sound of his mother's voice, the depths of her eyes.

Mercy pinned Dash down tightly with the bottom of his heavy boot and snatched a bandanna from his pocket and swiftly gagged him. *"It's past eight o'clock,"* he sang, electrified. The escapade was underway. Only now he wanted the game to have a more spectacular finale. More than the ending with Hazel Eyes and her running mouth, and the look of the pink barrettes in her hair when he held her underwater. Maybe not drowning this time . . .

Dash squirmed under the man's great looming shadow, gripped in a haze of terror. Had he entered another dimension and ceased to exist in the previous one? Or maybe what was happening to him now was just a recording of things that had already transpired. And in his hysteria, he saw himself sitting on the porch, staring into that hovering blue. He felt a sharp pain in his chest and started to cry, fearing his mind was playing yet crueler tricks on him. Because somewhere in the jumble of his ordeal, he thought he heard the howl of a wolf.

"I know you saw it," Mercy said calmly, pressing down harder, as if scolding Dash for running across the street without looking both ways or refusing to eat his vegetables. "And that's why you've been chosen. You know that, don't you?" He thought of the things he could do now and shook with anticipation. Something inside was getting worse. Or better.

Mercy rammed his boot harder into Dash's chest and listened to him whimper, thrilled once more by the sensation that acts of cruelty wrought. He planned to toy with him for a long time first, then let him go and hunt him down again, until the sporting came to an ending according to his wish. Exuberant, he glanced from one wild expanse to the other and back at the boy and laughed a laugh of glee into the Void. "Don't you worry!" he thundered. "I am not a beast!"

METAMORPHOSIS

Amber reached the edge of the forest. It was a fortification of growth that looked much larger than it seemed from the church grounds, now that she was standing before it. The dream flashed in her mind once more, and she was overcome with a sinking feeling. "Dash!" she called into the tangled wood. But it was like her voice was muffled by the barrier. She turned to look at the church tower, which now seemed more remote than it had been just moments before, and back again. *This is the forest*, she thought. A squirrel ran by her feet and crossed into the nebulous undergrowth and disappeared. She stepped forward and plunged in. Sunshine quickly disintegrated into gloom, and she looked from one unknown point to another, disoriented. "Dash!" Now her voice boomed through the darkened bois, and she heard creatures skitter at the sound. *Where could he be?* she wondered, choking back tears. And at this thought, a narrow pathway appeared out of the dimness.

She followed the path. The passage of time seemed different as she trekked through the shaded greenery. The seconds felt like minutes, the minutes like hours. The wildwood pulled at her hair as she struggled through the foliage. She could no longer tell if she was still walking the pathway, for the ground thickened with each step and fret. And every time she looked down to watch her footing and looked up again, the trees seemed to have multiplied. She began to cry. The thicket supped on her bitter tears, and the timberland grew denser as she went deeper into it. She trudged on through the semidark weald, tripping over rocks embedded in the ground and stepping into hidden burrows and unseen trenches. She was hot and tired now, wishing there was water nearby, and just at that thought she came to a pond, shallow and placid.

She went over to it and dropped to her knees, splashing her face. Her sweat swirled with the water and into the earthen bed beneath it, enriching it with her worriment. "Dash . . ." She sat back and looked from one measureless tract to the other. Nothing. Now there was no sign of any living thing, neither critter on the ground nor winged fowl. But the sound of her heartbeat was loud in her ears, and she said to the forest as if it were listening: "I am his and he is mine and I will die only if he lives." She began to cry again, then felt a sudden breeze.

Startled, she wiped her eyes and looked at the pond. Now ripples were forming on the surface, one ring flowing into another, without limit, without number, further distorting her reflection. And as she stared, she had that same strange sensation upon awakening sometimes, when she sensed that she'd left her bedroom to go into another, but could not remember leaving the room where she'd been, nor what the room she next entered looked like.

She shook the sensation away, feeling hotter, and she leaned closer to splash her face again. But now she saw something beside her reflection on the surface. *What is that?* She looked deeper still, and she thought she saw the faint vestige of some other face, with a nose elongating into a snout and ears sliding from the sides of the head to the top. She jumped back. *Stop it*, she thought. *Calm down and find Dash*. She looked around. Nothing. But the trees seemed closer than they were before, the branches splayed like great fingers reaching toward her.

She heard a gurgling sound from the pond and she inched back to the rim and looked in. The other face with the nose and ears was still there, but now her own reflection was gone. There was a great rustling of the multitude of leaves; now she heard every cricket and slug. Every leaf quiver and rodent skitter. Her mouth felt crowded with teeth and her gums ached. And in her wonder, she could not control her tongue, nor could she stop the saliva that pooled and spilled from the sides of her mouth and slid down.

And the harder she tried to look away from the pond, the more she wanted to look into it again. She turned back and stared into the water, each blink in the time drip slower than the last. And then two goldenrod eyes appeared beneath the surface of that sable basin, and as she gawked at their glimmer, the eyes grew wider.

She jumped back, spooked. But now everything seemed sharper. The wooden realm was enlarged as if under a magnifying glass. Faraway things looked very near. Each color looked like every other, and things once concealed in the dark stretches were exposed as if in light.

Now she felt a twitching in her muscles and her back bending into an elegant curve. But when she peered down, she did not see her legs. Nor did she find her arms. Another breeze blew, and she felt its gentle brush against the pelt that now covered her. Her ears pivoted like antennae, and through the ranges of the forest she heard a human voice: "I am not a beast!" She tilted her head at the curious sound, for now it was something she seemed unable to discern. And as she stood in the myriad of sights and sounds of the acreage, she tried to remember what had brought her to that moment and why she was there.

And then she smelled it on the air.

One odor among the pheromones of unseen millions in that forested interior, the singular scent of her young. She stood rigid, concentrating. The scent grew stronger, and in it she smelled danger and the pungency of fear. Now a growl emitted from her throat, vibrating her whole body like the rumblings of a quake. She let out a great howl and charged into the wilderness.

GOOD KILL

Red told Find Out about his supernatural experience down below and took him to the mouth of the abandoned coal mine. In the end, he led him there without much protest or pause, tired as Find Out was of not knowing what had happened to his wife. Desperate as he was to kill the single question consuming his mind.

Find Out stared into the portal of blackness. "I been knowing everything . . ."

"But not this," said Red.

"Everything. Everything been happening . . ."

"Except this."

They said no more and parted ways.

Find Out's news from Anacostia rang in Red's mind the whole way back through the territories as he walked parts of the way and hitchhiked others. He wondered what the tracker's color in the crystals might be. Would he find his answers? He didn't know. But he tried to balance the equation of years spent erasing himself with the message that he'd left a part of himself in someone else. Amber . . . Amber and a boy. His boy. Every now and then he looked around expecting to see the one who was always there, a reflex that remained even though he knew that she was gone. But the weight of what he'd done pressed into him still, and he tried to understand how he could take someone's child yet be given one of his own. He thought about such things as he traipsed from the northeastern territories and down into the Kingdom of Maryland.

And it was in accordance with constellations, circumstances, and events that he reached the edge of the imaginable forest of Suitland Parkway on the afternoon of Juneteenth. Cars whizzed by intermittently as he stood on the side of the road and looked into the blackened province he once inhabited. From the corner of his eye, he saw a deer navigating across the parkway, and it too came to the perimeter and looked in, and then it leaped forward and disappeared. Red stared into the woods. *Why am I stopping at the forest and not going straightaway to the quadrant?* He didn't know. But he needed to find the words first; to figure out what he could and couldn't explain to Amber, once he went down the hill and knocked on her door at last.

He longed to see that solitary place where he once slept, not with a wish to live there again, but to return to a point where he might somehow start over. *I'll know what to do from there,* he thought. He stepped forward. The sun vanished above the dense canopy, and it was like he had plunged into evening time. But even after ten years, the forest seemed exactly as he remembered, since the woodland formed according to the inclinations of his mind without him ever realizing it. He began walking through the forested pathways, and they turned and twisted according to his cogitations. And the deeper into the landscape he moved, the deeper he wanted to go, for he had a feeling that something else awaited him besides his solitude.

He sped his stride, moving quickly through the mazes teeming with growth. *I'll know what to do from there,* he told himself again. And just then, his woodsman refuge appeared up ahead, just as he'd left it, and he went over and sat down. He looked at the big rock where he once spread his clothes to dry and the stone mound where he built his campfire. He spotted the wild wintergreen he once loved and plucked a tender leaf and put it in his mouth. But Find Out's cryptic news about Amber's death dream and the boy crept into his mind once more, and he was spooked by that daunting feeling again: fear for someone else.

Because it meant that his boy was going to die, marked by his own mother's visions. He wiped the sweat from his brow and put his hand on the ground and the forest sampled his growing rancor. More and more, he wondered what doom could be awaiting his son and by what hand. And just as he was ruminating, he thought he heard something . . .

The powerful sense of her nose led her on, and she followed the scent through the forest, negotiating the convoluted pathways with ease and haste. Through the ranges she heard the sound again, and she stopped and stood rigid and listened, the hairs of her black pelt bristling. She held her head up and sniffed the air. The scent was stronger and now seemed to commingle with some other carnivore, the reek of an enemy. And there was the faint odor of something else on the wind—a familiar smell she couldn't place in the olfactory order of her hunt. The wind shifted and the scent of her young sharpened, muffling the others. At that, her blood coursed hot and swift and her chest rumbled. She broke into a sprint.

Red stood up at the sound. In all his time in the imaginable forest he had never heard another person there before. But now he was sure it was a man's voice somewhere in the distance. The hunting skills he'd learned in his years in the territories took hold, and he went off into the greenwood, following the utterances. They were still unintelligible in the prodigiousness of nature. But curiously, some of it sounded like singing . . .

At last she came upon her young pinned under the foot of some other animal, and she slammed the threat onto the ground with one leap. She watched her young wriggle away and scamper off to hide behind a fallen tree. Satisfied, she turned back to the threat, circling and growling. She leaped again, and in a single bound was on her target's chest. Every cell of her being issued one command: *Bite.* She opened her mouth wide and clamped down. Blood spewed forth and the forest thirsted more and drank deep of her wrath.

He braced against the bite with his forearm, shouting out in pain when the teeth went in. Great skeins of saliva dripped into his eyes and he clenched them shut. He felt another bite in his neck and kicked frantically, flinging his attacker into the trunk of a tree. He stumbled to his feet, gawking and bewildered, trying to understand what he was seeing.

She landed hard at the base of the tree, a sharp pain in her back. She righted herself and regained her footing, panting wildly. A bloodlust filled her and she knew only that the flesh before her had taken something of hers, and now that flesh was hers to take. She lunged forward again and was at her enemy's neck, tearing parts of it away.

Reeling from the assault, he seethed with anger at the turn of events. The boy was gone and now he was dealing with this . . . *thing*. Furious, he dealt heavy blows to his combatant's head with his fist. He felt its jaw slip from his neck and he rolled sideways. He grabbed a thick stick on the ground and scrambled to his feet. When his opponent came at him once more, he charged with the stick. Quickly, he shifted his body behind his antagonist and hoisted upright, clamping the stick tight against the neck.

Suspended by the choke hold, she growled and clawed the air, struggling to break free. Air was being cut off second by second, her back straightening like a board. Her bladder emptied and the soil drank of her release, growing by cubic feet with each of her gasps. She writhed as time slowed, the forest disappearing into the nothingness from which it was born, the glimpse of her young with it.

* * *

He clamped tighter, listening to his challenger gag and flail with the strangling. Exhilarated by another's suffering, oblivious to his injuries as the woods gorged on his bleeding neck. The forest multiplied, each kilometer compounding another, the sounds of the growls and grunts and whimpers booming ever louder. He reveled in the ruckus, thrilled by the act of dragging a creature into the waiting waste of the Void, until a knife in his back stopped him cold. Instantly, he lost his strength and the stick dropped from his hands and his subject slipped from his grip. Shocked, he turned around to find a man.

Red stood looking at the person he had stabbed, his hand still ringing from the feel of the knife going in. Because when he walked up from behind and saw him choking a wolf in one blink and a woman in another, he stopped thinking, for something else had taken hold. Now he looked again at the injured wolf (woman?) on the ground. And then from the corner of his eye, he saw something move and he pivoted. It was a boy hiding behind a fallen tree, and when he met the child's eyes, a chill went through him and he knew who he was without having to be told. Because the boy looked just like him, an unmistakable trace of himself. Many years later, when Red accepted what was now happening and placed it on the point of the time continuum it was meant to be, the boy would ask him what he had the right to ask: *What's your real name?* And Red would say it at last: *Edward Joseph, after my father.*

Red stood in the forest clearing, looking from the bleeding man to the injured woman (wolf?) to the boy and back again. And it was then that he knew—as all men do—that protecting his own was worth killing for. The wind picked up and rustled the leaves, a swishing sound that reminded him of the hunting grounds in the Kingdom of Oregon. *It'll be a good kill this time,* he thought. Not like in the jungle. Not like *her*. He took another knife from his pocket.

* * *

Mercy was leaning grotesquely to one side, his back crooked from the stab wound. Blood ran from the deep gashes on his body, and the forest floor widened, gorging on the glut of will and fear and desire. His injuries surprised him and he looked at the stranger as if he might explain a part of a scheme. "Who are you?"

"It doesn't matter who I am."

"You part of my game?"

Red spit out the chewed-up wintergreen. "Guess so."

"Well, my name is Mercy, and this ain't what I had in mind."

Red flicked his knife. "Mercy, huh? Well, ain't that too bad. I'm feeling good, though. 'Cause I know this thing is gonna end just like I mean it to."

Blood was dripping in heavy rivulets down Mercy's back and into the subsoil, where it dried quickly in order to suck in more. And it was then that he saw the boy crouched nearby, and he looked back at the man and smiled weakly.

"Ah . . . So that one is yours, is he? After all this time, you sure can pick a day." He laughed and it quickly turned into a violent cough.

Red flicked the knife again. "Dead man laughing. What the fuck is so funny, dead man?"

Mercy smiled. "It won't matter, yours or not. Ain't no one safe and can't nobody be saved. Everything's raw and sitting for the plucking. Didn't you know that?"

Now Red moved closer. *Bare hands,* he thought. *I need my bare hands.* He threw the knife to the ground, and the earth tasted what he was about to do in the perspiration on its handle. "I know I got something for that neck of yours."

Mercy stood still, for he felt the imminent pull of the Void. "Raw and sitting."

Red moved closer and put his hands around Mercy's throat.

"Sitting for the pluck—"

Red squeezed Mercy's neck like a sponge. He watched the

man's eyes roll and loll and gripped harder, until a vein on his forehead raised high and turned purple, until his body slumped and Red let it drop from his hands.

There was a great cracking sound of the forest contracting from the release of his kill, and he stood staring at the body for a long time, satisfied that he'd brought something to an end. Or made a beginning. He turned to the mystery on the ground. "Amber?"

Amber was cresting from the black depths of unconsciousness, the soil a luxurious pulp cradling her. She could smell the relief of her young and her heart calmed. But she was unsure of the state of her body, and she felt numb, unable to move. She listened to the gulp and burp of the wooded grounds, the bracken now thick and satiated. And then she smelled wintergreen and crushed leaves and firewood and she heard a voice: "Amber? Amber . . ." It was the tenor from the satin pouch, the one inside the vault of her mind, and she knew who it was without having to be told. Which was just as well, she was thinking as she blinked and blinked again. Because she couldn't see a thing.

VELVET

When the people who had volunteered to go looking for Dash walked into the scene in the imaginable forest of Suitland Parkway, there were no words to describe it, and they beheld the enigma that the forest presented without understanding how they'd found it. But they knew what they were seeing was too big to fit into their minds. Some parts might be forced, they reasoned, but the rest wouldn't make it in. Because every time they tried to believe their eyes, the slickness of it all kept slipping from their grasp.

They saw Mercy Ratchet in a puddle of blood on the ground, dead and smiling, and they tried to understand if that was the Mercy they knew; the one who gave them tissues at funerals and held them up in the pews when the spirit overtook them. They tried to comprehend if that was the same Mercy who worked at the elementary school and made sure the sidewalks were salted before the first snow. Wasn't he the one who bought all the fish for the fish-fry dinners (perch *and* trout)? And the one who made the best lemonade this side of heaven? They stared at the ghastly sight, trying to figure out if the smiling mess was really Mercy Ratchet or someone else. They looked at the man in the clearing standing over him, covered in blood. They saw Dash peering out from under a log, his face a painting of shock, relief, and wonder. And when they spotted a mound of velvet on the ground, which in one blink was a shimmering pelt and in another was a heap of dark skin and hair and impossible eyes, the women swayed and the men ground their teeth, and they tried to understand how big the thing that wouldn't fit was.

* * *

Rosetta emerged from the shadows of the forest and into the clearing like a woodland creature. From the distance that feeling like she could never go home invoked, she'd watched in puzzlement as her mother tallied the whereabouts of the children of others and followed the searchers there. When she saw Mercy Ratchet dead on the ground, a fugue slowly rose inside of her. She began circling the clearing, balling her fists and pulling at her hair, half skipping at times and marching at others.

And bit by bit, what Rosetta had been holding inside of her swelled and gushed forth in a Pentecostal wave of words from her own soul and the souls of other children like her, and even the lost soul of the boy who had once been Mercy Ratchet, and a pestilent surge broke the dam of her affliction and she said: "Dead marigolds me and the marigolds dead and nobody saved me from the peep-show box and wasn't no butterflies at the club only rats and vampires and snakes and spiders and walking across the bridge and that water calling me and you calling me I thought you were just being nice and I knew you and you knew me and why would you because school and how could you because milk if I knew what was really happening if I understood what we were really doing in that hot house damn you those nights on the corner and demons on mattresses and hunting and preying and breathing and seeing I hate you forever you took my life die I want you to die and I want to die you stole me and destroy because trash and syrup and you are evil and I am evil you took it away from me you took me because . . . shit!" And here Rosetta stopped, panting and dizzy, because she knew—as all the abused do—that there were no nouns or verbs or grammatical constructs to describe the depths of her outrage and pain.

When the spate was finished, what Rosetta said pooled thick and stinking where the people stood, and they struggled long to breathe. And in accordance with the dark irony with which creatures of passage live, a man with a slave surname from a lineage that bound him to wood traveled through the pages of time when none other could. So it was no surprise that the professor, who could find no terms of his own for the happening, searched the bookshelves of his mind and the words of W.E.B. DuBois appeared in his thoughts and he said: *"Herein lies the tragedy of the age: not that men are poor,—all men know something of poverty; not that men are wicked,—who is good? not that men are ignorant,—what is Truth? Nay, but that men know so little of men."*

No one else spoke. In congruence with an ancient law that they had never been taught yet understood, there would be no deliberation or adjudication, no purification through the burning of the corpse or burial rites performed, and the people agreed on this without saying so. The forest surmised this collective design, and out of the ground a great crevasse appeared. They threw the body in.

The Anacostia River flowed on, moving along in swift currents of industrial waste. The undead at Earl's Scrapyard came alive at sundown just as before, and patrons sailed the barge at Sonny's Bar. And every Sunday the holy flock of Saints of Eternity turned out in rain-forest splendor. But beneath the things the people remembered and the swaying and teeth-grinding they wanted to forget, they tried most of all to fathom if the passage of their lives was fate or wish. And without ever speaking of what was seen blinking on the ground in the clearing that day, the people thought of the velvet in the woods as a way to explain the inexplicable. With it, they named the unnameable, the preposterous, and the miraculous in the kingdoms of the land, for there were many happenings in the lives of black people that they found difficult to understand. So it was no surprise that such things came to be called "velvet," and they spoke to each other from one day to the next in the code that the happening in the forest inspired.

Girl, believe me when I tell you it was all velvet.
The velvet will find a way.
Ain't enough velvet in the world for that man.
Let's keep this velvet between us, you understand?

SEEING AND BELIEVING EYES

At the kitchen sink, Amber moved her hands around, probing for her drinking glass. When she found it, she held it under the running faucet until she felt the water hit the tip of her finger. She drank it down and eased the glass onto the windowsill where she could find it quickly again later. A colander of plum-sized grapes rested near the drain, and she moved her fingers through them, feeling for grit. Although the kitchen was in the back, she could hear the indiscriminate chatter of Red and Dash somewhere in the house, new sounds among the many she found could exist. She discovered that there were other things too, different ways of looking through a house that was now an image only in her mind. She could still see things when she closed her eyes: the blue cloudcap; how the garden looked under moonlight; the granules of salt collected on the shelves and the algae in the table grooves; how her dresses floated on doornails in the drift. But when she opened her eyes there was nothing. Now her days were like her dreamless nights, black and quiet, and in that velveteen calm her melancholy faded.

She centered herself in front of the window over the sink and listened. Even in this new darkness, she felt as if something were staring back at her, waiting. She moved her eyes to where she remembered the trees were. Every gnarl and knob remained in her mind, the places where lightning had written its name on the bark. She recalled the lily patches dotting the ground at the base of the trees, there since her mother had planted them.

And then she saw him.

Framed by the window that framed her mind's eye, she saw a man leaning against one of the oaks. He wore a cloak that shimmered about his tall frame. His hair hung down in ropes. And when he pushed the thick tendrils aside with his hand and she saw the half finger, she knew who he was.

Osiris stood among the stand of trees that faced the kitchen window once more. He shook away the carbon atoms in his hair and watched them bond and diffuse and settle again. It seemed like there was less of the carbon now. The feeling that he was vanishing seemed to be getting stronger, and he worried about what it could mean or not mean. But he wanted to see his daughter again. He kneeled and picked a lily. There was so much he wanted to tell Amber since his death. How he thought of her even as the river current took him. How each time he looked at her, this woman who was once his little girl, he saw his wife. *Where was Gola now?* He was thinking about this when he glanced up and saw Amber smiling at him

Amber opened the window and waited.

Osiris stood up and came to her.

Face-to-face, they took some time to see one another, to blend the images of who they were and who they had become.

And after a while Osiris said, *Been gone, baby cootuh.*

Amber nodded.

So sorry I been gone.

Amber shook her head, her eyes tearing. "In the dream, I saw you and the shark. But I didn't know what it meant. Not at first."

It ain't your fault, baby cootuh.

"The dreams got worse. So much worse . . ."

It ain't your fault.

"I didn't stop it. I couldn't stop it."

Lots of things can't be stopped.

"And Nephthys . . . Auntie blamed me."

Osiris sighed. *She blamin' herself.* He would have said more, but he was interrupted by the sound of glass shattering, for Dash had dropped his drink when he walked into the kitchen and saw them.

In the silence that ensued, Amber turned away from the window where her father was standing, and the world vanished from view once more.

Dash looked from the River Man in the window and back to his mother, as if he might laugh. Or cry. "Mama?"

Amber listened to the crack in her son's voice and smiled. "Meet your grandfather."

Nephthys stood alone at the top of the hill, staring into the thick blue cloudcap obscuring the valley below, unaware that the pieces of a family she'd helped salvage were just beneath her. In her travels from one quadrant to the next since that Juneteenth day, she heard the talk of her passengers about Dash's ordeal in the imaginable forest. And Captain told her about the return of the man from the war; it seemed that Find Out, wherever he was, had come through after all. She heard about the happening within another happening that involved her niece, for there was no end to the whispers about the velvet. And people spoke in fables about a child-eating monster who once lived among them but was now gone.

She stepped away from the edge and went back to sit in the Plymouth, the white girl silent in the trunk. Her half finger throbbed, and she ached with the inertia of one. *What to do now?* She didn't know. She stared into the dashboard at the hands on the clock, no longer comforted by the surety of those hands, uncertain as she was of her own passage.

ENCRYPTION

Osiris tarried in that place where dreams come true even when people don't want them to for a long time. He rejoiced at the reunion outside the window with his daughter and Dash. But now it was difficult to come anywhere but the river, and even on the banks he had an inexplicable feeling that it was getting harder to stay. What troubled him more as he stood thinking about the lingering that his state allowed was his sense that he was supposed to do something. Not just be. He felt for the prehistoric rock in his pocket. *And where was the boy?* He didn't know. He felt strained and closed his eyes, and when he opened them again the wolf was there.

The wolf was warming his belly on the blighted grass, and he looked at Osiris as if picking up a conversation from where they'd just left off. *You're almost there.*

Osiris was tired, too weary of the living-death quandary to spar with the wolf now, and the more he tried to understand each coded rendezvous, the more perplexed he felt. He looked at the wolf and sighed. *Wuh are you?*

The wolf's eyes twinkled. *The great question at last.*

Well, wuh are you?

The wolf swished his tail with a grand flourish. *Not many ask, you know. They sense that it will be hard to hear the answer. But since you ask . . .*

Just tell it.

The wolf rolled over to scratch his back on the parched ground and settled back again. *I am the All. The happenings of the ages.*

Meanin'?

Your happenings. Your ages.

My happenings?

Every moment that brought you to this point. Everything that makes the path for what comes next.

Osiris looked into the river.

And now that you know, what do you think?

'Bout wuh?

The reason. Your reason.

Don't know.

But you do.

Osiris looked at his half finger and the answer formed from the nebula of his thoughts. *To not be lost. To keep pieces of me.*

Yes.

To be 'membered in hate.

Yes.

To be 'membered in love.

Yes.

To be 'membered in lessons.

And now?

Osiris stared at the river current, so different from when he first emerged from it; a reddish-black slag in the infrared night. *I . . . I . . .* And here Osiris stopped, for that was easier than saying what was next.

The wolf nodded as if he'd heard his thoughts. *Move on you must.*

Osiris turned away from the river and back to the wolf, incredulous. That couldn't be all, there had to be more. Because if there wasn't more, there was only this leaving; only an absence remaining after his departure. And he knew—as all ghosts do—that his greatest fear was being forgotten. He looked at the wolf, feeling helpless. *But . . . but that be like I never was.*

The wolf sighed. This was what they all said. *Don't you see? You'll be here after you're gone.*

Osiris shook his head. *No.*
You're in your daughter's eyes.
No . . .
You're in your grandson's mind.
No . . .
And you're in your sister's heart.

PASSAGE

From her vessel Nephthys looked out at the uncharted sea. And lo, she saw bits of something drifting toward her, one piece and then another . . .

Nephthys sat in the 1967 Plymouth parked on the street in the watercolor of dawn. She had the windows rolled down, waiting for the fog. Even at that hour, there was the distant sound of sirens wailing and dogs barking, the pneumatic air-brake hiss of buses, the remnant happenings from the night before, and other white noise that places like Anacostia wrought. A stray cat crept by and stopped to stare at her with its holographic eyes and moved on.

Nephthys took a sip from her flask and listened to the white girl in the trunk drum the spare-tire rim. She closed her eyes, and when she opened them, she sensed that there was someone in the passenger seat next to her. She did not rush to turn her head. A strange and familiar feeling grew. If it was him, she had to think about how it must have been him all along in the mirror. And it was him moving her bottles. Was her brother here to judge her now at last? There was much she owed him as kin, a debt she felt she would never be able to pay. So it was no surprise that for a long while she did not look, and she tried to gather her strength to face what it was time to face. Finally, she turned her head slowly and let her eyes see.

And after a long and sacred silence, Nephthys greeted the one she saw sitting in the passenger seat with the dignity of one twin born thirty-nine seconds after the other.

At last they spoke in the symbiotic language of twins and each looked into the soul of the other.

Been hebby, said Nephthys.

'Gree, said Osiris.

Been haa'd.

'Gree.

They talked more, and Osiris shared all he'd seen and learned in the places he'd been since he was dumped into the Anacostia River, and Nephthys shared the happenings of her sojourns from one quadrant to another.

And after a while Osiris gazed at his sister and said: *But don't worry, Nephie.*

'Bout wuh?

Wuh de woman said ain't true.

De Lottery?

Yaas. It ain't blank.

After dreamin'?

After dyin'.

True?

True. De blank be full and more full.

And now Osiris was beginning to understand what he was supposed to do. He looked at his half finger. It carried the flame still, and he held it out to her.

Nephthys understood the gesture without having to be told, and she held out her half finger too.

They were conjoined once more, one passing the fire to the other, and Osiris said, *Oonuh push on through to tomorrow, Nephie.*

Cyan?

Cyan. And after that too.

Minutes moments chronons after he departed, Osiris would enter the deepest of carbon-black darkness, a raven expanse that emptied into yet more blackness and in its absoluteness was of a substance that formed all others. And out of that aspect would shine the distant light of yet more spaces. But he had no way of knowing this as he gave his sister the last of his fire. What he knew was that it was time to go. Maybe Gola was out there somewhere too?

He held his hand to his sister's heart. *Carry me there.*

Yaas.

Always.

Yaas.

Osiris smiled at his sister then, and he began to sing:

Indigo swirlin' round de vat
No beginnin' and no end
Circlin' round de ring shout lap
No beginnin' and no end . . .

By the last verse, her brother was gone. His voice hung in the car and Nephthys listened to it dissipate as she'd listened to the songs fade in the hallway of her apartment where there were other doors, other lives. She stared at the empty seat. *Where did Osiris go?* She didn't know. But now she looked at her half finger. It was aglow again, as it once was in those black Sea Island nights, and she remembered what it felt like to look out at a dark world through the fearless, hopeful eyes of a child.

And after a while the fog drifted into the car and she had that feeling that made what she did with the Plymouth possible. She looked down the street, past the four-thousand-pound mahogany Big Chair and out over the bridge at the Acropolis and beyond the outer rings and out to the edges of the world. She turned the key in the ignition and listened to the engine gather its power. *Who would it be today?*

She looked at the glowing tip again. She would need that light now more than ever to guide wandering hearts through the darkness. Because she knew—as all ferrymen do—that the fret of people was not how they would move around the streets of cities or across the currents of seas or through terrain and sky from one destination to the next. Rather, the worry of man was the worry of all creatures; the Great Fear of all souls seeking passage through the empires of the world, of all travelers of the labyrinthine byways of one existence to another. The dread that before they became shadow and mist, they would never find the place where they belong.

ACKNOWLEDGMENTS

Sometimes when you have so big an idea and so small a vehicle to convey it, it takes the belief of others to sustain you on what feels like a dark and endless path. I thank my editor, Robert Mooney, who raised his lighter high, never once wavering in this long journey, and reminded me of what a story must demand and relinquish along the way. I thank my publisher, Johnny Temple, a fire-breather at heart, who with his daring gave this novel a chance; and Alex Verdan for his valuable editorial support. I thank my husband, who has always been my first ear, reviewer, and conscience, all through the many chords of this book over some seventeen years of its writing. I thank my father, who was my first protector in this world, and stands behind me yet with sword and shield. I thank my mother, who from the stardust she must have become has whispered her poetry and wisdom in my ear. And I honor my grandmother, who really did drive a DC cab through the twists and turns of an era, for leaving me with her fighting spirit and a compass.